FALL LINE

Kate Leonard

For Jacqui

CONTENTS

.

PROLOGUE

She came to an unsteady stop by the orange-tipped pole. The round black sign attached to the top read 'Schlucht' in white letters, with the number one below. Translations flew into her head unbidden, each one more terrifying than the last: Gully. Canyon. Ravine. Abyss. She looked down the black run as it fell away beneath her, as narrow and steep as a ski-jump ramp. She knew this run. She had done it once before, all those years ago. It had been hell. She had fallen again and again. She'd been younger and much fitter then. Could she do it now? She hesitated on the lip of snow, paralysed with indecision. The run was dangerous, but wasting time here was more so. She had to get away while she still had a chance. The weather had started to change. A breeze was whipping needles of ice into her face from the slope above. She glanced up. Mist was beginning to creep over the sun. The jagged mountains peaks, which had looked benign and protective only minutes before against a radiant blue sky, were now turning grey and menacing. This was bad. The mist would take away all definition from the bumps and slopes, making it harder to judge her way down. Her gloved fingers were clamped rigidly onto her sticks. Her shoulders were raised and stiff. Her knees were shaking badly. Her breath came out in short puffs of panic. She had to relax. She forced herself to breathe deeply and drop her shoulders; she would never make it if she was tense. But should she even try? What if she injured herself? Wasn't it better to take the long, easy blue run that wound lazily through the trees? But the black was the quickest way down. Each minute was vital. Again she hesitated, unsure. Should she get help instead? Attach herself to a party of other skiers for safety? She looked around desperately, but the only other skiers were far below, five or six bodies following a red-clad ski monitor with ease and confidence. She would never catch them up. There was silence. Think! Quick! You're wasting time! Then she heard a noise that pushed all doubts out of her head - the swish of skis carving the snow somewhere above. Oh God, oh God, oh God! Was that him? Could he have caught up so fast? She had given herself away by running. Now he knew that she knew. He had killed them. All of them. He was close behind her and he was going to kill her. She had no choice. She had to go, and go fast. Find the fall line, the most direct path. She pointed her skis downhill and launched herself into the void.

PART 1

1

'Damn Facebook! Damn, damn, damn it to hell!' Kat swore silently as she struggled to keep her umbrella from turning inside out. She hurried across the street, keeping her eyes down to avoid the puddles. What had made her do it? Jesus, what an idiot. It had taken her so long to forget him. She had blocked him out for the last, what, almost thirty years? Then last week the Friend Request had appeared. Her finger had automatically gone straight to Delete. Then she'd hesitated. Curiosity had niggled at her. What did he look like now? What had he become? He'd been such a screw-up, full of tension but silent, unreadable. So attractive with his skinny, undernourished-looking body and sharp cheekbones. Could it be possible he'd become some fat middle aged banker with five kids? Or perhaps he'd got into drugs, done time. Maybe he'd gone into the army. She couldn't decide which was most likely. One click and she'd know. It would be remote. A virtual friendship. It didn't have to go anywhere. Just a click.

 'Fuck, sorry!' she said as her umbrella tangled with an elderly woman coming the other way. They smiled at each other and Kat felt briefly better. It was OK; she didn't have to do anything. She'd had another message from him that morning. The third one. She didn't have to answer. She'd seen his profile picture. She'd found out a little bit about him. Now just unfriend him and forget he ever existed. But why had he got back in contact? He must have gone to some pains to find her; there were dozens of Kat Williams on Facebook. Why now? She'd opened a door a crack and now here he was, stuck in her head like a virus, multiplying, relentless. Stupid, stupid girl.

She pushed open the door of the coffee shop and turned to shake out her umbrella in the doorway before placing it in the cast-iron stand. The warmth and smell of fresh coffee immediately made her relax. She looked around and saw her friend sitting at a small table, head turned and deep in conversation with the woman at the next table. Kat felt a mean little spike of irritation. Ellie could strike up a conversation with anyone. It was one of her gifts. But today Kat needed Ellie all to herself. She walked over and took off her wet coat.

'Sorry I'm late,' she said. 'I'm a bit away with the fairies today.'

Ellie turned round and gave her a beaming smile. 'Oh, don't worry! I need a second cup of coffee. Sit down. You're soaked! I'll get the drinks in. Shall we have cake?'

'Why not?'

Kat gazed after Ellie's retreating back as she made her way to the counter. She was dressed, as always, in the uniform of comfortable middle age. A forgiving jumper, stretch jeans and flat boots. A mass of curly brown hair, streaked with grey. Ellie's body had changed a lot over the years, but her hair was as wild and exuberant as ever.

As she watched Ellie weighing up the different cakes, rocking back slightly on her feet as she considered, Kat had a sudden flashback to the first time she'd seen her. That same rocking motion. It had been the first week of lectures, once the torture of Freshers Week was out of the way. Ellie was in the centre of a group of girls, waiting outside the lecture theatre, talking with animation, using her hands to reinforce her words. She was short and slim with a wild mop of tawny brown hair. Kat had looked on with envy and vague dislike as Ellie seemed to draw more students around her. She was obviously one of the cool girls. The 'in' set. Not my type at all, thought Kat as she'd hovered in the background, worrying about who she would sit next to, and what she could say to them. She'd felt slightly sick.

How was it possible that this girl had become her closest

friend? Was it just the fact that they both had broad Yorkshire accents and discovered they'd been brought up in mining towns a few miles away from each other? That was the start. It had set them apart and given them a connection. They used to ham up their accents to confuse their home counties classmates – 'Ey up, duck! Ow do? Gor any snap? Aye, I do. Wang it o'er then.' Kat smiled at the memory. She'd lost her accent since then. Ellie's remained as broad as ever.

Or was it that intense second year out in Berlin? Both out of their comfort zone but determined to experience everything. They'd gone to seedy jazz clubs packed with American soldiers, joined protest marches, crossed Checkpoint Charlie into the East. They'd taken crazy risks, hooked up with the strangest crowds, partied all night with existentialist fervour. Kat still thought of the Berlin year as the most exciting of her life. They'd been young and free and invincible. Such a long time ago.

Ellie looked round now and mouthed 'carrot cake?' and Kat gave a thumbs up.

As Ellie walked back with the tray, Kat debated whether to tell her about the text messages. She was used to dumping all her problems at Ellie's feet. Usually they came back magically transformed into positives. In the past it might have been 'I cocked up that job interview!' and Ellie would reply: 'Well it obviously wasn't the right job for you. There's a better one waiting.' Now it was more likely to be about the children. John split up with his long-term girlfriend? Well, better to find out now than later. Sarah had no idea what to do with her life? So much wiser not to limit your options. Ellie always made her feel better. Always saw the positive. But would her advice be impartial now? She had a blind spot where he was concerned.

Ellie sat down and pushed the tray between them. Then she gave Kat a searching look.

'You look tired. Are the children OK?'

'Oh, yes, they're fine! Did I tell you Sarah passed her driving test? It was the fifth attempt. I thought it was never going to happen.'

'That's great! She'll be really independent now. You won't need to ferry her about so much.'

'Yes, I know,' said Kat, a little sadly. She wanted her children to be independent, but each little step towards that made her more aware of the gaping hole in her own life. She gave herself a mental shake and said brightly: 'What about your three? What are they up to?'

'Oh, Dom's thinking of quitting his job.' Ellie's eldest was working in sales – and hating it. 'He ought to try and stick it out for a year though; it looks so bad on your CV if you don't.'

They talked about their children for a few minutes, then about work, the latest political scandal, last night's episode of Strictly.

'Have you read any good books lately?' asked Ellie. 'I'm having a dry spell. I need a recommendation. The last ones I've read have been utter rubbish.'

'Oh, I love Deborah Moggach. Have you tried her? I'm racing through all her stuff at the moment.'

Kat looked around her. Two walls of the coffee shop were covered in second hand books. Customers were invited to browse or borrow – or just sit in a quiet corner and read. Kat recognised many of the titles. She'd provided boxfuls of books herself, when she'd felt strong enough for a good clear out. There were her aga sagas. Her airport edition holiday reads. That was her Joanna Trollope collection. Then her eye caught the spine of a different sort of book. Walter Mosely. One of Peter's. She caught her breath, felled by an intense wave of sadness. How he'd loved his American noir. It was one of the few things they'd argued about. He wanted the house to be teaming with books and she wanted clean surfaces and minimalism. God, what she wouldn't give now to see him coming through the front door with another armful of thrillers and an apologetic grin.

Ellie noticed the tears welling in her eyes immediately. She reached a hand across the table and held onto Kat's, saying: 'It's OK. It's OK. I know.'

'But it's been two years!' Kat croaked, her eyes pleading and the desperation making her voice crack. 'When does it start getting better?'

'It just takes as long as it takes. Don't worry. There's no rush.'

'But it's not fair.'

'No, it isn't. It's shit.'

They sat for a few minutes, not speaking, Ellie holding her hand and Kat letting the tears fall.

The young waitress paused behind the counter and looked over at the two older women. She had barely paid them any attention before today, although they'd been coming in for years. They must be, what 55, 56? Dull, average middle-aged housewives, she'd thought. Good at her job, she knew their order before they spoke each visit: a milky coffee and a builder's tea. A slice of lemon drizzle. Or a piece of million-aire shortbread. But today they were immobile, holding hands, the blonde one was crying. Interest piqued, she assessed their appearance: one slim with carefully cut and coloured blonde hair, nice clothes, dresses young for her age but looks tired, lines around her eyes. The other shorter, overweight, dressed for comfort or to disguise the extra pounds, an untidy mop of curly brown hair streaked with grey. Less attractive on the face of it, but with a buzz of energy which actually made her the one you looked at most. 'Lesbians,' she thought, with satisfaction. 'That's it! And they're breaking up!' and she turned again to the expresso machine.

Kat wiped her nose with the serviette and forced a smile. 'Sorry,' she said.

'Don't be daft. Tell me. What are you thinking?'

Kat paused, trying to make sense of her emotions. 'It's not just losing Peter. I mean, that's bad enough. But it's like my life has lost its balance, I'm drifting off.'

'How do you mean?'

'Well, with you for example. We used to be a foursome. It was comforting. You, me, Peter and Nigel. We were always in step. Had our kids at the same time, bought our houses at the same time, went on holiday together... I thought it would always be that way. You know, I just assumed that we'd be in our seventies, the men would be out playing golf and we'd be sitting in the garden, drinking wine and nattering about our grandchildren.'

'We can still do that!'

'But it's not the same. We're not in sync anymore.'

'Yeah, I can see that.'

Ellie nodded thoughtfully. She knew without asking that Kat found it hard to see her and Nigel together at home, sharing domestic chores. It had been her idea that they meet at the coffee shop every couple of weeks. Neutral ground, less memories.

'Anyway. That's enough whinging!' said Kat, pulling herself together. 'Try Deborah Moggach. You'll love them. Start with Big Little Lies.'

'Didn't they make that into a film?'

'A TV series. That's good too.'

They talked for a while about whether it was worth getting Netflix. Then, in a lull, Kat decided to take the plunge.

'Something strange happened the other week. I got a Facebook friend request from Neil,' she said.

'Neil who?'

'Neil Adams.'

'Neil?' Ellie paused to think. 'You mean Neil the shit? From Uni? The one you went out with?'

'Yes, that's the one. It was right out of the blue. Took me by surprise.'

Ellie took a moment to digest this news. 'You didn't accept did you? I always thought he was trouble.'

Kat was taken aback. She'd forgotten how much Ellie disliked Neil. Distrusted him.

'Err, well...' she began.

'Oh Kat, you didn't..?'

'Well, yes, I did. Just for the moment I was so curious. I

sort of thought I could find out what had become of him without actually having to talk to him. You know, like I do with a lot of my other Facebook friends. Just swapping likes. But now he keeps messaging me.'

'Does he? What does he want? Does he want to meet up?'

'No, nothing like that, he just, I don't know, wants to reconnect with some people he lost contact with I think. He's back in contact with Sean too it seems, and he's trying to find Silvio.'

'What does he actually say in his messages?'

'Nothing dramatic, just, you know, he hopes I'm well, would like to get back in touch. He seems lonely, I think.'

'Huh. Don't fall for that crap. Have you messaged him back?'

'No, not yet. I can't decide whether to answer, or block him.'

Ellie was decisive. 'Block him. You know, there's always a reason we lose touch with certain people. They weren't the right people. We manage to hang on to the ones who really count. And it's so long ago! Who knows what he's like now.'

'Yeah, you might be right. He was my first love though. That still means something.'

'Block him.' Ellie tried to lighten the tone. 'But before you do, let's have a look at his profile picture. Is he still hot?'

Kat groped for her mobile phone in her overstuffed bag, brought up Neil Adam's profile picture and passed it to Ellie.

Ellie took her time. She pinched the screen larger and held the phone in her outstretched arm.

'You really must get varifocals,' Kat nagged, waiting for a reaction.

'Hmmm, oh yes. Those eyes. Shifty. Thin lips. My mother always says never trust a man with thin lips. Definitely serial killer potential. Avoid at all costs. But I must admit he's aged pretty well!' She handed the phone back with a smile. 'God, do you remember that skiing holiday we all went on in Switzerland? When was it?'

'Yeah, I do remember. It was in the Easter holidays. Just before finals. But I try not to think about it. It was awful.'

'Really? I remember it being pretty good. All that snow. The chalet. Telling jokes.'

Kat didn't reply. She had never told Ellie what happened on the last but one day of that holiday. The day everything changed. She tried to push the memory away now, before it overwhelmed her.

Ellie prattled on, for once not noticing Kat's darkening frown.

'Oh it's all coming back to me. Do you remember? We used to play the murder game!'

2
Back then

Kat stood at the top of the dry ski slope and thought, not for the first time, what the hell am I doing this for? What had made her think she might be able to ski – she couldn't even ice skate when she was a kid. All those skating 'parties' which she'd spent clinging miserably to the edge while her friends whizzed by whooping and yelling. Part of her considered skiing as a life skill though, like riding a bike or being able to cook Bolognese. It was a target she had set herself to conquer and she wasn't ready to give up just yet.

She had tried to persuade Ellie to sign up for the sessions. They had been sitting on Ellie's narrow bed in her tiny campus room, ostensibly there to work together on a joint presentation on East German Kaderpolitik. Neither of them really had a clue what Kaderpolitik was. Kat was worried, had been to the university library and found a couple of useful books. She'd skim read a few pages and wanted to see what Ellie thought. The presentation was in three days' time and they really should be making a start. Ellie, however, never worried about deadlines. She trusted herself to come up with something half decent at the last minute; they could pull an all-nighter and it would be fine.

Ellie was a miner's daughter. The first person in her family to go to university, to the immense pride of her parents, Ellie considered the whole thing to be a global experience, the social side just as important as the study side. She wanted to see and do everything. University was a revelation. She was thrilled by the variety of people, the freedom, the huge choice of activities. Work could wait a little.

Kat, on the other hand, had always expected to go to university, just as her parents had before her. Her mum and dad had painted a golden picture of university life – and for their generation it had been golden, a glorious release after the austerity of war. They had adored their university years and still went on reunion weekends to this day. It was assumed without words that Kat would be clever, go to university, have a wonderful time, meet exciting people, make a big group of friends she'd keep for life, probably find her ideal life partner. So far though, Kat had found university a bit underwhelming – like school but with more possibilities to drink. She had expected the students to be more radical, in dress and in politics. Instead she found most people she met quite ordinary. Maybe it had been a mistake to go to a red-brick university in the south. Lots of students went home to mummy and daddy for the weekend, and the proximity of London seemed to bleach the life out of campus.

Now, back in Ellie's little room, Kat's army surplus bag sat unopened on the floor. The heavy – in all senses of the word – tomes on Kaderpolitik remained untouched. They both knew they should be working, but instead they sat on the narrow bed threading beads onto silver wires to make earrings. Much more fun.

'Did you see that thing about the ski club in the newsletter?' Kat asked as she rummaged into the jar to choose a final bright red wooden bead. 'Ten sessions on a Thursday evening at the dry slope, minibus and equipment provided. It's quite cheap. We should go!' She was sure Ellie would be up for it, as she was for anything new.

'Oh, I'm not really bothered. I can ski a bit already. You go!'

Kat looked up from twisting the silver wire to clamp tight her multi-coloured beads. She was astonished. 'How come you can ski? I thought your folks were poor? That's a bit middle class isn't it?'

Ellie was a bit put out by the 'poor'. Proud to be working class, she nevertheless didn't want to be thought of as under-privileged. 'There was a school trip,' she explained. 'Subsidised for us *poor* kids,' she said with an emphasis that was an obvious dig. 'We went to some place in Italy. It was fun actually. You should definitely try it.'

Kat thought back to her own school days. She'd won a scholarship to an independent girls' school, luckily, as the fees were high. Or was it lucky? Maybe she would have felt more at home in a comprehensive, like Ellie. Would have learnt how to speak to boys more easily in a mixed school. Would have developed a thicker skin. Some of the girls in her school had got cars for their eighteenth birthdays, for God's sake. There had been ski trips but somehow she'd never found out about them until too late. Saw the golden car-driving girls coming back after the half term break with tanned faces and a little more continental polish. Maybe that's why she wanted to ski so much now.

'Oh go on. You could probably do with a refresher course. Let's go together.'

But Ellie was not to be budged. 'I'm not fussed. Besides, Thursday is film club night, there's some good stuff this term. A Clockwork Orange, Halloween, The Conversation. Jaws! How could I miss seeing Jaws again! It's a classic!' The subject was closed and they returned to their task, picking up the stray beads that had fallen on the floor.

So Kat, who was nervous about doing new things alone, had screwed her courage to the mast and signed up to ski every Thursday night with a bunch of strangers. The local dry slope was very small, with one button lift and a couple of floodlights. It still looked huge to Kat. The hexagons of bristles were hard and unforgiving. The other students seemed to get the hang of things quickly, but Kat was not a natural. After four sessions she was able to do a slow snow plough down the slope, but turning was a nightmare. She didn't trust the weight transfer theory – she knew she had to swap her weight to the turning ski, but somehow it never felt like the right time, so she ended up stopping or falling over. Getting onto her feet again laboriously by dragging her skis parallel, trying to push herself upright with her sticks while stopping the skis from sliding away under her, all the time aware of the others in the group making what looked really easy turns around her.

Now here she was again, at the top of the slope. She was going to do it this time. She set off, as slowly as she could, going across the slope. As the edge approached she made herself do it – she threw all her body over the right ski. It worked! She turned left, rather jerkily, but was now facing in the right direction and she hadn't fallen. This was progress. Just do the same again with the other leg now. She half snow-ploughed, half slipped down towards the bottom of the slope where it was a bit flatter to make a right turn. Just do the same again! Maybe she didn't have enough momentum. As she threw her weight on the left ski she came to a stop and fell heavily onto her bum, skis in a tangle. Her energy deserted her and she lay back on the matting, defeated for the moment. She shut her eyes tight to stop the tears coming. 'Crap,' she thought. 'If anyone dares laugh I'm not coming back again.'

When she looked up there was someone standing over her. She saw blue eyes, smiling, but in sympathy. A thin face with prominent cheekbones. Longish black hair that curled to his shoulders. From her prone position he looked tall but skinny, dressed in a dirty combat jacket and badly patched jeans. He still had his skis on – how the hell had he managed to come uphill to her with his skis on? He leant down and dragged her skis parallel, then held out a hand to yank her up onto her feet.

'Hi,' he said, 'I'm Neil. And that was a belter of a fall!'

3

Kat turned her key in the lock and let herself in to her house. It had been a satisfying day at work. She was finally getting somewhere good with her latest bunch of students: a mixed group of mainly Afghans, Syrians and North Africans, whose determination to succeed in their new country made them fast learners of English. They generally picked up the vocabulary well. Kat was now concentrating on pronunciation, which she thought much more important than grammar. She loved teaching. When she was in front of a class she was back to her normal self - assured, relaxed, fun. She could forget all the bad things. She threw herself into her job as an escape, planning her lessons with far more thought than was strictly necessary. It was when she stopped working that the problems began.

Opening the door, she allowed herself to imagine for a moment that Peter was still there, sitting on the sofa in the back room watching something relaxing on the TV like Bargain Hunt. He would call 'Hi! Did you have a good day?' and lift himself off the sofa to shamble into the kitchen and put the kettle on. She would dump her bag on the floor and reach up to hug his solid warmth. Smell his special smell on the shapeless cotton jumper. Relax.

But no, the house was just as she'd left it. Everything untouched. Its stillness was a rebuke. She felt as if the house didn't want her or protect her anymore, as if it blamed her for not being enough to fill it. They'd bought this pleasant semi-detached place twenty years ago, thrilled to be moving on from a flat. It had been a good family home – a solid 1930s build, with bay windows in the dining room and main bedroom above, a square, extended kitchen, and a living room with French doors leading onto a paved patio. It had been perfect when the children were young, with a swing and climbing frame in the garden, overflowing toy boxes in the cupboards, other young children in the street for theirs to play with, school within walking distance. Now the swing and climbing frame were long gone. The toy boxes were neatly stacked in the attic ready for potential grandchildren. The neighbouring children had long since grown up and moved away, and the street no longer echoed to the sounds of play. The house was too clean, too sterile, too quiet.

She opened the fridge, peered inside and shut it again. Looked through the couple of letters that had arrived on the mat. Put the kettle on, then changed her mind and poured a glass of wine. She turned on the radio for company, but the sounds coming from so far away into her kitchen somehow made her feel more lonely.

It had been two years since the cancer took him, and time was not the great healer it was supposed to be – at least not yet. 'Kat and Peter'. 'Peter and Kat'. The two names twined together for eternity, or so she'd thought. Unconsciously, she twisted the ring around and around on her third finger. It had been such a good marriage, full of mutual support, laughter, tolerance. Their home had been welcoming and open, with friends and family coming to stay often. They'd brought up two happy, well-adjusted children. Well, there had been the usual rows about school marks or staying out late, but nothing drastic. She and Peter had always made the big decisions together – she providing the grand ideas, and Peter filling in the details and working out the budgets. Now she didn't have any idea where to begin on her own.

She knew she ought to be making plans for her future. Should she move to a smaller place, a new start? Somewhere without all the memories? But that wasn't fair on John or Sarah; even if they were both independent now, with their own flats, they needed their reassuring home to be there for them for the odd weekend or for Christmas, needed to find all the belongings which hadn't made the cut to their own flats still where they always used to be. So much else had shifted in their lives over the past couple of years; she didn't want them to have to adapt to any more changes. And this house was precious to them precisely because of its memories of Peter.

Should she decorate, finally get around to some of the projects she had talked about with Peter? Update the kitchen? Before he got ill, they had pretty much settled on a plan to rip out the old wooden units and replace them with cool new concrete effect ones, with brass light fittings and an island with inbuilt cooker. Money was not a problem; the mortgage had been fully paid off when Peter died and she was quite well off with his work pension to supplement her smaller salary. They had been so excited about the prospect, but now it seemed pointless. Why bother when it's only me to see it? she thought.

Maybe she should get a cat; a little living creature to welcome her when she got home. To jump onto her lap when she sat on the chair. To look after. But no, she might end up like a sad old spinster who only talked to her cats and whose house smelt of cat piss.

People made helpful suggestions – Join a choir! Go on a singles holiday! But she just didn't have the energy. They urged her to be positive – You've got such wonderful children! You had such a good marriage! Or the worst – You're still young! You will find someone else! Kat wanted to scream at them. She didn't want to forget and she didn't want to distract herself. She wanted to dig down into the heart of her misery. She knew she was driving some of her friends away. They thought she was being self-indulgent and should make more of an effort. Invitations had started to dwindle, but she found she didn't care. Ellie was the only one who didn't push her to move forward. She allowed her time to wallow, and encouraged her to talk about Peter. 'Give it time,' Ellie had advised. 'You grieve as much as you need to. You'll know when it's right for you to make some kind of move.'

Kat imagined the scene in Ellie's house right now. Chaotic, messy and frankly not very clean. The TV would be on in one room, the radio in another. Piles of books and challenging board games would be strewn over the coffee table, together with a selection of mugs that should have been washed up days ago. Nigel would be in the kitchen creating something inventive using herbs Kat had never heard of, and using every possible kitchen gadget known to man. The dog would be chewing someone's shoe, un-noticed, in revenge for a missed walk. In the garden the half-built patio would be sprouting weeds. Shit, she was jealous. She was so bloody jealous of the mess, the dog drool, the mould in the coffee cups.

Was it envy or jealousy? She could never remember which one was OK and which was bad. As an English teacher, she should really know these things. Whichever one it was she felt, it was caustic.

She went through to the living room, sat down with her wine and switched on the TV, flicking through the channels. Same old stuff. Nothing caught her interest. People had lent her dozens of box sets – she could start 'Borgen' or 'Mad Men' or even 'Game of Thrones'. It all seemed too much effort to even choose. Instead she sat, staring out into the garden, watching the birds on the fat balls.

Then a chirpy little whistle snapped her out of her lethargy: her mobile phone signalling a message. She fished it out of her work bag and tapped on the icon: one new message: Neil Adams. She clicked it open and started to read.

4

Back then

Kat stood at the crowded bar in the students union, waving three empty glasses and trying to get the attention of one of the bar people. It was Friday night and she felt like getting drunk, then going down to the disco and letting off some energy with Ellie and the girls.

She'd been in a strange mood for weeks, ever since that night on the dry slope. She'd lost her appetite and couldn't concentrate in lectures. She kept looking out for a figure in a dirty combat jacket. She thought she'd spotted him a couple of times but it wasn't him. Neil. That's all she knew about him, a name. She'd dragged her friends off to different campus events each evening – he must show up somewhere. He wasn't at film nights; he wasn't at the Stranglers concert – she thought everyone would be there, as it was being televised and tickets were free. He didn't appear at discos in the Downstairs Bar. She'd even gone to a folk night and sat through some excruciating finger-in-the-ear pretentious warbling, hoping to catch him. He was nowhere. Maybe he wasn't even a student. Maybe he was a builder or unemployed. Maybe he'd wangled his way onto the ski lessons through a friend or something. He hadn't shown up for the last two skiing nights, maybe he'd been found out and chucked out? He'd had a Scottish accent. Did that make it more likely he was a student? He certainly wasn't a local.

Why did she even care? She had a boyfriend already, back home – down-to-earth, loyal, real Kevin, who she'd managed to stay faithful to for almost three years at university. A boyfriend who thought she was wonderful and sent her thoughtful little presents before exam week. She'd been perfectly happy with him for all this time, avoiding temptation, gently putting men off when they hit on her. He was coming down south to visit her next month, what was she doing daydreaming about blue eyes and a Scottish accent? But she knew without a doubt she didn't want Kevin to come anymore. How was it possible to change so quickly?

This was hopeless. The bar staff looked around her or through her as if she was invisible. She wished she was taller. There was some bloke pushing right up beside her now, so close she could feel the pressure of his elbow, and effortlessly getting the attention of the nearest barman. She looked up, really annoyed now, ready to tell him to piss off and wait his turn. Instead she froze. He took the glasses from her hands and put them on the bar. He took one of her empty hands in his and said in that lovely soft accent: 'Shall we go somewhere else then?'

And just like that she followed him out of the bar, without a word, leaving Ellie and the others wondering what had happened to their drinks.

As they left the students union, he slipped their joined hands into the roomy pocket of his combat jacket, his thumb gently rubbing the length of hers. They wandered down the hill towards the lake and began to walk around it, not talking, perfectly in step. It was a lake Kat had taken for granted for three years. She had had picnics there, taken her revision notes to sit under the trees. Played cricket with a gang of friends. But she'd never really noticed it properly before. Suddenly it seemed the most magical place in the world; ethereal and silent, with weeping willows bending over to touch the moonlit water, and reeds swaying gently in the breeze. A couple of ducks swam towards them, hopefully. More ducks dozed along the shoreline, their heads tucked into their chests. She shivered as the cool air penetrated her thin jumper. She'd left her coat in the bar. Neil immediately stopped and took off his jacket, wrapping it round her.

She felt the heaviness of the material on her shoulders and smelt the slightly musky male smell of the cotton. He stood in front of her, pulling the zip up to her chin, fussing with the collar. Then he kissed her. It was a slow, deliberate kiss. His two hands still held the collar, pulling her gently towards him. She felt the instant response of her body. A deep answering need. She was amazed. This was new. This was wonderful. He broke off, planting a last small kiss on her nose, and smiled down at her. She gazed up, trying to commit his face to memory. His blue eyes now looked grey in the darkness. His untidy black hair curled onto the ragged collar of his jumper. A thin face with sharp cheekbones and a pronounced dimple in one cheek. A pale, thin-lipped mouth and a hard chin, free of stubble. He was the most beautiful man she had ever seen.

'What's your name, anyway?' he asked.

'Kat. Kat Williams. And you're Neil.'

'I am.'

'Do you want to come back to my room?'

She lay awake on the narrow single bed, her head lying snuggly on Neil's chest, rising and falling gently with his sleeping breaths. Pale sunlight started to seep through the thin curtains, lighting up the sparse room. The washbasin with its single toothbrush. The desk with her files lined up neatly. Her pens, upright in the mug with the university logo. Pencils sharpened. The chair, pushed against the desk, out of the way. Everything orderly, everything normal. Except for the floor, littered with their discarded clothes. Che Guevara gazed into the distance from the poster on the wall. He looks a bit like Neil, she thought. Same hair. Same intense look. She felt utterly astonished at herself. Who was this girl she had suddenly become? The way she'd behaved last night would have shocked her in any of her friends. Asking a man back, only knowing his name. Pulling him into her room, not even locking the door. Acting with complete abandon. It wasn't just that she had wanted him, badly, urgently. It was a kind of inevitability. A realisation. Ah! This is what it's supposed to be like! This is the right one! She had had no doubts at all as she pulled off her clothes between kisses. My God! This is amazing! Incredible! The real deal.

She'd always suspected she wasn't particularly keen on sex. With Kevin there had been boundaries. She had preferred his kisses to be light and sensitive, pulling away if his tongue became insistent. Sex had been nice, but for her it had been more about the cuddling, the caring, the gift that she was giving to him. It was never about her needs. Last night had been an awakening. After they'd made love, they lay together, naked, exploring each other's bodies with their hands.

'What's this?' she'd asked, as she found an angry v-shaped scar on his forearm.

'Oh, it's when I fell off a bicycle when I was a wee kid. My mum had sent me to the shops for a bottle of Irn Bru. I was carrying it in one hand and steering with the other, then I hit a pothole or something. Fell on the bottle side, and it smashed into my arm. I cycled home, crying my eyes out. My dad fainted when he saw it! What about this one on your leg?' He ran his fingers down a long, thin scar just under her knee.

'Squash injury.'

'Really? What happened?'

'I fell over a bench in the changing room!' They both laughed.

'And this?' She touched the small hollow in his cheek lightly. 'Is that a dimple or a scar?'

'That's a rugby injury. I got a spike in the face. I used to play a lot at school.'

'You're too skinny to be a rugby player, surely?'

'Ah, but I'm fast.'

'Do you play for the university team now?'

'Nope. I did a try out, but they're all ex-public school types, loud, macho, into drinking games and all that. Not my scene at all.'

'Whereabouts are you from in Scotland?'

'Near Glasgow. Have you been to Scotland?'

'Yes, we had lots of family holidays there when I was young. We used to go caravanning. Ullapool, Skye, Oban. I loved it! I've never been to Glasgow though.'

'It's a bit different from the bits you've been to. It's not the same since the steelworks shut down. There's unemployment, violence.' He shrugged. 'It's supposed to be coming back up though. Where are you from?'

'Yorkshire. Not the nice bit, either. Near Wakefield. The people are great though! What course are you on?'

'Chemistry. Third year. And you?'

'Linguistics. German main. Third year too.'

Neil traced a languid finger between her breasts and down to her naval, making her shiver. 'OK, now for a really searching question. Are you ready? What… is your favourite colour?' he asked, imitating the voice of the Keeper of the Bridge of Death in the Monty Python film.

'Blue!' Luckily she caught the reference, as it was one of her favourite films. She continued with another question from the cult movie scene. 'What .....is the airspeed of an unladen swallow?'

'Do you mean African or European swallow?' he answered without hesitation.

This is great! she thought. We're on the same wavelength. 'OK, time for another searching question. Do you prefer cats or dogs?'

'Dogs, no contest. Favourite band or musician?'

Kat thought for a minute. She was a bit embarrassed about her mainstream musical tastes. Should she admit to loving REM, Soft Cell, having a soft spot for Abba? Or should she lie, try to be a bit more interesting. In the end she compromised.

'King Crimson. I used to listen to them all the time when I babysat for my dad's friends.' That much was honest at least. 'Free. Steve Winwood. Hendricks.' She'd racked her brains to remember the record collection belonging to her father's artist friends. They had always seemed such cool people, and she had really tried to get into their music.

'Thank fuck for that. I thought you were going to say Sheena Easton or Abba.'

'Would that have been a no-no?'

'Totally! I'd have been out that door in a heartbeat.'

I dodged a bullet there, thought Kat happily, snuggling closer.

They talked nonsense together, between kisses, until sleep eventually caught up with them.

Now it was morning. Kat felt ridiculously happy. Euphoric. She had woken up with Neil's arm still slung around her waist and his head turned towards her. She didn't want to move, didn't want to break the spell. It was Saturday morning. The whole weekend was ahead of them. Lots of time to discover more about each other.

'Hey you!' Neil was awake. He lifted himself up on one elbow to look at her. He said her name, kissed her lightly then sat up. 'I'm gasping for a fag. Is it OK if I smoke in here?'

'Oh!' Kat had always been a non-smoker, getting quite cross when people lit up next to her. But this new Kat seemed to be a different creature entirely. 'Yeah, go ahead!' As Neil reached down for his jacket and retrieved his cigarettes, she tipped the pens out of her mug to use as an ashtray. She watched distractedly as the pens rolled along her desk and some fell on the floor. Neil took a long draw on his cigarette, the inhalation making his cheekbones look sharper than ever. Then he exhaled, making a series of little smoke rings.

'How do you do that?'

'It's easy, I'll show you.'

'I don't smoke.'

'Sensible girl.' He crushed the cigarette against the side of the mug and stood up, searching for his clothes.

'You're not going are you? I thought we could do something today.'

'Sorry. Got things to do.'

'Oh.'

Kat felt her happiness melting away into doubt and confusion. Had this just been a one-nighter? Had she totally misread the signs? Assumed that he felt the same way she did? She watched as he pulled on his jeans and laced up his ancient Green Flash tennis shoes.

Neil shrugged into his jumper, shoved the cigarette pack into his jeans back pocket and headed for the door.

'Don't forget your jacket,' she managed to say in a casual voice.

'You keep it for a bit. You look cute in it. I'll get it back next time.'

With a last smile, he left the little room. 'Next time'. The words danced around in her brain. There would be a next time. She pulled on a t-shirt and opened the window to let the smoky air out. Gazing down she saw Neil crossing the courtyard below, his stride long, his hands in his pockets and his shoulders hunched against the cold morning air. Next time.

5

Ellie was late. She was supposed to be coming straight off the London train, and should have been here by now. Kat checked the text message again. Yes, the 3.10 from Kings Cross. Must have been delayed.

Her tea was getting cold and she finished it with a gulp. The café was busy today. The fine weather had brought people out. Young mothers filling time before school finished. Pensioners chatting over cake. Kat felt suddenly self-conscious and too visible. She looked at the phone lying on the table. Should she have another look? No, it was becoming unhealthy, she'd already looked far too often. But the phone would shield her, make her look busy, as if she was checking important emails. She traced the pattern across the glass screen to unlock it. Opened Facebook, touched the little magnifying glass icon and typed in Neil's name.

What could you tell from a profile picture? A single friend had shown her a popular dating app recently, trying to persuade her to get back on the horse. She had resisted of course, but had been fascinated by the photos men chose to display. What they inadvertently or purposely revealed about themselves. The tight t-shirt moulded to abs, screamed 'I'm fit, sex will be great!'. The puffed up peacock posing in front of a sports car proclaimed 'I've got the money to give you what you need.' The moody, unsmiling face, staring into the distance or hidden behind sunglasses shouted 'I'm a challenge, I'm artistic and cool.' She had flicked through dozens of photos, writing each one off with a scathing comment before handing the phone back to her friend, saying 'That's not for me I'm afraid.'

She looked at the photo Neil had chosen. Slightly out of focus, unprofessional. He was staring away from the camera, unsmiling. He looked younger than he would be now, possibly in his forties. Did that mean he has no vanity if he hadn't updated the photo in years? She tried to read his expression. Determined. Maybe a bit grim. His jaw was firm and there were lines around his mouth. The background was just cloudless blue sky. No clues there. He was wearing a black jumper, round-necked. Unostentatious. She pinched the photo out larger, looking for a designer logo. Nothing.

Frustrated, she began to scroll through his posts again, looking for something she'd missed previously. There weren't many. A lot of them referred to medical advances. Some related to Brexit, and further back, the Scottish independence vote. The same people writing on his timeline every birthday. He hadn't replied to them. Here was one interesting photo though. He was posing with work colleagues, receiving some award. He was smiling in that one, and looked much more like the man she remembered. He was at the centre of the group, and seemed to be the focal point. One or two of the other people were looking at him instead of the camera. Was he their boss? Was he respected? Liked? Feared?

She looked again at his basic profile information. Place of birth. Works at. University – that she already knew. There was nothing about relationship status. She knew he was divorced but was there anyone in his life now? She scrolled down his posts as far as she could, looking for photos of his ex-wife. Nothing. Had he removed them all? She looked at his friends list. Fifty-two friends. None mutual.

OK, she thought, he doesn't really use Facebook. He joined a while ago but doesn't post much. There's nothing strange about that – in fact it's sensible. She opened her own page, wondering what impression he had formed of her. There weren't many posts in the last two years. Mainly of photos of John and Sarah, the 'proud mum' posts that embarrassed them so much.

Then further back there were the family shots. Christmas. Holidays. Peter brandishing a barbeque fork. Peter and herself on a Hebridean beach, the long stretch of golden sand going on for miles behind them, the wind whipping her hair into a frenzy. She stared at that photo, remembering, wondering how she could ever be that happy again.

A thump made her look up. Ellie had dumped her bag on the floor and was standing at the table, grimacing in pain.

'Oh my God, these shoes are killing me. I've got to take them off. Can you go and order for me?'

'Of course! Sit down, I'll get us the usual.'

Back with coffee and cake, Kat took in Ellie's appearance. She had her best suit on – well-cut, sensible, sober, adaptable for everything from a business meeting to a funeral, with a turquoise silky blouse underneath. The shoes that now lay abandoned beside her were surprisingly fabulous. High, elegant but understated with a tiny bow detail at the back. A man's brown leather briefcase, a bit battered at the edges, finished off the look.

'How was London?'

'A disaster!'

This surprised Kat and she couldn't stop a tiny flutter of satisfaction to think that everything was perhaps not perfect in Ellie's life. She'd always felt just a little bit jealous of Ellie's high-profile job, as if Ellie had left her behind. A little mean-spirited part of Kat wished Ellie was still the part-time office assistant. She squashed the feeling down.

'Oh no! Why, what happened? Didn't they go for it?'

'No, worse than that. I got the train OK, got the tube, had just got up the escalator and onto the street when the bloody heel of one of my shoes fell off! Have you ever tried walking with one shoe on and one shoe off? It's like that, and it's impossible. I felt such an idiot! I had to hobble along for two streets before I found a shoe shop, which was way too expensive, bought these horrible things, practically the only things they had in a wide fitting, and they bloody kill me!'

'But they're gorgeous. You should definitely wear them in, it might take a week or two but they lift your whole look.'

'Bugger that, I'll just go to Marks and Sparks and get another pair of the old ones.'

Typical, thought Kat, fondly. Ellie had no vanity about her appearance. If only the shoes were in her size...

'But how did the meeting go, was that a disaster too?'

'No, that went fine actually. Although I was late because of the shoe thing, and didn't have time to read the proposal through again properly. But she was actually really nice, quite normal, and I think they're going to fund the project for another five years'.

Ellie worked for a mental health charity. She'd started part-time as an admin assistant to stop herself going mad when the children were small. Gradually she'd worked her way up to regional director, in charge of managing budgets, writing grant applications, generally figuring out how to squeeze enough money out of various organisations and spend it wisely enough to keep things going. She'd just been to London for a meeting with the Junior Health Minister.

'I had to wing it a bit, and I forgot to mention that whole demographics thing, but she seemed to get what we're trying to do'.

Kat could well imagine the scene. Ellie was full of confidence and bluster, she was not intimidated by anyone. At university she'd once improvised a whole off-the-cuff fifteen-minute mini-presentation in Otto Schwartzman's class, and he'd actually applauded afterwards. When it was Kat's turn she'd slaved over it for days with only a nod of recognition from the lecturer.

'Well that's fantastic. Did you get anything concrete out of her?'

'Not yet. She's got to read everything through again, but she was making all the right noises. I'm pretty sure we've got it. How about you, how's work going?'

'Actually, pretty good too. You know I told you about

Faisal, from Syria, three kids? He's just got a permanent job. He's going to be driving taxis and he's so happy. They must have thought his English was OK. It's a bit shaming really, you know; he was a doctor back in Syria, he lost his parents and his brothers, went through hell to get here and yet he's just over the moon to be working, living in this crummy town, making enough money for the family, getting his kids into school. It makes me feel a real wimp sometimes for complaining about my life.'

'Yeah, it puts things into perspective. We don't realise how good we've got it in this country. Well I think that's brilliant too! I just crunch the numbers and spout a load of buzz words. You're at the sharp end actually seeing real results.'

They spent the next half hour talking about politics, menopause and fad diets. Finally Ellie asked the question she'd been dying to ask.

'So, I want to know about Neil. Did you block him?'

Kat felt her face getting hot. She wasn't sure she wanted to talk about this just yet. It was some private little nugget of something that might not survive if brought into the open daylight. Brought under Ellie's sharp-eyed scrutiny.

'Yeah, um...I know you're not going to approve, but I didn't block him. We've swapped emails and texts a couple of times. And we might start Skyping.'

'Really? Oh!' Ellie's eyebrows shot up. Then she composed her face into an expression of calm concern. 'Look, you know I always want the best for you, don't you? If I give you advice it's because I love you.' Ellie was using her 'reasonable' voice, the one she'd always used when talking to her misbehaving children. Kat could imagine her next saying 'I'm not angry, I'm just disappointed'.

'Yes, I know that.'

'It's just... I think you're a bit vulnerable just now. Emotionally. He might exploit that.'

Kat felt a stirring of rebelliousness. What did Ellie know, with her perfect husband, her perfect job? She decided to dig her heels in.

'I'm not an idiot, Ellie. I can look after myself. I can make my own decisions.'

'OK, OK. Sorry, I didn't mean to patronise. But please think about it. What's the point of stirring up the past again? You've come so far. You're getting stronger all the time. I just don't want you to jeopardise that now.'

'Oh, give it a rest will you! You're being over-dramatic. It's just a really normal, boring chat between very old friends. To be honest it's nice to have a bit of company when he messages me in the evenings.'

Ellie lifted both hands in a helpless gesture, admitting defeat. 'Yeah, OK. I suppose it must be. So go on then, tell me everything. What does he do? Does he have kids? Where does he live?'

'He lives in Shrewsbury, he's divorced, no kids, and he does something to do with writing up reports on new drugs for medical journals.'

'He did Physics at Uni didn't he?'

'No, Chemistry. And then he did a PhD, something about drug-cell interaction. I didn't really understand when he was explaining it, to be honest.'

'So what do you talk about in the emails or texts or whatever?'

'Nothing special. It's very bland. We talk about our jobs. He asks about my kids. We share a few memories from university days, talk about who we're still in touch with. I told him all about you.'

'So has he asked if you can meet up? Would you want to?'

'God no! I mean, I don't think so. It's just nice to talk about old times. It ended pretty badly between us and this is just a way of making up for that I think.'

'Ah, you mean 'getting closure'.

'God I hate that expression. But yes. It's like... there's always been this big question mark, some regrets. Things both of us should have done differently.'

Ellie sat back, narrowed her eyes and gave Kat a direct look. 'So why did you two split up? I mean I wasn't sorry when it finished, I never thought that much of him. But you seemed to be all over each other when we were on that ski holiday. What changed?'

'Oh, there was nothing in particular.' Kat shrugged and picked up her teacup, unwilling to meet Ellie's eyes. 'We were just very different people I guess.' She didn't want to explain more. She regretted not having told her the truth at the time, but the whole episode had been too painful, and with each passing year it had become more difficult to talk about. She gave Ellie a bright smile and quickly changed the subject. 'So did Nigel choose his company car? Is he really going for the Mercedes? It's a bit flash isn't it? What's he trying to prove?'

Ellie ran with the subject, poking fun at her husband's need for a status symbol, but Kat was barely listening. She was back in the crowded London station, the last-but-one place she'd seen Neil. She pictured him standing there, one hand raised in a tentative wave as she'd turned and hurried away from him as fast as her legs would go.

6
Back then

After that, it was as if Kat saw university in a whole new light. What had she been doing for the last three years, sleepwalking through the weeks and missing so much? She had been like a schoolgirl playing at being a student. She wrote a blunt and cruel letter to Kevin, breaking up and asking him not to come down. She didn't even feel particularly bad about it.

Neil lived off site in a run-down barracks town with two housemates and their rented house didn't have a phone. She never knew when she'd see him. He would suddenly turn up at the door of her campus room with a bottle and a grin. Or come into the communal kitchen when she was eating her baked potato with beans and say: 'Grab your coat, there's a party at a pal's house.' Each time she felt a surge of joy and left whatever she was doing to follow him. She never ran into him in the daytime; he was like a vampire. Did he not go to lectures? Maybe not – he seemed to spend a lot more time drinking than studying.

A couple of weeks after they met, he knocked on her door one night and said: 'Come to the bar with me. I want you to meet my flatmates.' She immediately abandoned the essay she was trying to finish and followed him to the students union. They made their way through the crowded bar and Neil pointed to a Formica table in a corner, where two men were sitting over pints of beer. They could not have looked more different. The first was olive skinned, handsome in a polished sort of way, with slicked-back black hair, a long, slightly hooked nose and a full, sensuous mouth. He was dressed immaculately in a crisp

white shirt. The other was more what Kat would have expected
– scruffily dressed in faded green U2 t-shirt. He had sandy coloured, badly cut hair which stuck up in all directions, and a stud
earring in one of his rather prominent ears. As Neil introduced
her, saying simply: 'This is Kat', he stood up, and Kat could see
that he was a giant, well over six feet tall, lanky and awkward.

'So you're the girl who's been keeping this bollix away
from his beer!' he said with a grin. He had a strong Irish accent.
'I'm Sean. The good looking one here is Silvio.' He pointed to his
seated companion. 'So what'll you have for a drink?'

'Thanks,' said Kat, 'I'll have half a lager.'

Sean disappeared into the throng at the bar and Neil
fetched a seat from the next table for Kat. She sat down, and as
Neil went off in search of a fourth chair, she tried to make conversation with the dark-haired man sitting opposite her.

'So, Silvio. Is that an Italian name?'

'Yes, it is.' His voice was slightly nasal and bored. He
looked at her coolly, and Kat could see no spark of interest in his
eyes. She struggled on, determined to like Neil's friend.

'What part of Italy are you from?'

'Campania,' he replied briefly.

'I'm sorry, I've never heard of it! Whereabouts is that?'

'It's in the south. You've heard of Naples?' Kat detected a
touch of condescension in his question.

'Yeah of course. Must be beautiful. So why are you studying here?'

'For my English.'

'Oh. Right.' And with that, their conversation ran dry.
Silvio looked past her and around the bar, as if searching for
someone more interesting, and Kat pulled nervously at the skin
around her fingernails. It was a huge relief when Sean came back
with her drink.

'Cheers!' he said. 'So, Kat-not-Kate-not-Cathy, what on
earth do you see in this eejit here?' He pointed with his beer
glass towards Neil, who was heading back to their table with a

precious chair. 'You look like a sensible sort of girl to me! You do know the man's a total bollix, I hope? Can't trust him at all.' He said it with a lopsided smile but his eyes were serious.

'Dunno really. Umm, maybe it's his wonderful fashion sense,' said Kat and they both laughed conspiratorially, looking at Neil's attire. The same dirty jeans and a cricket sweater that was starting to unravel at both elbows.

'Where are you from? Do I detect a northern accent?'

'I'm a Yorkshire lass' she replied.

'That's nice. Wild moors and sheep and all.'

'Nah, I'm afraid I'm from the industrial bit: shut-down coal mines, blackened mills and all that! What about you, where are you from?'

'County Clare, a small town near the sea, you'll never have heard of it. Lahinch. Ah but it's beautiful though! The wild Atlantic, the cliffs of Moher, the wildflowers on the Burren...'

'Why did you leave it to come and study here? It sounds like paradise!'

'Well it is and it isn't. Really beautiful and all. Everybody in the town knows everybody – but everybody also knows everybody's business. It can get a bit claustrophobic. To be honest I couldn't wait to leave the place! And you? Why did you come down south?'

'I wanted to see what the beautiful south was all about, have a change of scene. And I thought it would be a good idea to come as far away from home as possible – you know, learn to be independent.'

'And do you like the south?'

'Honestly? Not much. I find it all a bit antiseptic, a bit bland.'

'I know what you mean!'

As they chatted, Kat felt more and more at ease with Sean. He was loud-mouthed, irreverent but warm and straightforward. A strange thought struck her: she already knew more about Sean than she did about Neil. He hadn't told her anything about his background. He was a closed book. Did that

46

mean their relationship was just based on physical attraction? And why had Sean said he wasn't to be trusted? Had that been a warning?

Kat never really broke the ice with Silvio that night. He intimidated her, made her feel like a teenager all over again. She wanted him to like her, but she didn't know what to say to him. He was sophisticated, intellectual and grown up. She found out he had a sports car, and was even into jazz, which she'd always considered music for the middle-aged. He could have been from a different planet. Gradually she got used to him, but she often found herself looking at him, wondering what his cool indifference was masking.

Sean, Neil, Silvio, the three housemates. It took her a while to figure out what kept this trio of disparate people together. Eventually she realised that what they had in common was a love of pinball. That first night, she watched from the side-lines as the three of them played, shouting encouragement at each other.

Later, Kat was introduced to the game, and found she was surprisingly good at it. They spent hours in a corner of the Upstairs Bar feeding the juke box and playing the three garish pinball machines, winning replay after replay. Kat learned how to make the silver ball shoot to the target, how to hold it till the last minute with the flipper, how to nudge the machine just enough to stop the ball going out without causing a tilt. She loved to watch Neil play, his legs splayed, leaning backwards, cigarette hanging out of the side of his mouth. This felt just a little bit seedy - like the public bars she had glimpsed from the lounge bars when she first started going for bar meals with her parents. Smoke and noise and action. She loved it.

Kat had mainly done her socialising on campus up till now, suspecting that there was a gulf between the 'townies' and the students that would be hard to span. But with Neil she started to visit the pubs in town, playing darts or pool with the locals. Neil favoured the spit-and-sawdust pubs – he was much more tap room than lounge bar. Kat admired that too. It was honest. It was real. It was everything her parents would hate!

Neil encouraged her into petty theft. She regularly smuggled beer glasses into her handbag. One night, after being thrown out of the pub, they stole a road sign and carried it up the hill to campus. It now had pride of place in her drab little campus room, next to Che Guevara. Then there was that night they were kissing outside one of the student residences. Someone had heckled from a ground floor window and Neil had scooped up a handful of frozen snow to chuck at him. The window had smashed – there must have been a stone in the snowball – and as they'd run off, laughing, Kat had thought 'I'm changing!' with a delicious shiver.

He introduced her to smoking. She knew it was stupid to spend her grant money on cigarettes, and was aware of the health risks, but it gave her so much confidence, made her feel edgy and cool. She was young! Time to worry when she was older.

And then there was the sex. Real sex. Although he wasn't her first, he might just as well have been. This was so different. Unbelievably different, as if her fumblings with Kevin should not have been called sex at all. She couldn't get enough of him. Grabbing handfuls of longer hair. Tasting the cigarette breath. Squashing up together on the narrow little bed. Not wanting it to stop. Careful, considerate, tentative Kevin was forgotten completely.

Neil didn't say much. He never spoke about them as a couple, never discussed the future, he just assumed. And she assumed back. They were just a good fit. Occasionally he would take her hand and smile at her, his slightly hooded blue eyes looking deep into hers, and she would feel as if her heart was about to burst. They didn't need words; they had something that went deeper than words, didn't they?

Ellie on the other hand, was not at all sure how she felt about Neil. He was always polite to her, but never really talked. There was something closed off and secretive about him. She resented the way Kat was changing too. She'd started wearing more grungy clothes – ripped jeans and weird hats. She's stopped styling her hair, leaving it straight and natural. She was using lots of black eye-liner. Most strangely of all, she was now listening to edgy bands like The Sisters of Mercy and Joy Division, claiming to love them, when she'd always been a Spandau Ballet and Echo and the Bunnymen sort of girl. She had become unreliable too, and had stood her up with no notice a couple of times for film club nights and even for revision sessions.

This was their final year, the spring term. Next term would be a panic of exams and job applications. Ellie wanted to have fun with Kat as usual; to go to the disco at the Downstairs Bar, have long chats into the night about life, love and everything. Instead she felt Kat was veering off down a completely different track.

Ellie herself had had lots of boyfriends at university. Each very different from the other. There had been a squaddie from the local army camp. A pink-haired punk from town. A linguist from the French course. The relationships never lasted long, but always ended on good terms. Just now she had been going out with Roger for a couple of months, a rather lumpen civil engineering student into role-playing games. Not dressing up and having kinky sex, but rather playing all-night long tedious marathons of Dungeons and Dragons. Ellie was thinking about dumping him, but she wasn't sure, now that Kat was unavailable half the time. He wasn't so bad.

Here was Kat now, walking over to join her at the refectory table. She was wearing faded and frayed jeans and an oversized man's jacket bought from the Oxfam shop for next to nothing. Her hair was long and loose and Ellie had to admit Kat wouldn't have looked out of place on a 60s album cover. She smiled and pulled out a seat.

'Hey you, where've you been? I miss you! You weren't at Linguistics this morning.'

'I know, I was staying over at Neil's, and we had to wait till Silvio was ready to drive in – it took ages! Did I miss anything important?'

'No, I'll give you the notes but it was just more stuff about language acquisition. Nothing new. You've skipped quite a few lectures though; it's not like you. You're becoming a rebel!'

'I know, my parents would be horrified!' Kat sounded quite pleased though.

'It's just, you picked a funny time to do it, just before finals,' Ellie warned. Then she did a little double take. It was usually Kat telling her to shape up – this was role-reversal.

'Oh it'll be OK,' Kat said breezily. 'There's plenty of time before that. Time for some fun actually. What are you doing over the Easter break?'

'I shall be making a detailed revision plan and then completely ignoring it, as usual. Why ask?'

'We're going skiing in Switzerland!'

'Who's going skiing in Switzerland?'

'You are! I am! A bunch of us! Silvio's parents have got a chalet in a little Swiss ski resort called Felsenalp, and it's not being used this year, and it sleeps ten people. You've got to come! Neil said I could invite anyone.'

'Hang on, slow down. It's Silvio's place?'

'Yeah. Well, his parents' place.'

Ellie thought for a moment. She'd met Silvio on a couple of occasions and privately thought him an arrogant sod. He didn't even look like a student – he was polished and suave. Black polo neck and trousers with a crease instead of jeans. When they'd been introduced he'd looked down his snooty nose at her, then seemed to discount her as beneath his interest. As he'd said 'hello' he'd already been looking over her head, searching for someone better to talk to. God, what an arse! A bit scary too with his cool stare and perfect teeth.

'Hmm. I don't think so. Silvio's not really my cup of tea.'

'He's not so bad. Underneath all that aloofness he can actually be quite nice. Sometimes.' Kat didn't sound very convincing.

'What will it cost?'

50

'Nothing. Well just the train fare and ski hire and stuff, but nothing for the chalet'.

'How many days?'

'A week. Maybe ten days. I'm not sure.'

'And who's going already?'

'Neil, Sean and Silvio obviously, this girl called Gillian who's on Sean's course. I've not met her yet. You and me – you can bring Roger if you like.'

'Ugh, I'd rather not. He'd probably go skiing in a wizard's hat or something.'

'And have a couple of wands instead of ski poles.' They giggled.

Ellie was torn. She didn't fit in with Neil's lot. They were strange. Misfits. She couldn't work them out. She had a feeling she'd probably like Sean if she got to know him better. He looked affable and normal, not like taciturn Neil or creepy Silvio. But, on the other hand, this was a new experience and she tried wherever possible to stick to her philosophy of never turning down a new opportunity.

As Ellie hesitated, Kat delivered the killer argument: 'Besides, it's in German speaking Switzerland – it'll be revision without the sweat!'

'Hmm, that is tempting. But I don't know… I don't really get on with that bunch. It might be awkward.'

'Oh, please come. Neil said we can invite a couple more of our friends too – there's room for more. Then it'll be more of a mix.'

'OK, maybe I'll come! I'll have to check the finances, but it should be OK. So that makes three, four five, six. What about Bill and Helen?'

'I don't know Bill very well. Helen's OK though. We could ask Jake?'

They spent a the rest of the lunchtime discussing the relative merits of various friends and whittling down a shortlist. But as she made her way back to her campus room, Ellie felt a shiver of foreboding. Neil and Silvio. Could she really spend ten days with those people? There was a darkness about them, something under the surface. What had she agreed to?

7

It was Ellie's youngest son's twenty-first birthday. Nick was going to make his parents leave the house for the weekend so he could have all his mates over and go wild. But in exchange he'd been forced to put in an appearance on the Friday before, when his parents had invited a few friends and neighbours, uncles, aunts and grandparents to the house. Past the sulky teenager years, he thought he would be able to bear this with good grace, express adequate gratitude for gifts of money or Amazon tokens, be the perfect son for an hour or two before sloping off back to his room to play video games.

Kat arrived early with two quiches and a case of prosecco. As she struggled down the path to the front door she couldn't help noticing the abandoned vegetable patch now full of tall weeds, the peeling paintwork in the porch and the dead look-ing flowers in the hanging basket. The house was a good, solid, detached 1960s build, with the potential to be great. Ellie and Nigel had wisely done what estate agents always advise, and bought the worst house on the best street. The trouble was, they hadn't really done anything with it. Many projects had been started but left unfinished, through lack of time rather than money.

'Hi! It's me,' Kat called as she made her way down the hall.

'We're in the kitchen,' came the reply.

Kat dumped her quiches on the table, and gave Nigel a big hug. He hugged her back hard, lifting her off her feet and twirl-ing her round.

'Helloo,' he boomed. 'Mm, so good to see you! How the

devil are you?'

Kat was struck again by how similar Nigel was in character to her best friend. He was a bit loud, a bit brash, always cheerful, always quick to take up a new idea. Just a little overweight too. As a couple they egged each other on to ever greater heights of enthusiasm.

Kat turned to hug Ellie, but Ellie held up her hands covered in flour, so they did an ironic little air kiss instead.

'The cavalry has arrived,' said Kat. 'What can I do?'

'Have a glass of wine first,' said Ellie. 'Then could you do a quick tidy up do you think?'

'Of course!'

Kat was a bit of a tidy freak. In her own house everything was in its place, surfaces left clean and bare. A few chosen objects placed strategically for effect. Whenever she entered Ellie's house she was instantly itching to clear up; to tidy the papers scattered on the sofa into a pile, to pair up all the shoes thrown off in a jumble in the porch. But she also acknowledged that there was something deeply comforting about the mess. You could throw yourself into a chair, kick your shoes off, curl up, grab a magazine in this house without feeling you were disturbing the balance. It was a house made for living in. You'd invariably get up again with your black jeans covered in dog hairs, but what did that matter?

Kat spent a contented hour running the hoover around the living room and dining room, collecting odd socks, junk food menus, magazines and broken pens, which she shoved into a wooden chest out of sight. Then she went back to the kitchen to help with the food, slicing carrots and celery for a dip. She watched with envy as Ellie and Nigel moved around each other in the kitchen, opening drawers, finding cutlery, never colliding, the way birds never crash into each other when they fly. She breathed in the tantalising aromas. To Kat, whose most exotic dish was moussaka, they seemed more like alchemists, turning the ordinary into something different with a little twist. Chocolate in the chilli. Cumin in the dip. Coconut powder in the curry. The kitchen looked like a bomb site, but the food was going to be great.

'So where are you two off to tomorrow?' Kat asked.

'We've booked a B+B in York – not too far in case we have to rush back to the rescue if someone's in an alcoholic coma! And we can explore York a bit – it's ages since we went there.'

'Are you expecting the worst then?'

'No, not really. Last year's party was great, they'd cleaned up everything when we got back, we just had to take the empties to the bottle bank.'

'Ah but this is twenty-one, they might go a bit mad.'

'God, do you remember his eighteenth?' Nigel asked Ellie. 'Vomit in the flower beds, pizza on the walls. That poor girl we had to find who'd wandered off pissed as a newt. We gave him such a rocket for that. I think it made a lasting impression.'

'I do remember! And the loo was blocked. We had to get the emergency plumber out, cost a fortune! But lots of them will be driving this year so I'm pretty sure it won't get out of hand.'

They chopped and mixed in companionable silence for a while. Then Nigel went out into the garden to cut some herbs and Ellie took the opportunity to ask: 'So, have you heard from Neil again recently?'

This was something Kat actually wanted to talk about. She needed advice. 'Yeah, we talk about once a week on Skype and send texts every couple of days. Just casual stuff.' She paused, looked up from the chopping board and waited until Ellie turned to face her. 'Actually he wants to meet up. The kids are totally freaked out about it, they're sure he'll have turned into a serial killer or a pervert or something. Plus, he's, you know, he's not Peter.' Kat still called her children 'the kids', even at the age of twenty-five and twenty-seven. They were protective of their mum. A bit overprotective. When she'd mentioned the prospect of meeting up with an old ex-boyfriend they'd been horrified and tried everything to dissuade her.

Ellie could understand their reluctance. 'Of course

they're worried. And they're right to be. I mean, how well do you actually know him? You went out for, what, a couple of months? And it's over thirty years ago. People change. He was pretty strange even then, you must admit. He might be a right weirdo now. Well obviously you told him no, didn't you?'

'Well…' Kat took a deep breath and then blurted out, defensively: 'No, I didn't. I said I'd think about it.'

'Christ Kat, do you think that's wise?'

'I'm going to say yes.'

'Argh! What are you *like*!' Exasperated, Ellie wiped her hands on a tea towel and sat down at the kitchen table, pointing to a chair for Kat.

'Uh-oh' thought Kat, taking a seat. 'Here comes the lecture.'

But Ellie surprised her. 'Right. OK. If you really must do this, then let's do it sensibly. You need to meet on neutral territory, somewhere with plenty of people about. You need someone like Nigel to be there in the background in case things turn out badly. You need to have an escape route planned in case he turns up in a dirty raincoat with nothing underneath!' She was only half joking.

'Erm… the thing is, it's not exactly neutral ground. It's a bit odd. He suggested going back to Felsenalp again, getting the same bunch of people together, having a kind of reunion of university friends.'

'*What?* The ski resort? That's so creepy. Why would he want to go back there? That's where you broke up, isn't it?'

'Yeah. I don't know, maybe he wants to make up for things? To get things back to how they were before? Or just because it was the last time we were all together with that bunch of people. Afterwards we all left Uni and everyone went separate ways.'

'Kat, it's madness. Be careful. I hope you didn't agree to that.'

'I didn't say 'no'. I kind of want to go.'

'But why?'

Kat tried to explain. 'I don't think you maybe realise quite how... empty I've been these last two years. I just work, eat, sleep and I've had absolutely no desire or energy for anything else. Lots of friends have nagged me to join things or go for dinner and stuff, but I just couldn't be bothered, couldn't see the point. Well this is the first thing that's really... got me a bit interested again. I feel like I've woken up from a coma. I'm noticing things around me more. I'm enjoying music more. Enjoying the garden more. It's like... it's like everything used to be grey and now it's gone back to colour. I dunno, I'm not explaining very well.'

'No, I do get that, I really do. And that's all really good. But don't you think it's a risk to go back there? You'd be really cut off. I've just remembered - you can only get up there by cable car! You'd be in some chalet, no way to escape, with a man you don't know.'

'But I do I know him a bit now. We've been talking quite a lot online.'

'It's not the same though. People can hide things, put on an act.' Ellie looked at her friend, taking in the determined set of her jaw and the new spark in her eyes. 'I think you've made up your mind haven't you? You're pretty determined to go, whatever I say!'

'Yes, I think I am.' Kat took a deep breath. 'Ellie, will you and Nigel come too? Please, please? I'd feel so much better if you two were there. It'd take all the pressure away, make it just a friends thing. And you both love skiing. Please? Plus, you know, the kids would feel so much happier about the whole thing if they knew you were both going too?'

Ellie considered things. It didn't feel right. But on the other hand she hadn't seen Kat looking so animated in a long time. She had one last go at dissuading her. 'I think you're absolutely bonkers. It's a stupid idea. You should meet up in London or somewhere first, before you commit to something like that.'

'Please Ellie. It's the first thing I've really looked forward to for ages. I feel like it's kind of important that I go. Like it's closing a circle. Will you come?'

Ellie sighed and stood up. 'OK, I'll think about it. I'll talk to Nigel.'

As if he'd heard his name, Nigel came back into the kitchen carrying handfuls of thyme and mint. The conversation turned to cooking again.

Most of the guests had left, but a few stragglers remained in the living room, chatting with Ellie. Nigel and Kat began to ferry the leftover food back to the kitchen.

'Nick!' called Nigel up the stairs. 'Come and give us a hand, will you?'

There was silence from upstairs.

'Typical. He's probably got his headphones on – or pretending he has. I'll go get him.'

'Oh, don't bother,' said Kat. 'It's his birthday after all. I'll help you clear up.'

Together they started to put the best of the leftovers into Tupperware boxes and throw out what was unsalvageable for composting.

'Hey, that goes in the recycling,' warned Nigel, as Kat was about to chuck out a cake box. 'We're into saving the planet in this house.'

'Sorry. It's got cream all over it. Can they recycle that?'

'I think so. Anyway, they sort through everything at the new recycling plant.'

'How do you know? Have you visited it?'

'Yeah, I have! You should go, it's really impressive. The building itself is really innovative, with a living wall – you know, made of plants. And inside it's just incredible.'

'I should do more really. I'm good with plastic bottles and tins and stuff, but not so good with paper.'

They chatted companionably about plastic pollution,

the oceans, going zero waste. Nigel was quite an evangelist on the subject, and often made Kat feel rather guilty. Her love of tidiness made her want her rubbish chucked out of sight as quickly as possible, not collected in a corner to take to the tip at some later date. Nigel, on the other hand, had a whole garage full of various piles and loved nothing more than hitching up the trailer for a trip to the tip.

After the food had been dispatched into plastic tubs – Nigel was vehemently anti clingfilm – they made a start on the dishes. Kat washed and Nigel dried.

'So, Ellie tells me you want us to go skiing with you.'

'God, that was quick! She told you already!'

'Just that. I don't know the details. Where is it?'

'A resort called Felsenalp. In Switzerland. An old university friend wants to rent a chalet there. Ellie and I went there when we were students. It's very small, but it's pretty.'

'How many runs does it have?'

'I can't remember exactly. Not many though. Maybe twelve?'

'And who's going to be there?'

'I'm not sure yet. This old friend Neil for definite. And probably another old Uni friend called Sean. Maybe a couple of others. Dates to be confirmed. What do you think?'

'Yeah, possibly, if the dates fit. I've not skied in Switzerland before. It might be fun. Tell me more about these old friends. What are they like?'

'Oh, I'm rubbish at describing people!'

'Hmm. Have a go. Let's say you had to describe this Sean in four adjectives. What would they be?'

'Oh! OK...um... tall, Irish....um... funny and... chatty.'

'He sounds OK. What about the other one, Neil, did you say?'

'That's more difficult.' Kat thought for a moment. 'Taciturn, guarded, brooding and....sexy!'

'God! He sounds bloody awful. Like bloody Heathcliffe or something. You're not selling it. I don't think I'd get on with him at all!'

'Actually, you are totally and completely the opposite of each other.'

'Ha! You mean I'm not sexy?' Nigel flicked the tea-towel at her.

Kat dodged the tea-towel, laughing. 'No-one is questioning your undoubted status as a sex-God. But in all other ways you're different.'

'Oh. So how would you describe me then?'

'You really want to know?'

'Yeah.'

'OK, let's see. Loud, open, enthusiastic and... Can't decide on the final one.'

'Try sexy again.'

Kat snorted with laughter, scooped up a handful of soap suds and blew them at him. 'I've seen you in your swimming trunks, don't forget! So anyway, I would so love it if you and Ellie could come.'

'Tell me the dates when you know them and we'll try.'

Kat felt a huge rush of relief. 'You are stars, both of you.' She reached for the next plate and plunged it into the water. 'When are you two finally going to get a dishwasher?'

'Yeah, I've been looking into that. I've resisted for years, but the new ones are pretty energy efficient. They're supposed to be better for the environment than hand-washing, as long as you do a full load.'

Conversation turned back to the environment as Nigel happily expounded on the relative impacts of hand-washing and dishwashing.

Late that evening, Nigel pushed the dog off the sofa and sat down heavily. 'Come and sit down for a bit Ellie. God, it's been a long day. Let's watch something on TV.' He flicked through the channels, but not finding anything of interest, gave up.

'Kat seemed on good form today,' he said. 'She was quite jokey earlier on.'

'Mmm.'

'What, don't you think so?'

Yeah, I do,' said Ellie, 'but I'm worried about this whole skiing thing. I never liked that guy Neil when we were at Uni. I thought he was a bad influence on her – you know, she started smoking, drinking, missing lectures…I wouldn't be surprised if they were taking drugs.'

'But isn't that what you're supposed to do when you're a student? Experiment a little?'

Yes, but… I don't know. I've just got a bad feeling about it.'

'Are you sure you're not a bit jealous?'

'Jealous? Why should I be jealous?'

'That Kat's got someone else coming into her life? That you might be losing your number one spot?'

'No! I'm not that insecure! If it was anyone but him I'd be delighted!'

'Well then, don't worry. We'll be there with her. We won't let anything bad happen. I'll sort the guy out if he starts shooting up in the bathroom.' Nigel yawned and stretched. 'So have you got any photos of this Felsenalp place? Did you have a camera back then?'

'Um, yeah, I should have some. Let me see.' Ellie started to rummage through the bookshelves behind the sofa, pulling out photo albums, flicking through and replacing them. Finally she held up a plastic-coated album, the pages falling out and the photos faded.

'This is the one,' she said, settling back onto the sofa and putting the album between them. 'That's me on the chairlift. That's the view from the top. You can see the glacier, look. And that's inside the chalet. There's Kat and that's Sean.'

'Who's that girl in the corner with the dark hair?'

Ellie peered at the photo, trying to place the slight figure with the cool expression at the edge of the picture. 'Umm, I can't remember her name now.'

'Is she going to be coming to this reunion thing?'

'God, I hope not. I didn't get on with her at all. She was a cold fish.'

8
Back then

Kat and Neil dumped their bags in the entrance and tried to brush off the snow clinging to their legs. Little puddles started to form on the concrete floor.

'I thought I'd be OK with these moon boots on, but this is crazy! It goes right up to your thighs! I've never seen so much snow!' Kat said. Neil was trying to get his Doc Martens off, but his fingers were too cold to deal with the iced up laces. They'd had to dig a little path to the chalet by kicking the snow away. Then do the same along the side of the chalet to locate the key, hanging from a nail under the low roof. One side of the building was almost completely covered by a drift.

'Yeah but think how good the skiing will be.'

'I'm nervous about that. I've never skied on real snow, I might be terrible at it.'

'You'll be OK. Everyone says it's a lot easier,' Neil reassured her. 'And it's nice and soft when you fall,' he added with a grin, 'as you have been sometimes known to do.'

Felsenalp was everything Kat had imagined on the long train journey. It could only be reached by a lengthy, spectacular cable car ride from the town in the valley below. Arriving at the end station was like stepping into a scene from a tourist brochure or a jigsaw. Too charming, too typical, too Swiss to be true. It was a very small village, with about sixty or so traditional wooden chalets and a couple of medium sized hotels. The car-free streets were slippery and blue-tinged with packed ice, and each chalet roof was insulated by at least a metre of snow. Long icicles hung from the gutters. All around loomed the jagged peaks of the Bernese Alps. It was quiet, a little old-fashioned, and meant to be perfect for beginners with mainly blue runs and just one black. For the more adventurous you could link up to the next village for a wider range of runs.

The chalet itself sat about a hundred metres from the centre of the village. It was small, unpretentious and very traditional. The bottom half of the chalet was made of uneven rough stones but the top half was constructed from wood, darkened over the years to a rich dark brown. A small balcony ran the length of the upper floor. It reminded Kat of a cuckoo clock with its carved wooden shutters and deeply overhanging triangle of roof. She half expected a little dancing figures to pop out of one window and waltz round to the next as the hour struck.

She took off her charity shop ski jacket and hung it on the nail next to Neil's and they both took in their new surroundings. The front door opened into a bare concrete room with racks on the walls to hang skis, and rough benches to sit on while putting on boots. A big boiler stood silent in one corner and logs were stacked neatly in another. They crossed this room and opened a small door, finding a narrow staircase leading to the first floor. Orange pine floor, walls and ceiling. The furniture was also pine, rustic and sturdy. Red and white checked curtains hung from the windows, one of which was completely blacked out with snow. A huge empty fireplace took up most of one wall, with a couple of old squashy sofas around it. There was a little kitchen in the corner, with a basic oven, sink and fridge. A rudimentary bathroom. Two more doors opened onto small single bedrooms with tiny windows and red and white checked duvets. Another staircase led upstairs to a big open dormitory style loft with four single beds against one wall and four against the opposite wall. Pillows, sheets and blankets were folded and piled on each bed. Everything smelt musty, as if the chalet hadn't been used in quite a while.

'It's quite basic isn't it?' said Kat, as they went back downstairs. 'I expected Silvio's folk to have something a bit grander.

Isn't his Dad a count?'

'Yeah, but I don't think they're loaded,' said Neil. 'I mean, they used to be, but I think they've had to sell off some of their land and paintings and stuff to keep the castle going. Anyway, Silvio wouldn't have invited us if it was really posh. Let's grab one of the downstairs bedrooms. I'll fetch our bags up.'

'Hang on. Don't you think we should wait for the others? It is Silvio's parents' place – he might have other ideas.'

'First come first served,' Neil replied, carelessly.

He ran down to fetch their bags, then, dumping them on the little bedroom floor, pulled Kat close and kissed her neck.

'We're all alone here. What shall we do to pass the time?' He backed her towards to bed but she pushed him away.

'Oh no you don't. We're here first so we should get things ready for the others. Build a fire, go to that little shop we passed and buy things like milk, eggs, cheese and stuff. Come on, let's find the wood pile.'

'Don't be boring. There's loads of time, the others won't be here for ages.' He put his hands on her hips and pulled her body close. 'It's just you and me. Live a little! You're freezing and you need warming up.'

Later, they lay gazing at each other on the single bed with the duvet wrapped tightly around them. He stroked her hair and she felt a rush of intense belonging.

'Tell me about your family,' she said. 'You never talk about them. '

Neil had been winding a lock or her hair around his fingers but now his hand froze. 'What do you want to know?'

'Just the usual, you know, brothers and sisters, parents.'

Neil paused for a long moment. Finally he spoke. 'I've got a younger brother, Gordon. He's a trainee mechanic in Edinburgh. We don't really get on so well now. Haven't seen him for ages. My dad was in the army so we moved around a lot when we were kids. We lived in Cyprus and Germany and Hong Kong. That was great. Loads of freedom to mess around. We got into all kinds of trouble. Then my dad was posted to Northern

Ireland. He was killed by a remote controlled bomb when he was out on patrol. I was eleven and Gordon was ten. After that everything was different. Mum got depression. She sent us off to a military boarding school. She thought that was best.'

'Oh God, I'm so sorry about your Dad.' Kat was overcome with compassion. This is why he never talks, she thought. He's had such a tough life, no wonder he keeps it all in. 'Was boarding school awful?'

'I loved it actually, I was well into all that running, shooting, climbing stuff.'

'Shooting? You mean real guns?'

'Yeah, they taught us how to shoot. They had a whole shooting range. And how to fly a plane. And to march. We had a proper parade uniform. Kilts and jackets. Church on Sunday. You either learnt to play the pipes or the drums. Most people at school went on to join up.'

'Why didn't you?'

'I thought about it. I fancied doing something like military intelligence for a while.'

'You mean like spying? You'd make a good spy. You're very hard to read and you keep disappearing.'

'Do I? Well you've got me now for a whole ten days. I'm not going to disappear. Anyway, what about your family? What are they like?'

'Oh, super normal. There's my mum, my dad, and one brother, one sister. We all get on OK, and we never argue. We're always very nice to each other. A bit like The Waltons but less numerous.'

'That's not normal, that's weird. Arguing is a fact of life. Don't you ever disagree?'

'Oh yes, but you have to read the signs. A look. A silence. A sigh. Nothing is ever put into words. We sing round the piano at Christmas and invite the neighbours for dinner parties. Mum went through the roof when I got my ears pierced – of course she didn't say anything, she just didn't speak to me for a week.'

'Would they like me, do you think?'

Kat paused, wondering how to be truthful without causing hurt. 'I think they always imagined me with a nice, polite boy who is parent-friendly, has good prospects and short hair. So… you'd come as a bit of a shock I think.'

'Did they like Kevin?'

'They certainly didn't like his motorbike – that was another huge silent battle. But they never really took him very seriously. We were together for over three years but they always thought I'd meet someone more 'suitable' at university. Mum used to say 'Play the field! There's no hurry!' Kat pursed her lips, remembering how angry this used to make her. 'What about your mum? Would she like me?'

'She would totally love you. She'd think you're much too good for me.'

'That's because I am,' said Kat, planting a kiss on his nose to show she was joking. 'Come on, let's build that fire now.'

❖ ❖ ❖

The rest of the party arrived later that evening. Silvio showed them round with a proprietorial air, telling them to be careful with the few ornaments and not to use the good plates in the kitchen. He went down to get the boiler started and the little chalet gradually started to warm up. When everyone had nosed around and claimed a bed, they all set off again through the snow to a restaurant that Silvio said did a reasonable fondue.

Kat and Ellie brought up the rear, arm in arm, walking slowly so they could gossip.

'So who's this Gillian girl? What does she do?' Silvio and Sean had driven most of the way here with the mysterious Gillian - a small, slim, dark-haired girl with sharp features, eyes permanently narrowed as if puzzling out some great mystery. She had an air of total self-possession, and addressed all her comments to the boys without really acknowledging any of the girls. Kat took an instant dislike to her.

'I think she does Politics and Economics, same as Sean. They can't be great friends though cos I've never seen her with him before. She's a bit stand-offish isn't she?'

'Yeah, she's a bit full of herself.' They both gazed down the road and considered Gillian, who was walking between Neil and Silvio. She'd linked her arm through Neil's on the pretext of having unsuitable boots. 'Let's hope she's totally crap at skiing.' They giggled. 'We're a really mixed bag of people though aren't we?' Ellie continued. 'Silvio is like some Italian aristocrat or something and Rob and Sue are pure 'cor-blimey-mate'!'

'Bleedin' 'ell, they got shooters!'

'Wipe yer plates and let's 'ave a cup o' Rosie'

Kat snorted with laughter. She liked Rob and Sue. They were Home Economics students who lived on the same floor as Ellie on campus. They were both Londoners, laid back and cheerful. Sue's parents ran a pub in the East End, where Sue had worked a few shifts as a teenager. As a result of fending off drunken advances, she was unflappable and had a good line in repartee. Rob was quieter, with a baby face and curly fair hair. He was the son of a jeweller, who ran the type of old fashioned shop where you could repair watches and reset stones in rings. He'd been initially expected to follow into the family business, but his father advised him against it, saying it was becoming too dangerous an occupation these days. Instead, Rob planned to open a gastro-pub with Sue when they got their degrees. Both had learnt to ski on school trips, to Kat's amazement. How come comprehensive school kids got the best school trips? she wondered.

'How do you think everyone will get on?' Ellie continued.

'Well Rob and Sue have said they'll do most of the cooking so that went down brilliantly! No, seriously, it's a godsend – Sean's been threatening to cook his Irish stuff which is basically a mush of potatoes, carrots and cabbage that stinks the place out. They're really chilled. I think they'll get on great with everyone. And Silvio's not so bad when you get to know him. He's actually quite kind.'

'If you say so. Can't see it myself. Well, we'll have to get on. The chalet is pretty small and we'll all be squashed together on the sofas in the evening – we won't be able to get away from anyone we don't like.'

Kat watched Neil hold open the restaurant door for Gillian to walk through. A shudder of unease passed through her and she pulled her scarf tighter.

'Come on, I'm starving. Let's go practice our German on the waiters.' They hurried to catch up with the others, catching the door before it closed.

The warmth and the smell of bubbling gruyere hit them instantly. The little restaurant was very traditional. The panelled walls were decorated with pitchforks and other farming implements. Cow bells hung from the low, exposed beams. The chunky tables were partly covered with red and white checked tablecloths. Giant pepper pots stood on each one, and the chairs had little hearts carved into their backs. They found a table for eight and stripped off their jackets. Ellie and Kat, being last to arrive, found themselves at the end of the table, next to Rob and Sue. That left Gillian at the other end of the table, exactly where she undoubtedly wanted to be, surrounded by the three other men.

After a short discussion, Ellie ordered fondue and a couple of bottles of crisp, dry white wine, happily engaging the waitress in conversation about the different cheeses used. When the waitress returned with two fondue burners, one for each end of the table, Kat felt irritated. That means there will be a nice cosy group of four at the far end, huddled around their burner, with their backs to us, she thought, sourly. She gave herself a little shake. Never mind. Our fault for being last to get here.

As Ellie chatted to Rob and Sue about the long train journey, Kat sat back in her chair and contemplated Gillian. It was rare for her to take a dislike to someone. Often she didn't get on with people, but she usually blamed herself, thinking it was her fault for being socially awkward. Gillian reminded her of the posh girls from her school days. She looked groomed, with her sleek dark hair and fine-boned features, as if she would be more at home sipping Pimms at a polo match. Although she was small, she was delicately built, with long slim fingers and a tiny waist. She was dressed in jeans, ankle boots and a crisp white cotton shirt, which had somehow survived the journey without a crease. But above all, it was her posture that intrigued Kat. She held herself very upright on her chair. Each movement seemed to be considered, measured, controlled. Kat watched as she tilted her head and frowned slightly, before spearing a piece of bread with her fondue fork. She watched her turn to Sean with a narrowed-eyed look. She seemed to pause before she spoke, as if weighing each word for maximum effect. She reminded Kat of a bird of prey, sitting imperiously on a high perch, surveying its surroundings with tiny precise head movements. Alert, sharp-eyed. Ready to pounce. 'These are my three men,' thought Kat. 'Get your claws off them!'

She gave a mental shrug and turned back to her attention back to her end of the table. She took a long gulp of the deliciously sharp wine and leant forward to spear a piece of bread. Stop being paranoid! They were in Switzerland! This was going to be great!

9

'What about this one?' said Kat, holding up a royal blue all in one ski suit.

'I'd rather have a jacket and trousers,' replied Ellie. 'So much easier when you need a pee. There's not much choice in my size though.'

They had gone to the big out of town retail park in search of bargain ski wear. Kat found what she wanted quickly but Ellie was struggling.

'Why do they think everyone is a stick? It's so demoralising. The average British woman is size 16, so God knows who they expect to sell all this stuff to.'

Ellie had changed a lot over the years. When they first met she had been as slim as a boy, a little stick figure with an out-of-proportion mass of curls. Married life, contentment and a fondness for savoury snacks had added several stone, and she now dressed to disguise the weight gain rather than follow fashions.

'What did you wear last time you went skiing? It wasn't that long ago was it?'

'It was three years ago but I've put on weight since then. I tried it on yesterday and Nigel starting laughing.'

'Oh that's mean. It's not as if he's exactly a Slim Jim himself. What about snowboarder style stuff, that's generally baggy and it's really trendy.'

They continued looking along the aisles until Ellie at last found a parka style jacket with fur hood in her size. 'This'll do. Come with me to the changing rooms?'

'OK.'

Kat sat on the little bench outside the cubicle and listened to Ellie struggling with zips and swearing. She finally pulled back the curtain with a flourish, struck up a pose and gave a defiant 'ta da!' Kat couldn't keep her face straight. The sludgy khaki was not flattering.

'It looks lovely and warm,' she managed to get out at last in a strangled voice.

'It's horrendous isn't it? I look like a giant turd. I've had enough, let's go get a coffee somewhere.'

Half an hour later they were sitting on hard plastic chairs around a small table in the big open-plan food and drink area. Kat stowed her bulky bags under the table and massaged her fingers where the string had dug into them.

'I hate shopping,' said Ellie. 'I knew this would be a disaster. I should have looked for stuff online.'

'Yeah, but you can't always tell how things will fit, or if they're warm enough. You just need a coffee break, then we'll have another bash. We're not leaving here till you've got something you really like.'

'You mean something that *you* like. I am really past caring,' said Ellie. She took a sip of her coffee. 'Nigel's booked our flights by the way, the ones we looked at on Monday.'

'Oh great! Did he go for the Bern ones or Geneva?'

'Bern. And he's booked a hire car to take us up the valley. It seems a bit of a waste to me, when we have to leave the car at the bottom of the cable car for a whole week, but it worked out cheaper than the train. So where are we staying? Not Silvio's parents' place again I hope? Unless it's had a massive makeover? It was a bit shabby really.'

'God no! Neil's booked a really smart chalet. It looks ultra-modern inside. I'll show you, I've got it on my phone.

Kat found the site and flicked through the photos of the chalet so Ellie could see. No more oppressive orange pine – these wooden walls were pale gold, the ceilings high and beamed. Everything looked immaculate and fresh. Huge flower displays on the tables. Tasteful art on the walls. The bedrooms shared elegant grey-tiled bathrooms and the views from the enormous balcony looked stunning.

Ellie was astonished. She and Nigel had hired some beautiful chalets in the past, but this was in a different league. She wasn't looking forward to the trip, and was only going to provide moral support and maybe protection for her friend, but she was definitely going to enjoy staying here. But it also made her strangely uneasy. She knew the cost of a place like this would run into several thousands.

'Wow! That does look nice. Very nice. How the hell can he afford it? Is he a millionaire or something now?'

'I don't think so.'

'What did you say he does for a living?'

'Something about writing reports for drug companies.'

'Hmm. Are you sure he's not a drug dealer? Drug baron maybe? This must have cost a bloody fortune!'

'I know,' Kat laughed happily, not realising that Ellie was half serious. 'He is splashing the cash. He won't let us pay for anything. He must really want this trip to work out.'

But why? thought Ellie. Why is it so damned important to him? What's on his agenda? She changed the subject.

'So who's all coming in the end?'

'Neil, you, me, Nigel, Sean and Matt.'

'Who's Matt? I thought Neil was trying to get the old gang together, not find new people'.

'Matt is Sean's husband.'

'*Husband*? Sean's gay? Really? Well, well, well! We never knew! Ah, bless him!'

'Yeah, I know! We were so naïve, we didn't think. I hadn't met many gay people back then. Or I suppose people used to hide it more. I can see it now. All the girls used to fancy him and he never seemed to react.'

'I know. What was the name of that awful girl who came skiing with us? The snotty one? I was trying to remember the other day. She was in a photo I showed Nigel. She was really making a play for him the whole time. It's quite funny in hindsight. She was knocking herself out for nothing.'

'Gillian. Yeah, she was quite tenacious.' Kat's face darkened as she remembered the sleek, sly girl with the posh accent. A picture flashed into her mind: Gillian leaning against an orange pine wall, smirking. She changed the subject quickly. 'Why don't we go to T.K. Maxx next. They're bound to have something there.'

But Ellie was still thinking about the holiday. 'What about Silvio, is he not coming?' she asked, crossing her fingers discretely under the table. She remembered finding him arrogant and dismissive, although he'd been an excellent ski guide and an unpaid instructor.

'No, Neil's been trying to find him on social media but he seems to have disappeared off the face of the earth.'

'Well thank heavens for that! He was a total arsehole if you ask me. So there's just the six of us? This might turn out to be OK, I suppose.'

'Hah. You don't have to sound so enthusiastic. Is Nigel looking forward to it?'

'Oh yes! You know what he's like before a holiday, he goes completely overboard. He's bought maps of the region, a new backpack, avalanche kit, energy bars, survival blanket, fold-up knife and fork set – he's ready for an arctic expedition!'

'Go gadget man! Will he have room for any clothes though?' Kat joked. 'But seriously though, what about the skiing? It's a really small resort, there's only a dozen or so runs, if you remember. Is he not going to get a bit frustrated?'

'Not at all. We're all getting older – even Nigel. Gone are the days when we could ski all day. It'll suit him just fine. We'll ski in the morning, then sit on a terrace with a glass of wine - or in the chalet with a good book. Sit round the fire in the evening...' She broke off suddenly, as a memory stirred.

'Yeah that sounds so good. Come on, drink up and let's go back to the shops. You won't be going anywhere if we don't find a ski suit.' Kat picked up her bags and jumped to her feet.

Ellie followed, reluctantly, still thinking about her last

remark. 'Sitting round the fire in the evening' she'd said. That's what they had all done before. Talking about murder. Was that normal?

10
Back then

The first couple of days were fantastic. The weather was cold and clear, the sun making the snow sparkle as if covered in little shards of glass. The snow on the slopes was deep and soft without being slushy. The other skiers were mostly Swiss families, polite and careful. Silvio explained that this was why his parents had bought a chalet here: there were no kamikaze Brits haring down the slopes screaming, or Americans in loud outfits saying how 'awesome' everything was, or snooty Frenchmen pushing to the front of the queue. In fact there were hardly any queues at all. Some of the ski lifts were a little old and creaky, but you could often ski straight onto them. The village was intimate, the shops and restaurants were reasonably priced, and best of all, you could ski right back to your door.

Getting kitted out in the ski hire shop was a long, frustrating business, with boots being tried on and rejected, everyone trying to convert their weight into kilos, discussions about what made a beginner or an intermediate level skier. Kat and Ellie translated as best they could to the harried assistant. Eventually they all hit the slopes. Gillian, Rob and Sue headed off straight for the chair lift to take them to the top of the longest blue run, skis over their shoulders and anchored with one hand, poles in the other, boots flapping undone. Kat and Ellie watched them stride off with a mixture of envy and admiration. Annoyingly it seemed that Gillian was a very good skier. 'Hope she breaks a leg' thought Kat, unkindly.

Silvio took the others to the nursery slope, where he spent the morning showing Sean how to snow-plough, turn and stop. He was a generous teacher, very patient and genuinely keen to see his housemate able to ski with the rest of the group. Sean was picking things up well, in spite of his spindly arms and legs and high centre of gravity. He was not at all embarrassed to be learning with four and five year old kids. In fact he had gathered quite a fan club of little skiers who clustered around him, amazed to see this giant in the funny clown hat who couldn't ski as well as they could.

Meanwhile, Neil, Kat and Ellie went down the short nursery slope a dozen times to get used to the snow, at first tentatively, then picking up a bit of speed. Kat did in fact find it easier to control her skis than on the dry slope. She would have happily spent all week there, but was persuaded to try a blue run. At first she was terrified by the chairlift, swinging round to wallop her behind the knees and swaying jerkily skywards. She was even more terrified at the thought of getting off the lift at the top. Neil and Ellie sat either side of her, lifting the bar at the last minute, encouraging her to edge forward in her seat and promising to hold her upright when they touched the ground. Of course she fell, but at least she didn't cause a pile-up. The view from the top was magnificent. They edged close to the fence and took in the sight. Jagged white peaks in every direction. Lower down, forests that looked black against the snow. And right below them, the glacier. Huge and white and flat, but looking as if someone had pushed it together like a concertina, the snow wrinkling into rounded corrugations. It was breathtaking. And the run was actually OK. It started off as a path, difficult to negotiate being so narrow. Kat was relieved there was strong netting in place to stop skiers plummeting to the glacier below. Once she got her ski caught in the netting and fell, Neil and Ellie laughing as they tried to disentangle her. Then the run opened up into a wide, gentle expanse of deep, smooth snow. Ellie went first, making slow and careful turns. Kat followed, trying to turn in exactly the same places and sometimes succeeding, sometimes coming to a stop. Neil brought up the rear, lifting her up when she fell and collecting runaway skis. Gradually Kat started to get the hang of it. By the time they reached the lower slopes, winding through the trees towards the village, she was no longer falling.

'Wow, wow, wow!' she said, exhilarated. 'That was amazing!'

'Want to do it again?'

'Yes!'

◆ ◆ ◆

By the second day, the group had split into two parties. Sean was able to join them on the blue run. Not being the worst one there gave Kat the extra confidence to push herself a little harder, go a little faster. She started to really enjoy herself. Meanwhile Silvio joined the others, the more advanced skiers, showing them off-piste tracks through the trees, guiding them over little jumps and shepherding them down the steep black run.

When they returned to the chalet at the end of the day they all were glowing with pride and good health, recounting their falls, near misses and successes as they pulled off their boots, lined up their skis in the racks and applied after-sun to their pink cheeks and noses. Silvio looked on indulgently with a little ironic smile as they twittered on. He was the king of this particular castle, and that was just the way he liked it.

After dinner on the second night of skiing they sat around the fire drinking wine and talking. There were not enough seats and Ellie noticed how Gillian positioned herself on the floor, between Neil and Sean, with one arm resting lightly on the sofa as she looked from one to the other. She glanced at Kat and saw that she was staring at Gillian too. The three of them were talking about Thatcher's politics, privatisation and enterprise culture. Gillian was putting up a very good fight as the only Conservative voter amongst the group. She made her points clearly, with a ready supply of numbers to back them up, which was in sharp contrast to Neil's 'Don't talk bollocks, man!' and Sean's 'You actually voted for that gobshite?'

'Tax and spend didn't work did it?' Gillian was saying now. 'Look at the state the economy was in under Labour! You've got to motivate people to succeed, to build businesses and to spend the money they earn. It shouldn't be seen as a bad thing to make money. Aspiration is not a dirty word!'

'Bollocks. You've got to look after the weakest in society, not the rich. The gap is getting bigger and bigger. What about fairness? Equal opportunities?'

'If the rich get richer it benefits everyone. They spend money, create jobs. A strong economy is good for all of us.'

'That's crap - it only works if you live in the south. Have you ever been to Glasgow? We're talking real poverty there... And what about the super-rich that hide all their money abroad?'

So the argument continued. Kat and Ellie had both grown up in mining communities, and had witnessed real suffering in their northern hometowns as pit after pit was threatened with closure. Ellie's dad was worried that his colliery was on the hit list. He hated Thatcher with a passion and was prepared to strike if necessary. What Gillian was saying was anathema to them, but even so they had to admire her tenacity in the face of opposition. She was holding her own easily. Eventually Ellie couldn't take it anymore. She pulled Kat off the sofa and said, 'Enough politics. We're on holiday folks. Who wants to play Trivial Pursuit?' But it was Rob and Sue who jumped up to fetch the board game. They set it up on the pine table, leaving the others to continue their argument about trickle-down economics.

Later that night, sitting on the single bed, taking her socks off, Kat asked Neil: 'Do you like Gillian?'

He shrugged. 'Yeah, she's OK.'

'Really? She gets on my nerves. She hasn't said a word to me or Ellie all holiday so far. She only hangs out with the men.

Doesn't her politics annoy you?'

'I don't agree with it, but it doesn't bother me. She's probably just a product of her upbringing. Typical Surrey girl. It's fun arguing though.'

'Mm. She's always looking at you. I think she fancies you.'

'No, you've got that all wrong. It's Sean she's got her eye on. She kept touching his knee all night.'

'Did she? I didn't see that. Does he like her do you think?'

'To be honest I don't think he even noticed. Don't worry, there won't be any bed hopping tonight. Now hurry up and get in here. I'm freezing my bollocks off.'

11

Nigel steered the car into a space in the free car park, pulled on the handbrake and sat back with a sigh. He loved driving, but he didn't like this hire car at all, and was glad to be seeing the back of it for a fortnight. Next to him, Ellie woke up with a start.

'Are we here already?' she asked.

'Yep, just arrived.' said Kat from the back seat. 'There doesn't seem to be much snow though,' she added, wiping the condensation from the window and looking up at the mountains.

'That's global warming for you,' said Nigel. He had studied Geology at university and was an expert on geo-morphology - the creation of mountains, valleys, volcanos and other landscape features. 'They say the glacier up there has receded by a thousand metres.'

Kat found this deeply depressing. She remembered the abundance of snow thirty odd years ago, and how huge the glacier had seemed as it snaked along the valley floor. How could anything that massive be destroyed by man? She hoped this wasn't a bad omen. They pulled their bags out of the boot and set off towards the centre of town.

The six of them had agreed to meet up in a bar before getting the cable car up the mountain. Kat's stomach was churning. All those emails and Skype sessions didn't seem to make a difference, she was wretched with nerves. What would it be like seeing him again? Would they shake hands? Hug? Would she feel anything? And if she did, was it disloyal to Peter? What on earth would Peter think if he was here now? He'd be horrified. In the

MacMillan hospice, when he knew there was no hope for him, he had urged her to move on, not to stay sad for ever, to meet someone new – but not like this. Not with the person who'd hurt her so much in the past.

She had been honest with Peter about the Neil episode. When they'd first started going out she'd felt it necessary to tell him about her past: that she'd been in love with someone who turned out to be a shit. She'd explained that she'd built up a shell of detachment to avoid being hurt again, and had developed a reputation as cold and aloof. Frigid even. She warned him that she still found it really difficult to let herself become dependent on someone else.

Kind, generous, patient Peter had not been put off. He gave her space when she needed it and, little by little, managed to break down the wall. After two years of dating she had been secure enough to say yes when he proposed. The wedding had been happy, if chaotic. Ellie, chief bridesmaid, had turned up late – she'd followed a group of cars and ended up at the wrong wedding, sipping champagne with the wrong mother-in-law. Kat had roared with laughter when Ellie eventually pulled up outside the church and ran across the churchyard to her side – it was so typical. Ellie had also brought her new man, Nigel, as her plus-one. As he strolled more slowly towards them, she confided to Kat that this one might be a keeper.

Marrying Peter had also meant gaining a large and affectionate new set of in-laws, teasing, jokey and tactile. Kat loved them almost as much as she loved her new husband. Gradually she succumbed to the warmth that encircled her, and discarded her shell of cynicism. Two children followed, the first with a potential pregnancy scare of spina bifida that turned out to be a false alarm. A beautiful, intelligent, thoughtful little boy. Then a girl, a bouncy, joyful bundle of fun. Peter had been a fantastic father, often sacrificing career kudos for the sake of being home in time for the children's' bedtime. Throughout the ups and downs of parenthood, house moves, career highs and lows, Peter had been her rock, solid, open, big-hearted and loving.

And now she was going to meet Neil, her first real love, as different as it was possible to be. For a moment she wished she was back at home, surrounded by familiar objects, anywhere but here. She held back a little, then stopped on the pavement, unwilling to go on. Ellie turned round, dumped her bag and came back to take her arm. 'Come on,' she said, 'You can't wimp out now! Don't overthink things so much, just let go and see what happens. It's probably just a couple of weeks of skiing with old friends, nothing more.'

Minutes later they pushed open the door of the brasserie they'd researched on TripAdvisor. Leaving their cases behind the large reception desk, they went through to the bar area. It had a warm and welcoming atmosphere. The walls were wood panelled and the tables were set discretely into alcoves with padded corner seats in gold coloured plush. Kat saw Sean immediately, sitting at a round table in the far corner, and felt a rush of affection. He hadn't changed that much. He still had his untidy hair, now grey, and prominent ears. The same goofy smile and eccentric dress sense. He stood up and hurried towards them, arms wide open. Kat hugged him tightly, her nose pressed up against his bright orange polo-neck.

'It's so good to see you again,' she said.

'I know, it's mad isn't it? You haven't changed a bit. I'd know you anywhere!' he replied.

Sean gave Ellie a big hug, shook hands with Nigel, then led them back to the table.

'This is my husband, Matt,' he said with evident pride.

Ellie and Kat had been speculating about Matt on the flight, trying to guess what he would be like. He was not at all what they expected. He was of small, compact build with a shaven head which showed off his deep tan. Most surprisingly, he was a vision of elegance! His pale blue sweater looked like cashmere and a cream silk scarf hung from the back of his chair. When he stood up they noticed the impeccable cut of his jeans. But the deep laughter lines around his eyes and mouth gave an indication of what had brought these two unlikely-looking men together.

Introductions made, they sat around the table with mugs of beer exchanging news, trying to catch up on the missing years. The talk flowed naturally and Kat relaxed into her seat. She explained briefly about Peter, giving the bare bones and keeping her voice unemotional. Ellie talked a bit too long about her charity work – she was rightly proud of it, but 'she does go on a bit' thought Kat, fondly. Smartphones were brought out to show photos of the children.

Sean and Matt were both accountants and had met in the same London accountancy firm ten years before. Sean said that telling his Irish Catholic parents he was gay was the hardest thing he'd ever done. He'd put it off for years, claiming that Matt was just a flat-mate, or asking him to leave the flat whenever his parents came to visit. It had taken him a long time to realise he had the right to pursue his own happiness. His parents were still trying to come round to the idea of their marriage. They came to visit them in London fairly regularly, tried desperately hard to say all the right things to Matt, but they'd asked the pair of them not to return to their small Irish town, for fear of the gossip, and Sean had refused to visit his hometown without his husband. It was an unresolved dilemma, and obviously still a source of sadness for them both.

'What about your parents?' Nigel asked Matt.

'Oh they're totally fine with it – very liberal. They kept pushing us for years to adopt – ugh!' He gave a rather camp shiver. 'Other peoples' children are bad enough, why on earth would we want one of our own?' He paused. 'Ah!' He clapped his hand over his mouth theatrically and added as an afterthought: 'Of course I'm sure your children are all perfectly delightful!'

Over a second beer the chatted easily about houses and travels. Nigel was telling a convoluted story about a disastrous holiday he and Ellie had had in Ireland the year before – delayed flights, a car breakdown and a leaking roof in the holiday cottage. Kat had almost forgotten about Neil when she looked over Nigel's shoulder and saw him standing in the entrance. She suddenly felt intensely aware of her own body – her heartbeat, her hot face. Her beer glass felt too weighty in her hand and she put it down heavily on the table. He still looked so good. His hair was still slightly too long, receding and peppered with grey, but his features were even more pronounced than before. The same high cheekbones, the long nose, the slightly hooded blue eyes. He stood tall and straight. His shoulders had broadened and he'd lost the youthful slouch. He scanned the room, an impatient frown drawing his eyebrows together. She took in his black jeans, his cotton sweater, his expensive-looking black ski jacket. She tried to read his face. He looked assured, confident, maybe a touch arrogant. That was something new and unexpected. He's changed so much, she thought. Of course he's changed. What did she expect? It's been over thirty years. Her doubts intensified. He might as well be a total stranger. Suddenly Neil's expression softened as he spotted them. He came over to where they were sitting with a broad smile. Kat exhaled, unaware that she'd been holding her breath. He gave Sean a huge hug, slapping him on the back, shook hands with Nigel and Matt, gave Ellie a kiss on both cheeks. Then he looked straight at Kat. She found she couldn't speak.

'Hello Kat,' he said.

Neither seemed to know how to react. They stared at each other awkwardly, until Neil eventually leant forward to kiss her cheek. As they sat down again, Kat was aware of Ellie giving her a thoughtful look.

Sean broke the silence. 'So do we want another beer here or shall we go and take the cable car now?'

12
Back then

The weather changed the next day. The sky was yellowy grey in the morning, and by breakfast time the snow was coming down in enormous flakes. They waited a couple of hours to see if it would stop, but by lunchtime there was no change. Silvio, Rob, Sue and Gillian wrapped themselves up, put on goggles and set off down to the lifts, their bodies quickly disappearing into the curtain of white. Sean and Ellie decided to stay in the chalet. They planned to build a couple of snow walls outside so everyone could have a giant boys versus girls snowball fight later.

That left Kat and Neil. 'Come on,' he said. 'We know that blue run off by heart by now, even if it's chucking it down we can't go wrong with that one.'

They pulled on their gear and trudged through the fresh snow towards the chair lift. It was still running but there were no other skiers to be seen, either waiting for the lift or coming down the run. The silence was disconcerting. They snapped their skis on and pushed themselves into position to take the next chair, wiping inches of snow from the seat. Once they'd pulled the bar down over their knees, Neil took off a glove and fished for his cigarettes in his inside pocket. He offered one to Kat and lit it, their heads close together as he cupped the flame protectively with his gloved hand. They smoked together in silence as the lift creaked and shuddered its way up the mountain.

Then it stopped. They were used to this – it happened each time someone fell at the top or bottom, and usually started up again after a minute or two. But this time it didn't start again. They sat there, swaying slightly in the wind as the snow swirled around them.

'Must be mechanical problem, it'll start again soon,' said Neil. But after five long minutes they were still stuck.

'I spy with my little eye something beginning with S.'

'Snow.'

'Yep, your turn.'

'I spy with my little eye something beginning with M S.'

'More snow.'

'Yep.'

They gave up the game and returned to their silent thoughts. Five more minutes passed. Kat listened to the rather worrying creak of the metal seat as it swayed backwards and forwards in the breeze.

'This would be a great place to murder someone,' said Neil, out of the blue.

'*What?* We're hanging twenty foot in the air in this rickety old seat and you come out with that? Is that supposed to make me feel better?'

'No, I was just thinking, you could make a brilliant thriller set here. You know, there are so many ways you could kill someone in a ski resort. Imagine, like now for example. The lift starts off again, you can't see anything, then at the top you see a figure emerging through the mist, holding a gun, the lift continues inevitably towards him...'

Kat caught on with the game. 'No, not a gun, an ice pick! And as the lift comes in he raises it slowly. You can just make him out, you get closer and closer, there's no escape, then...'

'Yeah. Splat. What about that poor guy at the top of this chairlift, for example, he must get so bored on a day like this. There's no one here. He's like John Tracy in Thunderbird 5 – he never gets any real action.' Thunderbirds was Neil's favourite TV show. Kat smiled at the comparison, although she couldn't for the life of her remember there having been a John in the Tracey family. 'Imagine he's gone mad with boredom and starts a murderous rampage.'

'Or you arrive at the top of the slope, there's no-one around. He comes through the fog towards you and pushes you over that fence and you go crashing down onto the rocks.'

'Nice one! Or you fall into a crevasse in the glacier, never to be found for a hundred years, when the glacier melts back.' Neil seemed delighted with this idea. He looked at the snow which was beginning to build up on the fir trees, weighing down their branches and making them bend towards the ground. 'I wonder if you could start an avalanche on purpose? You could wipe out a whole bunch that way!'

'Yeah, but it would be very hit-and-miss. You'd probably kill the wrong people. What if you tampered with the chair-lift so that it tipped up and the victim ends up dangling upside down from it, trying desperately to hang on.'

'Or you could sabotage someone's ski boots, loosening the screws on the flaps so they come open when the victim's skiing down a really steep bit.'

They spent the next few minutes thinking up all the horrific ways someone could die on the slopes before at last, with a jerk, the lift started up again. As they continued to the top of the slope, Kat replayed their conversation in her mind, finding it a bit odd that the subject and object has subtly changed places. How had they started out wondering how a theoretical murderer would act, and ended up discussing how they themselves would commit a murder?

At the top of the mountain, all was white silence. Skiing through the snow was completely different. The visibility was limited and Kat stuck as closely to Neil's back as possible. She only recognised small parts of the run, and couldn't trust herself to get any speed up. Her goggles steamed up constantly and her face was frozen. But when they made it to the end of the run with no major falls she was again filled with pride. 'I've got the bug,' she thought as they skied down the street right to the door of the chalet.

13

'Has anyone got a phone signal?' asked Matt, with a worried frown.

They had just arrived and were all tired from lugging their cases the two hundred or so metres uphill to the chalet. The snow was patchy and lumpy underfoot, making it hard going even with wheeled cases. It seemed like a stunning place though. Set in an elevated position overlooking the village, it was built on three levels. The ground floor consisted of a massive boot and ski room, and also a boiler room with a washing machine and a space for drying wet clothes. Wooden steps led up the side of the chalet to the main entrance. The huge living space was open plan, the walls and high ceilings covered in traditional pale pine. In the middle of the space was a stone chimney breast, in front of which stood a Scandinavian style wood burner. A basket of logs sat next to it, with more logs stacked neatly in a lean-to outside. The leather sofas were piled high with cushions and sheepskins. The kitchen area was ultramodern with gleaming white units and granite worksurfaces. A massive oak table stood in the dining area with a bottle of wine and a basket full of traditional biscuits and cakes set on it as a welcome gift. Folding glass doors lead to a large balcony overlooking the village and the peaks beyond. Upstairs, the bedrooms were simply decorated: pine walls, big windows, crisp white bedding and fur throws.

'This must have cost a small fortune,' thought Kat. Neil had insisted on paying for the two weeks in the chalet himself. 'How long has he been saving up for this?'

They stood together now in front of the glass doors in the living area, watching the setting sun slowly turn the snow from pink to indigo on the mountains.

'I don't have a signal.'

'Nor me.'

'Oh great! What a good start!' Matt complained. 'At least there's supposed to be Wi-Fi. I'll see if I can find the code.' He went off to search in the drawers and cupboards.

'I don't remember the mountains being so beautiful,' said Kat. 'You can see everything so clearly.'

'Well, we never had a view like this last time. We were much lower down. And most of the week you couldn't see a damn thing for all the snow,' said Ellie. 'Let's go out onto the balcony.'

She opened the glass doors and they stepped onto the wooden decking, leaning out over the railings.

The peaks were losing the last of their red glow as the sky darkened. They looked down at the village, where the lights were starting to come on in the chalets and a few late skiers were still making their way home. The village didn't seem to have changed much. They had noticed a second little supermarket on their way, and the two ski lifts they had passed seemed brand new. There was much less snow though, and a few patches of grass and rock stood out at the bottom of the runs.

Neil lit a cigarette and offered the one to Kat. 'No, I gave up years ago!' she said. 'When I got pregnant. You should really give up too, you know. Have you tried the E-cig?'

'I did try but it's such a pain to charge it up all the time. If you run out of charge you end up just buying a packet of fags again.' He took a deep drag, hollowing his cheeks as he inhaled, and Kat gasped, instantly felled by the familiarity of this gesture. He might have changed a bit physically, but here he was, screwing up his eyes against the smoke, just the same. She wondered if he still blew smoke rings.

'Ooh, hooray, another smoker,' said Matt from behind

them, as he joined them on the balcony. Neil offered his pack of Marlboroughs, but Matt preferred his own brand. He lit one with a heavy silver lighter. 'Guess what,' he said. 'The Wi-Fi signal is so poor it keeps cutting out. I thought this place was supposed to be high end! A decent Wi-Fi is a must these days. We are officially unconnected! Out of touch! There's no *way* I can survive two weeks of this I'm afraid!'

Neil's face darkened, annoyed that his beautiful chalet was being criticized so soon. He ground his cigarette angrily into the wooden flooring, then immediately lit another.

Sean noticed Neil's frown and tried to smooth things over: 'Come on! It might be good for us!' he encouraged, 'Like a digital detox! It's just what we need. Especially you, Matt. You're always on that bloody phone of yours. Let's have a two week ban on electronic gadgets. Think of the benefits: less eye strain, better sleep, more concentration... We can have proper talks instead.'

Ellie agreed. 'I think it'll be wonderful. No depressing news, no Facebook alerts about housework.'

'What? Your friends write posts about housework?' asked Matt, horrified. 'What kind of friends do you have?'

'Very annoying old schoolfriends mostly – how am I going to survive a week not knowing the size of Helen's ironing pile?' She paused, looking now a bit concerned. 'But actually I don't want to be out of contact with the children for two weeks. Not that they'd worry at all...'

'Me neither,' said Kat. 'I promised I'd send them both a photo every other day or so just to let them know I'm OK.' Her two children had insisted on this, still not at ease with their mother meeting up with 'some random guy'.

'I've got an idea,' said Nigel. 'Why don't we have breakfast in a different hotel or restaurant every day? They're bound to have free Wi-Fi and we can all use theirs to check our emails and stuff, and then the rest of the day we can do a total detox.'

'Sounds like a plan.'

Matt and Neil stubbed out their cigarettes and everyone

went back into the living room. They examined the stove, opened up the kitchen cupboards and tested out the sofas.

'Look,' said Kat, who'd been exploring the shelves above the wood-burning stove. 'There's Uno, Scrabble – although it's German, two packs of cards, Jenga, tons more. We can be really old-school and play all these games. Relive our childhoods!'

Matt put a hand to his chest, dramatically. 'Oh my! What a time to be alive!' he said with heavy sarcasm. He picked up his case and carried it up the stairs to the first floor. 'Ooh, bags this bedroom, it's divine!' they heard him call down.

Later that evening, after eating raclette in the nearest restaurant – where Matt had blatantly ignored the detox rule – they did in fact sit round the beautiful oak dining table in the chalet, drinking wine or whisky, and playing Uno.

'I'd forgotten how much fun this is,' said Ellie. 'I haven't played since the kids were small.'

'Huh. It might be fun for *you*,' said Nigel, pretending to be cross. By some unspoken agreement they had all decided to gang up on Nigel, dumping multiple 'pick up 4' cards on him, or changing the direction of play when he was just about to put down his last card. They were all a bit drunk, and each time they got Nigel, they roared with laughter. Even urbane Matt was enjoying the game.

As the evening progressed, Kat started to feel more and more felt relaxed. She hadn't really spoken to Neil much, beyond a few general remarks, but it didn't feel weird, it felt warm and almost normal. She looked over at Neil and he caught her eye and smiled.

'This is going to be a good holiday,' she thought. 'He's the same Neil. Just older and a bit more self-assured.'

14

Back then

After that it became a game they all played: who could think up the juiciest, most grotesque murder. The rules were simple; it had to be connected to skiing and reasonably viable.

The weather continued to be disturbed, with frequent snow showers and low clouds obscuring the tops of the runs. They skied every day, morning and afternoon, determined to make the most of their short stay. Kat found it difficult; the lack of sunshine meant there were no shadows to show where the snow curved upwards or downwards. When the clouds came down she lost her sense of direction completely, and became dizzy. But she continued to ski, following Ellie, Neil and Sean, each one keeping the right distance from the other so that no-one became lost in the fog. Gradually they all improved and on the fourth day the four of them took part in a little slalom race organised by the ski club. They got medals for completing the course, which Kat and Ellie wore proudly round their necks.

But in the evenings it was all about death.

'We thought up a good one today,' said Sue. They were sitting around the fire with the lights off. The flames from the burning logs lit up their faces, and cast strange flickering shadows onto the pine walls. 'Listen to this: It's early evening, the last run before the lift closes. You're alone and it's just beginning to get dark. Someone comes up behind you and knocks you out. When you come around, you're buried up to the neck in the snow. You can't move. You shout and struggle but it's no good. Then you hear an engine. The piste-basher machine is coming towards you with its flashing lights and its warning noises. It gets nearer and nearer, you can see the blade approaching. You shout but no-one can hear you over the noise of the engine, the driver doesn't notice you until it's too late. Your head is sliced clean off and the caterpillar tracks have mashed you into the snow. The driver feels the bump, stops the engine and looks back up the piste. By the light of his machine he can see a patch of red in the snow. But he doesn't see a figure, all in black, outside the circle of light. It's the killer.'

'Yeah that would work. Brilliant! But better if the killer has injected some kind of immobilising drug so you're awake when he buries you, but you can't move.'

'Ugh, gross!'

'We've got one, we've got one,' said Kat. She and Ellie had thought this one up while they sat on the chairlift earlier. She paused, leaned forward and began her story. 'You meet this really hunky ski instructor in a bar. You know, gorgeous, muscly – the silent type. You get chatting and he asks you to go for a walk. It's dark. You walk around a little reservoir and he kisses you. Then suddenly he puts his hands round your neck and strangles you. He cuts up your body and throws the parts into the reservoir. That night the snow machines come on. The water sprays out and turns to ice crystals. At first the crystals are just pink, then gradually the snow on the ground becomes redder and redder as the water is fed from the reservoir.'

'Hmm. Why would he bother to cut up the body? Why not just throw it in? And wouldn't the reservoir be frozen? Your body parts would just sit on top.' said Gillian. 'Anyway, I don't think snow machines work like that. I bet they're just connected to the main water pipes, so you couldn't get a body into the circuit.' She spoke with confidence and authority.

Kat was pissed off. She had a clear vision in her mind of the red arc spewing over the white snow and she didn't want details like water pipes to make her murder impossible. A carpet of red snow. Perfect. Trust Gillian to burst her balloon she thought, sourly. She probably wasn't even right. I bet there is a reservoir somewhere!

'What about this?' said Sean. His long face, normally so amiable and open, looked strangely distorted in the firelight as he spoke. 'The killer is a crazy old man. A loner. He's grown up in the mountains and has a cattle farm. He doesn't talk to people but he knows the name of every cow, and he talks to them. He hates skiers. The pastures where he grazes his cattle in the summer area all bare and eroded and he finds rubbish like empty bottles and biscuit wrappers dumped under the trees. His cattle aren't thriving and he can't make a living any more. He decides to take his revenge. One winter he sees a forecast for low cloud and fog. He goes out at night with a head torch, climbs to the top of a run. Then he starts moving the piste markers. The next day, a thick fog comes down. A group of skiers heads up on the lift with an instructor. They can't see a thing. They ski from piste marker to piste marker following the instructor, who's following the numbers – 15, then 14, then 13. But then they disappear. Then the instructor sees one, it's number 12, but it's not where he expected it to be, it's way off to the right. They head towards it anyway, then go crashing over the edge of the cliff.'

'Or better still, what about a different ending?' This was Rob's contribution 'The group follow the marker number 12 but it takes them over a strangely flat area. One by one they lose their momentum and come to a stop. Then they hear a loud crack. They look at each other, confused. Another crack. Then the instructor realises they've been skiing over the frozen lake. He tells them not to move. They stand stock still, trying not to make the situation worse, but slowly the cracks get wider and wider until at last the first person, the heaviest, the one they've been teasing, drops through. The others look at each other, terrified. Another crack and two more fall into the freezing water. They scatter and try to ski off in different directions, but the cracks are multiplying all around, too fast for them. The instructor almost makes it to solid ground; he's the last one to fall through...' Usually quiet, Rob surprised them all with this macabre twist.

They voted this top murder of the night. But Neil was less impressed. 'Your murders are all too complicated. There's too much preparation involved. I think the secret to a good murder is to keep it simple. Why not just push someone off a chairlift? It'd be dead easy, and in the fog no-one would know. There's a great stretch on the blue run we've been doing where the lift goes over a kind of ravine. One well-timed push. You'd never find the body!'

'Too easy!' they shouted him down.

'Boring!' teased Kat.

'No, I think Neil's murder is the best,' said Gillian, smiling up at him from her place on the rug. 'Much less chance of things going wrong.' She stretched her legs out on the floor and arched her back, like a cat. 'Even a girl could do a murder like that.' Kat caught Ellie's eye and they shared a little grimace of dislike.

Silvio was sitting in a corner, a book on his lap. An old-fashioned fringed standard lamp cast a weak light onto the pages. He looked over at the group huddled round the fire, their expressions alive with sadistic glee. Right now they disgusted him. He thought the game was childish and somehow disrespectful of these magnificent mountains. This was his chalet, his holiday and they were behaving like a bunch of boy-scouts round a camp fire. He snapped his book shut.

'Don't be so fucking stupid, all of you,' he sneered. 'These mountains are dangerous enough as it is. You could get lost in the fog, you could get caught in an avalanche, you can break a leg so easily or even your neck. You don't need to invent killers – the mountains are the killers.' He got to his feet. 'I need some fresh air.'

They watched Silvio leave the room and go downstairs, gaping with surprise at his vehemence.

'What's got up his nose?' asked Rob. 'That was all a bit dramatic!'

'Sense of humour bypass,' said Gillian, smugly. 'He's such an old woman!'

But Kat felt chastised. They were only here thanks to Silvio. They should all show him a little more respect. How dare Gillian, the newcomer, criticize him? She went out to join him outside, lighting a cigarette and offering him one.

'Are you OK?' she asked.

'Of course,' came the short reply.

'I'm sorry if we're behaving like a bunch of idiots. I hope you don't regret inviting us. We do really appreciate being here you know, it's amazing.'

Silvio gave a dismissive shrug of his shoulders. 'It's not so amazing really. It's just a little chalet. We used to have a huge one in Val d'Isère in France. That was really something.'

This was one of the longest sentences Silvio had ever spoken to her. She felt an unexpected stab of sympathy towards him. 'What happened to it?' she asked.

'We sold it.'

'How come?'

Silvio sighed and looked at her properly for the first time. 'We have a beautiful castle, we have lands. We have olive groves and orange trees. But you know, a title means nothing. It brings no wealth. And olives are hard work. They don't bring much money. And a castle needs millions of lira in maintenance. We've had to sell off a lot of assets just to stop the estate falling into ruin. The chalet had to go.'

'Shit! I didn't know. I never really thought about that. And you're going to inherit these problems? Are you the eldest?'

'I am. My job is to find a way to stop it crumbling to the ground.'

'Bloody hell! What are you going to do?'

He shrugged again. 'Open it to tourists I suppose. Get rich Americans to come and eat dinner with the count. But I can't stand the thought of fat idiots in loud clothes crawling all over my home. Maybe it will be better to just abandon it. No-one asked me if I wanted to spend my whole life fighting for it, after all.' He gave a sad, ironic smile and turned back to re-join the others.

Kat stared after him, speechless. She had always just assumed that he was rich, and therefore had a life of ease and luxury. What kind of a stupid inverse snob had she been? He had more on his mind than any of them. No wonder he found the murder game childish. She went back into the living room, glad to see that the others had changed the subject and were now discussing the next day's skiing.

But the following evening murder was on the menu once again..

15

They skied as a group the first morning, doing the gentle blue runs in slow sweeping curves. The snow was icy and a bit thin in places, but the weather was cold, crisp and sunny. Kat hadn't been skiing in a long time, but found it was coming back to her. 'It's true what they say,' she thought. 'Just like riding a bike.' Matt looked like he'd been skiing all his life, and Sean was unrecognisable from the gangly, uncoordinated skier he used to be. Once again Kat found herself the worst in the group, but she didn't mind. What she lacked in technique she made up for in fitness. She could see Ellie and Nigel beginning to flag, but her legs were still going strong. By lunchtime Ellie's thighs were burning, and she and Nigel decided to pack in and return to the chalet. Sean and Matt carried on for another couple of hours before they too decided to stop and have a few beers on a sunny balcony.

It was the first time Kat and Neil had been alone. They skied on in companionable silence for a while. Then, when they found themselves alone on the four-person chairlift for a change, they finally began to talk.

'Tell me more about your job,' said Neil, wanting to start on safe ground.

'OK. Well, I love it. I teach mainly refugees and migrants. It's not well paid or glamorous in the least, but I really love the students – they're a constant source of inspiration.' She told him a couple of stories about her favourite students and their backgrounds. 'It's great fun actually. We do lots of realistic role-plays, you know, like calling the doctor for a sick child, or going to a parents evening at school. And we do some cultural stuff too – we talk about Henry VIII or Christmas, or Bonfire Night. When they get good we actually go out into town and I give them challenges.'

'What like?'

'For instance, to go to an estate agents and find a list of flats to rent. Or to go to a café and ask everyone how to make the perfect cup of tea.'

'That sounds fun. I can imagine you'd be a great teacher,' he said. 'You've got a lot of empathy. And what about your husband, was he a teacher too?'

'Peter? Yes he started off as an English teacher, then went into teacher training. He was head of department in the training college.'

'What was he like? Tell me something about him that sums him up.'

Kat thought of Peter and a little smile softened her face. Rather than the miserable memories of illness and loss, she found the happy memories flooding back. She desperately wanted to convey the essence of Peter to this man.

'He bought me flowers every week. He just loved flowers. He was a hopeless cook, he burnt everything. Especially on barbeques. He was much more generous than me, we used to argue about that a bit. He'd always pick up the bill when we went out with friends. He'd drop anything for a friend in trouble or if one of the kids needed something. He loved old war films and American crime novels. He used to wear baggy jumpers and off-the-arse jeans to work. He was brilliant with children and loved playing with babies. He always put me first. He was just, oh, bloody perfect.'

'He sounds perfect. I'm so glad you had each other.'

Kat felt a surprising stab of happiness. She had been lucky. The knot of bitterness she'd been carrying around for two years begin to untie itself a little.

'What about your wife? When did you get married?'

There was a long pause 'Oh… really late,' Neil replied at

last. 'I was thirty-seven. Anna was much younger.'

'Anna. That's a nice name. So what was she like?'

Neil tensed. He really didn't want to talk about her, but Kat had been so open about her husband. He could edit out the worst of it. Give her the cleaned up version. 'I'm afraid I wasn't as lucky as you. We should never have got married,' he began. 'We had pretty much nothing in common. We met at a medical conference in Portugal. She was a pharmacologist, very pretty, beautiful really. Intelligent. She was interested in me, and in my work, and I was flattered. It's a cliché, but I suppose I'd reached an age where I was getting bit desperate to find someone to settle down with. And she was a real catch on the face of it. We got together at the conference and it was fantastic. Four days and nights of, uh... well, fun.' He gave an embarrassed laugh. 'After that, though, we lived miles apart and the long distance thing wasn't working, so stupidly we took the plunge and got married.'

'A whirlwind romance.' Kat was a bit ashamed to have used such a well-worn cliché. She rushed on. 'What did she look like?'

'She was very tall for a girl. Long curly red hair. Great legs. Things started to go wrong more or less as soon as we were married. I wanted to have kids and thought she did too, but it turned out she didn't. She said I was enough for her. We argued about that, and about money. She didn't like my friends, didn't like me spending too much time with them. She was always criticizing them to me, saying they were no good for me. I felt she wanted to change me, make me into her idea of a perfect husband. I stayed out late at work more and more often. She got very jealous, thought I was having an affair – I wasn't. I just didn't want to go home. It all got a bit dramatic towards the end, you know, she was checking my emails, following me in her car, accusing me of getting it on with her friends. She was so unpredictable – one minute accusing me of all sorts, screaming at me, then the next minute clinging to me, begging me not to leave her. I just couldn't take the drama any more. We had massive rows. It all got too much and I left. Left the house, left the town, left my job. Went back to Scotland for a while. Then the divorce. That was acrimonious. So anyway. Sad story.'

'I'm sorry. It's a shame. Did things calm down with time? Are you still in touch?'

Neil's eyes turned cold and hard. 'No way. She's right out of my life. Expunged. I destroyed all the photos. That period of my life is over. Closed. I will never set eyes on that woman again as long as I live.'

Kat was chilled by the expression on his face and the suppressed anger she could hear in his voice. She sensed there were things he wasn't telling her, but knew that the subject was closed – for now. She turned to face the slope again. The chairlift clanked as the cable reached the final supporting tower. They zipped their jackets up to the chin and got ready to lift the safety bar.

16

Back then

They all skied together on the last but one day. It was bitterly cold and the wind was whipping little needles of ice crystals onto their cheeks. Despite their different levels, Silvio kept the group together and herded them on like a duck with its ducklings. He watched the beginners with a critical eye, appraising their progress.

'We're going to do the black,' he announced, after a couple of runs down the blue. 'It's not a real black, it's not too hard. You can all do it fine.'

Kat glanced at Ellie nervously, who pulled a face back at her. She then looked at Neil for support but he was gazing up at the run, excitement shining in his eyes.

'Neil!' said Kat. He didn't turn. 'Neil!' she tried again, 'We're not ready for this are we? We can't just go from blue to black.'

Neil shrugged. 'If Silvio thinks it's OK then I'm sure it will be. We've been doing the same runs all week. Let's end with a high.' With that he turned away to follow the others, making their way to the lifts.

'Jesus!' said Kat under her breath. She'd expected a bit more from him.

'Come on,' said Ellie. 'We've got no choice now. We'll stick together, even if we have to do the whole thing on our bums.'

By the time they reached the chairlift, Neil was already sitting on a chair with Gillian, Rob and Sue.

'Fuck's sake!' said Kat to Ellie. 'He didn't even wait for me!'

Was he annoyed at her for being such a wimp? Sitting next to Gillian, for God's sake! Was he trying to act cool to impress her? Kat felt miserable and exposed, as if someone had pulled a nice warm blanket away from her. She got on the lift with Silvio, Ellie and Sean, her heart thumping with fear and frustration.

'Silvio, are you sure we're up for this?' asked Ellie.

Silvio looked down at her, surprised. 'Yes, I'm sure. Don't worry, I wouldn't take you down it if I didn't think you could do it. There's only one tricky bit.'

At the top the others were waiting for them. The start was a nice easy blue, which they all did together. Then after a hundred yards there was a branch off. One by one they stopped beside the ominous black piste marker. Kat couldn't even see the start of the run as it dipped away sharply under a lip of snow. She and Ellie exchanged a grim look.

'It's not as bad as it looks,' said Silvio. 'The first bit is tricky, but we'll take it steady. Then it gets much easier. I'll go last.'

Rob and Sue pushed themselves off easily and disappeared over the edge. Then Gillian. Then, to Kat's dismay, Neil followed. Kat felt another stab of misery. Tears of self-pity welled in her eyes. Just at that moment she hated him.

'Shit, shit, shit!' she breathed, as the four of them edged towards the start of the run. She looked down to see the four others disappearing round a bend. Then, pulling herself together, she decided to forget about that arsehole Neil and just concentrate on getting down without killing herself.

'Who's going first?' she asked Ellie and Sean.

'Go for it!'

And so she did. It was not enjoyable. It was a teeth-gritting, painful test of endurance. The start of the run was narrow, and curved up at the sides like a half-pipe. The snow had been carved into rounded humps and hollows. Kat felt she was skiing like a total beginner again, frequently stopping to look for a safe place to turn. She fell often, but picked herself up each time with dogged determination. The next bit was wider and easier, to their great relief, but as they rounded a bend, Silvio halted them and told them they had to go as fast as they could over the next downhill stretch, in order to get up the incline that followed. This was something new and frightening. Speed until now had been something they avoided. Speed usually meant out of control! They glanced at each other nervously, then looked at the piste, noticing how smooth it was. No zig-zag tracks, no lumps – it was like a narrow motorway.

'Follow the fall line,' said Silvio. They looked at him, perplexed. 'Imagine where a snowball would roll down the hill, straight down, taking the shortest route. You do the same.'

Kat clenched her jaw. She would show Neil she was no wimp. She would do this. She put her skis together and for the first time headed straight down, not once trying to turn. She just about made it, pushing herself up the last bit with exhausting stabs with her sticks. She looked back and saw Ellie and Sean side stepping doggedly up the hill, having run out of speed too soon. The run continued like that with horrendous gradients that looked to be about forty degrees, followed by more gentle bits. They fell time and again, but Silvio was there to help them up and encourage them on.

When at last they reached the end, Kat felt grim satisfaction. It was over. They were alive. No bones broken. A first black run done.

No thanks to Neil. She was going to bloody well kill him when she saw him.

17

They fell into a nice easy routine. They got up late and had breakfast in one or other of the restaurants, taking the opportunity to check emails and send messages to family. They skied at a gentle pace over lunchtime until about 2pm, then stopped for mulled wine or beer before doing a last couple of runs. Back in the chalet they took turns to cook, and afterwards worked their way through the different board games. German scrabble was a revelation – ten points for a Y! They laughed as their ordinary English words scored crazily high points. They got down on the floor to play Jenga, with Matt cheating, trying to blow the tower down. One night they even played the kids game Twister. Ellie was crying with laughter as she watched Nigel trying to reach round Matt to touch a blue circle. Kat dropped out quickly - she had brushed against Neil, her arm touching his shoulder. The contact felt like a burn and she collapsed on the mat on purpose to sit out the rest of the go.

After each different game they chatted easily, sitting around the wood burner with the lights down low and a glass in their hands. It felt intimate and safe. The conversations flowed easily. Often they reminisced about university life: 'What was the name of that fantastic burger bar on the high street?' Or 'Do you remember the rugby club dos in the Downstairs Bar? The state of the place at the end of the evening!' and 'Were you there that night the hypnotist came to do a show? Making people bark like dogs or pretend to make love to chairs. It was awful.' Matt and Nigel, the two outsiders, would fake yawn and roll their eyes until the subject was changed. Sometimes they talked about politics, the European Union, the environment. Sometimes music or film. They hadn't, until now, talked much about their personal lives, and Kat was glad. Ellie gradually lost some of her reservations about Neil and began to warm to him. Even Matt had to admit there was something really restful about not being a slave to phones or laptops.

Ellie and Nigel cooked the first night - a wonderful concoction of pork loin, cream, wine and mustard. The following night it was Sean and Matt.

'Is it cabbage and potato mush?' Neil had teased. 'That's all Sean knew how to cook back in the day. It was vaguely edible I suppose. Made a change from chip butties.'

'I have moved on since then,' replied Sean, with mock dignity. 'I'll have you know Matt and I have been going to cookery classes. We have private tuition at the Cook's Academy. Tonight we shall be creating chicken Marengo with tangy green salad, followed by classic crème brulée.'

'Bloody hell!' Neil was impressed. 'I'd better find a decent bottle of wine then!' He had gone down the stairs to fetch a bottle from the crate outside.

But tonight it was Kat and Neil's turn to cook and they were making a simple spaghetti Bolognese. They stood together in front of the kitchen work surface, chopping onions and tomatoes.

'Why do they call you Kat?' asked Neil. 'I never thought to ask you that before. Why not Kate? Or Cathy? You're real names Catherine isn't it?'

'Yes it is. Hmm. OK, I'll tell you why. I was quite overweight when I was younger – when I was about eleven or twelve. I just loved my food and it never really occurred to me that I was getting fat. Then when I got to secondary school, you know, everyone splits into cliques, who's cool and who's not. And I got teased for it. You know how bitchy girls can be – it was an all-girls school. Well someone came up with the nickname 'Fatty Katty' and that's what they called me all year.'

'That's not very nice. I got called Adamski at school for

some reason. No idea why! Were you traumatised?'

'I was a bit at first, but actually I think it pushed me into losing the weight. I'd probably still be a pudding if it wasn't for them. Anyway, the name got shortened to Katty, then to Kat, and that stuck.'

'Kat's quite cool. Do you like it now, or would you prefer if I called you Catherine?'

'God no! That's what the teachers used to call me when I got into trouble.'

'You got into trouble? I don't believe it! I had you down as a goody-two-shoes.'

'Oh, our school was really pretentious. You could get into trouble for all sorts. Sitting on a window ledge for example. Picking flowers in the school garden. Having the wrong colour socks. Not labelling all three parts of your recorder. What about you – were you one of the good boys or did you get into trouble? You went to a military boarding school didn't you?'

'Yeah that's right. Oh I got into plenty of trouble, that was the fun of it. Sneaking off to smoke, smuggling drink in. Bullying the younger boys. If you got caught you got the cane or the belt. The worst thing I did was shoot a sheep during rifle practice.'

Kat was shocked. 'That's horrible! Poor thing! Did you do it on purpose?'

'Yep. I'm ashamed to say.'

'But why did you do it?'

'Dunno really. To see what would happen I guess.'

'Poor sheep! Did they find out it was you?'

'No. We had a code of honour. You didn't rat on your pals so the teachers never knew.'

Kat shook her head, wonderingly. 'I thought my school was bad; yours sounds awful!'

'No it was brilliant. I loved it. There was lots of outdoor adventure stuff, so it was really cool. Well, apart from the paedo teachers.'

'*What?* Seriously?'

'Yeah. Some of them were a bit dodgy. You had to watch

your step.'

'Hang on a minute, this is serious! You really had paedophile teachers? That is so bad! What did they do?'

Neil shrugged, carelessly. 'Not much happened to me really. I remember one time I got called out of bed in the middle of the night to see a master called Perkins. Paedo Perkins. He made me take my pyjamas off and do press ups and touch my toes. He called it a medical examination. I remember he held my balls and got me to cough. Then I went back to bed.'

'Jesus! Was he wanking?'

'I don't think so. Maybe afterwards.'

'That is so gross. Were you not freaked out?'

'To be honest I didn't really think it was odd at the time. It's only now that I realise it wasn't exactly normal.'

'Do you think he was checking you out? Choosing his next victim?'

'I hadn't thought of that. Yes, you could be right. Shit, I wonder if... I wonder if it went a lot further with some of the boys? The quiet ones.'

'What about your brother? He went to the same school didn't he? Did he have any trouble?'

'I don't know. It's not something we ever talk about. I know he didn't like the school though.'

'Neil you can't keep this to yourself. You've got to go to the police with this. Or contact people though the old boys association or something, find out what really happened. People shouldn't get away with it. Not in today's world.'

'Nah, old Paedo Perkins will be dead by now. No point. I'm OK.'

'Maybe *you* are, but I bet some people are still traumatised. Your own brother maybe. He might still have issues. You could help him if you talk about it.'

'No. It was just the way it was. Didn't do me any harm. Best to forget it.'

For Neil it was obvious the subject was closed. But Kat looked thoughtful. 'I think I was nearly taken by a paedophile once,' she said.

'Really?' Neil's eyebrows shot up. 'What happened?'

'I was about eleven or twelve. I was staying with my friend Caroline on the Lancashire coast. We went cycling down this disused railway line one day. We came across this abandoned factory down an overgrown track. We were really into mysteries at the time, we thought we were the Famous Two! So we dumped out bikes and went to explore. There was a white car parked further up the track and a man sitting inside reading the newspaper. When he saw us he got out and said hello. He was middle aged, fat. He had an old, lazy Labrador dog and we stroked it. I still remember thinking: 'He's a nice man 'cos he's got a dog.' He offered to show us round the factory and we said OK. It was really dangerous inside – I think it was fire damaged. Part of the roof had fallen in and it smelt horrible, but we were dead excited. Well, he took us up some stairs; really dodgy, half the treads were missing and we had to jump over the gaps. It was dark, hard to see where you were putting your feet. He was holding Caroline's hand, and she was holding my hand. We went up and up, then at one moment Caroline must have had a doubt. She pulled away from him and we both went running back down the stairs, grabbed our bikes and legged it. I remember we were laughing hysterically. We felt really wicked for leaving that nice, kind man who was showing us round.'

'Yeah. Sounds like you had a lucky escape there. What other reason would he take you up there?'

'I know. But I didn't put two and two together for a long time.'

'But did it traumatise you? Did it put you off men when it clicked?'

'No, not at all.'

'There you are, you see. Bad stuff happens to everyone. You've got to just put it away and get on with your life.'

'But don't you think it's better to process stuff like that? Talk it through? Otherwise it can come back and bite you on the bum?'

'Nah. I'm not into that touchy-feely, navel-gazing shit. No point dwelling. Man up and move on.'

Kat was not convinced. She wondered just how well-adjusted Neil could be after losing his father, being sent away to boarding school, coping with paedophile teachers, murdering a sheep. A normal person would have needed years of therapy to come to terms with all that. He didn't seem damaged, but obviously he'd been a bit rubbish at relationships. His marriage had failed. When she'd first met him he'd drunk far too much as well – but that was just student life wasn't it? She felt a little shiver of unease. She didn't really know him well at all.

Something made her remember the game they'd played all those years ago.

'Do you remember the murder game?' she asked, 'We used to think up all those ways of killing someone when we were here last time?'

'Oh yeah, I remember it very well. The chairlift in the fog. The missing piste markers. Falling into the frozen lake. I still think new ones up sometimes. I half thought about becoming a crime writer! Making our ideas into a novel.' He laughed, self-consciously. 'I think I've got a warped mind. I love all those gory bits. Dismembered bodies. Blood and guts. Red stains on the snow. That's right up my street.'

Kat watched as he turned to get the meat out of the fridge, a thoughtful expression on her face. He passed her the pack of minced beef and Kat looked down at the packet in her hands, suddenly repulsed by the blood which had leaked out, staining the white polystyrene tray. Red and white. Like blood stains on snow. She pushed the thought away and decided to change the subject.

'So where did you do your PhD? Did you get a first?'

'Yeah I did. Incredible isn't it! After wasting so much time in the bar. I decided to knuckle down at the last minute. Found I was really quite good at Chemistry. What did you get?'

'Respectable 2:1. Same as Ellie.'

They talked about their early careers – a post-doc abroad

for Neil and an unsatisfactory first job in marketing for Kat. As the conversation turned to safer topics, Kat wondered why she'd had a twinge of doubt moments before. She imagined what Ellie would say: 'Stop overthinking! Don't analyse everything so much, just live in the moment.' She browned the mince and stirred in the tomato sauce, deciding to follow Ellie's advice.

❖ ❖ ❖

After dinner, Neil challenged Nigel to a game of chess. They set the board up on the dining table and were soon deeply involved in the game. Neil's frown of fierce concentration showed he was trying hard to win, but Nigel was no pushover – he also had a competitive streak.

At the other end of the open plan space, Ellie sat on one of the fireside sofas, with Kat lying across it, her feet in Ellie's lap. They'd broken the seal on a bottle of Highland Park whisky and were sipping the amber liquid with complete contentment. Sean and Matt came to join them on the sofa opposite and poured two more glasses.

The whisky had made Ellie less cautious about broaching touchy subjects and she was curious.

'How come we never knew you were gay before?' she asked Sean, without preamble.

Sean was happy to answer: 'I didn't really know myself. I just knew I didn't really fancy girls much. I tried. I went out with a few girls, but it was always just like mates. No chemistry at all. I was brought up a strict catholic, so it never entered my head I might be gay. I thought I'd just not met the right girl, to be honest. Then I met Matt at work, and we'd go out on a Friday after work and have good crack. We'd talk the night away, go clubbing, dancing. But it still didn't click.'

'So what changed?'

Matt took up the story: 'I fancied him right from the start. I knew he was the man for me but it took over a year before it entered his thick skull that I might be interested in that way. One day I just took him by the hand, looked him in the eye and said: 'Well then, what are we going to do about this? Shall we take it to the next step?' He looked at me like he didn't have a bloody clue what I was talking about.'

'And then what?'

'Well, at first I thought he was just talking bollocks,' Sean continued. 'Messing with me, having a laugh. Then when I realised what he meant, it wasn't so easy. Nothing was clear to me anymore. I had to reassess what I thought about a lot of things. My religion. My parents. My hometown. All my past. What I thought of myself. I had to weigh all that up against what I might gain if I went ahead. It wasn't easy. It's still not easy to be honest. My brothers and sisters are fine about it and Mam and Da pretend it's all fine. We've been married over five years now and it's still a bit strained when they come and stay.'

'But no regrets?'

Sean threw his arm round Matt and pulled him close. 'No regrets. You're stuck with me for good I'm afraid.'

'Do you get any trouble in London?' asked Kat. 'Any homophobic remarks? Are you completely open about it?'

'We're still a bit careful,' Sean replied. 'We don't hold hands when we're out on the street for instance. But things have changed so much. There are so many more gay couples on TV now, gay presenters, gay sportspeople even. It's becoming almost the fashion! We've had a couple of little things – we got turned away from a bed and breakfast place once, but on the whole it's fine. It's got a lot better since same-sex marriage came in.' Sean turned to Ellie and asked: 'Nigel's a great fella. Where'd you meet him, then?'

'We met in a folk club. I went through a folky phase after Uni; you know, real ale, wellies, did some conservation work in my free time. I met him at a ceilidh. He had a shaggy beard, a moustache, and his beer tankard was hanging from his belt.'

'Really?' said Matt, glancing over to where a neat-haired, clean-shaven Nigel was hesitating over the chess board. 'My God, what a style disaster,' he said, shivering in mock horror. 'And you were attracted to that?'

'Oh yes! Love at first sight! We used to spend our week-ends rescuing bats and cleaning out rubbish from rivers. When you've seen someone up to the arse in mud and you still fancy them, you know it's the real thing.'

Sean looked over at Kat. He knew that this conversation about love and partners was difficult for her, but he wanted to include her. 'How long were you and your Peter together?' he asked.

'Twenty-seven years.'

'And where did you two meet?'

'You won't believe it; in the Casualty department of the local hospital! He'd fallen off a ladder trying to hang a mirror in his hall. He was absolutely awful at DIY. He thought his arm was broken – turned out it wasn't. And I had cut my finger cook-ing. I was waiting to get stitches. We both ended up sitting next to each other, and waiting for hours and hours 'cos the nurses didn't think we were that serious, so we got talking. Ended up exchanging phone numbers. Went for a drink. And the rest is history!'

'Did he get any better at DIY after you married?'

'God no, he was so bad at it! Never got better. He used to cut through the cable of the hedge trimmers every year.'

'Remember when he tried to put those smoke alarms up that time?' said Ellie. 'It took him about two hours and there were only two screws to screw in. We all just watched him try-ing to figure it out and timed him to see how long it would take. He got so cross.'

They laughed, and Kat felt again that some of the bitter-ness was seeping away. It felt good to talk about him. 'Oh I know!' she continued. 'There was one time were trying to build a bed from Ikea together – it almost ended in divorce…' She happily told the anecdote, exaggerating some parts. Dear old Peter. Such emotional intelligence and such practical incompetence!

A loud shout went up from the dining table 'Yesss!' They looked over and saw Nigel doing a happy strong man pose with his fist up to his forehead, Bruce Forsyth style. He'd won the chess game. Ellie smiled fondly and turned back to ask Matt a question, but Kat watched a while longer. She was surprised to see the look of intense displeasure on Neil's face, as he swept the chess pieces into the box with an angry clatter. 'He's a sore loser,' she thought, shocked. 'I didn't know that.'

18
Back then

Kat persuaded Ellie to go for a quick drink before returning to the chalet. Partly to celebrate the black run, but mostly because Kat wanted to make Neil wonder where she was and start worrying. She knew it was childish, but she couldn't help herself.

'You lot go on ahead,' she called to Sean and Silvio. 'We'll catch you up.'

They hung back, then turned towards a quiet little bar. Jamming their skis into the piled up snow, they loosened their boots and went inside. It was more of a locals bar than a tourist bar. The chairs and tables were unapologetically plastic. The small TV on the wall seemed to be showing some kind of Swiss game show. A couple of older men sat at one of the tables, reading newspapers, but otherwise the place was empty. The barman was watching the TV with a bored expression as he lazily dried a beer glass with a cloth. He looked round as they approached and poured two beers, unsmiling, disinterested.

'God my legs are killing me,' said Ellie. 'That was really tough. We did it though. Aren't you proud of us?'

'Yeah,' said Kat distractedly, scanning the room for a seat that looked clean. 'I guess.'

'What's up? You sound pissed off.'

As they sat with their beers, Kat poured out her frustration. 'Neil's ignored me all day. He's hardly said a word to me. He didn't stay with us. He went off with the others without even a look back. Bastard. And the way he looks at Gillian sometimes… I think he likes her.'

'I think *she* likes *him*. She's made a play for Sean and that didn't work out so she's changed her game plan. She's one of those girls who needs male attention. But don't worry about Neil, he's not stupid.'

Kat took a long drink of her beer. Then she looked straight into Ellie's eyes, searching for honesty. 'Do you think Neil loves me?'

Ellie shrugged, helplessly. 'Oh God, I don't know. He's not very demonstrative is he?' she replied.

'You're not sure, are you?'

'Honestly? No. I'm not. But look, I don't know him well enough to say. Maybe that's just the way he is.'

'But when we make love he's so incredibly tender. That must mean something'.

'Don't confuse sex with love,' Ellie warned. 'Maybe he's just very good in bed. Anyway, more to the point, do you love him?'

'Yes!' Kat replied without hesitation.

Ellie raised her eyebrows and nodded thoughtfully, surprised by the strength of emotion. Then she added: 'But can you see a future? You know, marriage, kids, commitment, the works?'

Kat hesitated. She tried, but found it very difficult to imagine Neil in the role of dutiful husband and father. 'Maybe that's not what *I* want,' she said defensively. 'We're too young for all that anyway.'

Ellie considered this. 'You're right. We're both too young to think about settling down. Look, enjoy your time with Neil. You like him. You're having great sex. We're in Switzerland, for God's sake. Enjoy yourself. If it works out, then great. If not, there's someone better round the corner. You never know, you might meet your very own Roger one day!'

They both laughed at this reference to Ellie's rather nerdy on-off boyfriend. Kat felt her anger dissipate. Maybe she was being oversensitive. Ellie was right, she should just make the most of the holiday. They finished their beers, taking their time, then headed slowly back to the chalet.

They found the others sitting around the table. One bottle of wine sat empty, and another was half full. The conversation was loud and animated. Their entrance didn't make the splash Kat was hoping for. Neil looked up briefly and said 'Oh, hi!' before turning back to Sean. Kat felt all her insecurities returning to swamp her like a tidal wave. Did he care? Had he even noticed when she wasn't there?

She and Ellie pulled up chairs. Soon Ellie was laughing and joking with the others, but Kat felt more and more isolated and miserable. She felt like the outsider again, not able to fit in. Not knowing what to say. She hated herself for being so feeble. The others were talking about TV shows they had watched as kids. This turned into a game; one person would sing a theme tune and the rest would try and guess the show. Sue was singing in a surprisingly strong voice: 'Tra-la-lah, tra-la-la-lah » and the shout went up instantly: 'Banana Splits!' Then Ellie tried to sing the Wombles theme, but was so off-key that everyone was stumped. Neil did a decent attempt at the Thunderbirds theme – Kat knew he loved that show and could have guessed he'd choose that, but still didn't join in the game. Instead she watched Gillian, sitting at the head of the table, her back as straight as a headmistress in front of a class. She was inclining her head from one person to the other, orchestrating, controlling, bestowing her approval. Silvio appeared to be the only other person not under her spell. He sat at the opposite end of the table, looking bored. He caught Kat's eye and, with just the slightest movement of one eyebrow, told her what he thought of the game. Kat raised an eyebrow in return, feeling a little better to have an ally.

Later that evening, she and Neil did the washing up together.

'You're very quiet today,' said Neil.

Kat was silent. She kept her eyes down, concentrating on

the plate she was washing. She knew if she started to speak, she wouldn't be able to stop the flow of reproachful words.

But Neil insisted. 'What's up? You seem upset.'

'Oh, you noticed did you?'

'What do you mean by that? Are you pissed off with me?'

'What do you think?'

'What the hell have I done?'

'You really have no idea?'

'Stop being cryptic and just tell me. Look at me! If I've done something to upset you just tell me straight out.'

She let the plate drop back into the water and finally looked at Neil. 'Let's go outside; I don't want to talk where the others can hear us.'

They put their coats on and went out into the dark. Neil lit a cigarette and offered her one. Kat took a deep draw, then started to explain. 'You haven't spoken to me today. You left me on the black run. You knew I was scared and you left me.'

Neil gave an exasperated sigh. 'I just wanted to go a bit faster today, see if I could do it. I knew you'd be fine with Silvio. And you were fine, weren't you?'

'That's not the point.'

'Well, what is the point?' he asked, irritably.

Kat tried to marshal her arguments. She was hopeless at confrontations. She blamed her upbringing – she hadn't had enough practice at rowing with her family.

'You should be looking out for me,' she said finally, aware she sounded weak.

'What are you, some sort of helpless creature who needs a man by her side all the time? You were with Silvio and Sean and Ellie. I've been skiing with you all week. Just for once I wanted to go faster. What's the big deal?'

It all sounded so rational, Kat began to doubt herself. Was she being stupid? Did she really have the right to be annoyed? Or was Neil manipulating her, twisting things around to make it her fault? She tried another tack:

'You went off because of Gillian. You sat next to her on the chairlift. You're always talking to her. In fact you seem to hang on every word she says.'

'Now you're talking utter crap. You're imagining things. Of course I talk to her; how can I not talk to her? We're all in this tiny chalet together. I talk to everyone. You're being ridiculous.'

He went to put his arm round her, but she moved away, still not reassured.

'You know I don't like her. I don't trust her. Could you not just keep your distance a bit more, for my sake?'

'Fuck's sake, will you listen to yourself! You're really dictating who I can and can't speak to? Jesus, this is pathetic. You're doing my head in. I'm going back in.' He stubbed out his cigarette angrily in the soft snow and turned to go back into the chalet, leaving Kat shivering outside, feeling more miserable and confused than ever.

19

Ellie and Kat sat on the terrace of a little chalet-restaurant halfway down the longest blue run. The run snaked down through the trees to the next little village, Hindenalp, which was even smaller than Felsenalp. They had done it a couple of times and now felt they deserved to sit outside on the rough wooden benches with a mulled wine each. The sun bounced off the snow with such intensity that they had taken their jackets off and rolled up their sleeves. Their hats and gloves lay in a pile on the table and the snow melted steadily from their loosened boots. They watched the skiers coming down the mountain above in graceful curves.

'This is the life. Better than working any day. And there's another week to go!'

'Ugh! Don't mention the 'w' word.' said Ellie. 'I don't want to think about that. I've got a million things to do when we get back. It's going to be a nightmare!'

Kat was surprised by Ellie's words. 'But you love your job, don't you?' she asked.

'Mm, yeah, most of the time.'

Kat was sensitive about Ellie's more spectacular career. She wanted to know if it had come at a cost. 'Do you ever think you missed out,' she asked, 'working full time when your kids were small? You know, dropping them at the childminder's every day, not waiting at the school gates with the other mums?'

Ellie considered. 'No, not really. You make a choice and you stick with it. There's no point feeling guilty about what you choose; that's just a waste of time. I might not have been there for them as much as you, but I believe what they say about quality time with the kids being more important than quantity.'

Kat nodded thoughtfully. She herself had stayed with her children when they were small, just teaching a couple of evening classes once they were in bed. She'd always worked part time since they started school. Peter had been great too, making sure he was back from work for every bath- and bedtime. She sometimes wondered if she'd made her children an excuse to not push her own career. She'd never been ambitious. She really wanted Ellie to say something like 'Oh I wish I hadn't worked so hard' or 'You're so lucky you had that time with them.' But Ellie was having none of it.

'Look,' she said, 'we went to university to get a good education and to use our brains. I wasn't going to waste that. And why take a second role under some man when we're more than capable of doing the job ourselves – or doing it better? Besides, I really think I was a good role model – especially for Hannah. She knows she can do anything she wants to with her life.'

'Yeah, true.' Kat nodded in agreement, but then picked at the subject again: 'We're supposed to be the 'having it all' generation aren't we. But do you really think it's possible? To have a great career and good sex life and perfect children, just by being organised?'

'Well, no, it's a mad scramble. It's daily compromises and last minute solutions. I wouldn't claim to be well organised at all. It's just two seconds from chaos most of the time, but it's sort of exciting. And you definitely need a supportive husband to make it work.'

'Yeah, you struck gold with Nigel. You're so lucky he loves to cook.' Kat pushed a little further. 'Did he never resent you being the main wage earner at all?'

'Not a bit!' said Ellie, rather sharply. She was shocked by the question. 'Come on, what decade are you living in? Do you still think the man should be the breadwinner and the woman should stay at home, cooking and cleaning and looking after the kids, or else do some little part-time job for pin money?'

'No, of course not. Well, maybe I do, a little bit.' Kat realised that this was in fact just what she had wanted. She had been more than happy for Peter to carry the load. 'Maybe I'm just lazy!'

'No, you're definitely not lazy. I've seen all the effort you put into your lesson plans. Far more than I would. But did you never think of starting your own language school, or else writing a textbook or something, once the kids were older?'

'Honestly? I didn't want the stress. I wanted to have time for all the other stuff – the coffee with friends, the sneaky daytime TV, the Pilates class. Is that a cop out? Maybe. I don't know. If I'd had a more demanding job it might have helped me get through the last two years.'

'Hmm, yeah. But it might have made it harder too. Your choice was right for you, mine was right for me. It's not a competition.'

Ellie's words were placating, but secretly she did think Kat could have done more with her life. She knew that star signs were complete hokum, but had often thought that Kat was the typical Cancer. Like a crab, she was encased in a cosy shell of security, half tempted to break out, now and again sticking out a tentative claw to test the waters outside, but withdrawing back into her shell at the first sign of danger. Sometimes she really wanted to give her a shake and say: 'Wake up! You've only got one life! Take a risk! What have you got to lose?' She decided to change the subject. She looked up at the deep blue sky.

'I can't believe this weather.'

'It's fantastic isn't it?' Kat stretched luxuriously in the warm sunshine.

'It's been brilliant today. We've got to make the most of it. The weather's supposed to change tomorrow.'

'Is it? How do you know that?'

'It's on that board by the lift – they show the forecast for the next three days. It's going to be warmer but cloudy. Foggy on the tops. Poor visibility.'

'Oh no! What a shame! It's been perfect so far. I hate skiing in the fog.'

'Well we don't *have* to ski. We could have a day off like Sean and Matt. Just hang about the chalet being lazy. Or – I know! We could hire some snowshoes. I've never done that before. It looks good fun.'

'Snowshoes. That's an idea. Do you think that's what Sean and Matt are up to now?' Kat wiggled her eyebrows suggestively. Sean and Matt were very tactile and obviously still couldn't get enough of each other. They had had appeared at the top of the stairs that morning, arms round each other's waists, wearing nothing but their boxer shorts, saying: 'We're going to have a day off today.' Matt had blown a kiss to the others below, and winked lewdly as he followed Sean back to the bedroom.

'I very much doubt it. Honestly, I don't know how they find the energy after all that skiing.'

'You mean you and Nigel aren't at it like rabbits every night? I'm disappointed!'

'These days we're more likely to get our books out or do a Times easy crossword in bed. The most action I get is when Nigel rubs my feet. But I'm OK with that. Middle age pleasures!' She looked at Kat thoughtfully and asked: 'How is it going with Neil? Are you attracted to him? I must say he's mellowed a lot. I didn't like him much in the old days, but I think he's OK now.'

Kat pulled a face and sighed. 'I really don't know. Yes, physically I find him really attractive. And we have good chats. We talk really easily. But then he suddenly goes all weird on me.'

'How do you mean?'

'Well, we can be talking away normally, but when we touch on some subjects he just shuts down, goes silent.'

'What like?'

'Anything to do with his ex-wife. He told me a bit, but when I dug a bit further he just clammed up. His family in Scotland, that's another no-go topic. Even his house. He's happier talking about old times. He talks about student days a lot. And that first ski holiday. It seems to have meant a lot to him. He remembers stuff I'd completely forgotten. It's strange. I feel like he's holding some things back from me. I don't know if I want to get involved. You know how it was with Peter - we just told each other everything, no secrets. You've got to have that trust, don't you think, in a relationship?'

'Yes, I agree absolutely. No way he's anything like Peter. Nobody could be, really.' They both paused, remembering warm, generous, straight-forward Peter. You didn't have to second guess with Peter; what you saw was exactly what you got. Ellie moved the conversation along. 'But has he made a move? You know, gone in for a snog?'

'Ellie! Don't be crude! No he hasn't. Nothing like that. The only physical contact we've had is when he puts his hand on my back sometimes, when I go through a door; or grabs my elbow if there's someone skiing too fast near us.'

'What would you do if he did lunge?'

'I honestly don't know.' Kat knew she was blushing. 'Anyway, to change the subject, how do you think he's getting on with Nigel today?' Neil and Nigel had arranged to ski together that day, and were planning to race each other down the runs. They both loved a challenge. 'Do you think Nigel's winning?'

'I doubt it,' said Ellie. 'For a start he's at a huge disadvantage. He's got so much stuff in his backpack weighing him down.'

'Maybe the weight will make him go faster.' They all teased Nigel for setting off each day with his emergency gear, which included foil blanket, avalanche kit, energy bars, whistle, Swiss army knife, compass and first aid kit. But he insisted that it was better to be prepared for anything in the mountains. 'He's just dying for an opportunity to get his kit out, so to speak. Save the day! I think he's been watching too many extreme survival programmes on TV!'

Ellie felt she had to stick up for her husband. 'Well just you wait, tomorrow, when we're all stuck in the fog waiting for it to clear, we'll all be huddled under his emergency blanket and fighting over his energy bars! Anyway, he certainly won't be needing it today. I can't believe this weather. Do you want to do another run or shall we have another drink?'

'Drink! I'll get them.' Kat picked up her purse and clomped across the wooden decking to the bar. Ellie sighed contentedly and lifted her face to the sun.

20

Back then

They drank far too much that night. It was their last opportunity to get drunk. The next evening they would have to be reasonable if they wanted to pack up, clean the chalet and leave on time on their last day. The chalet was in a bit of a state, with a pile of empty bottles in the corner of the living room, a couple of singed holes in the fireside rug, smelly, overflowing ashtrays on the floor, dishes, plates and pans stacked haphazardly in any old cupboard. There had been a couple of breakages too, which Silvio was fuming about. They promised to leave some money to cover the damage.

When Kat had eventually walked back into the room, she found the others once again huddled around the fire with the lights off. All except Silvio, who was sitting a apart from the group again, looking at the mess and glaring at the others down his long aristocratic nose. Neil was staring into the flames, his jaw clenched. He didn't look up to acknowledge her return. Kat felt thrown off balance. They had just had their first real argument. A nasty one. But everyone argues don't they, she thought. It doesn't mean anything. She sat on the arm of the sofa and poured herself a big glass of wine.

Quiet, angelic-looking Rob was telling a story, but his words were slurred and his plot kept changing.

'A guy and a girl stay in a little log cabin, way up in the mountains. No, wait, two guys and one girl.' He waved his glass as he spoke, spilling wine on the sofa. Kat looked up to see if Silvio had noticed. He had. Rob continued, unperturbed. 'A snowstorm comes and they are snowed in. It's cold. One of the guys goes out to chop some logs but doesn't come back. After some time the other man goes looking for him. He doesn't come back either. The girl is alone. She hears something outside. A thump, thump noise. No, wait, she hears something scratching at the door, a long screech, as if a claw is tearing into the wood. '

'Make your mind up Rob! Is it a person or an animal?'

'OK, OK, thump, thump then. She opens the door and calls for them, and the noise stops. She goes back in and the noise starts up again – thump, thump, thump.' Rob belched loudly, and they laughed, breaking the atmosphere he was trying so hard to create.

Rob continued, undaunted. 'She doesn't know what to do. Eventually she puts on her coat and goes outside. No, she stays in the cabin and it gets dark. '

'You haven't thought this through, have you?'

Yeah, jush, jush wait.' Rob slurred. 'It's a good one, honestly. Ok. She goes out. She sees footprints heading towards the woodpile and she follows them. She hears the noise again. Thump. Thump. She sees a figure by the woodpile and runs towards him but it's not her friends. It's a stranger. He is stacking wood. 'Oh, maybe it's the owner' she thinks. Then she notices where he's stacking the wood. There is a hand sticking out from underneath the growing woodpile. He's burying the body under the logs. She notices the other guy, lying in the snow some way off, an axe planted in the back of his head.' Rob sat back and threw his arms out, looking round, expecting applause, but none came.

'Not your best murder, Rob.' said Sean.

Ellie agreed. 'Yeah. That was a bit rubbish, Rob. I think we're running out of ideas. Let's talk about something else. I've had enough of murder for a bit'. It had been fun at the start, but the game was getting stale now.

'What do you suggest?' asked Sue.

'I don't know. You choose.'

'Anything but politics,' said Kat, giving Gillian a false

smile.

'I know, I know!' said Sue. 'Tell them that story you told me, Ellie. Tell them about that guy, you know, the one at the party. Your most embarrassing moment.'

'No way!' said Ellie, going red. 'I told you that in confidence.'

'Oh, go on!'

The others began chanting: 'Ellie, Ellie, Ellie!'

Finally giving in, Ellie began telling a long and drawn out tale that Kat had heard before. She blocked out Ellie's voice and let her mind return to the argument she'd had with Neil, replaying their hurtful words and trying to decide if she had a right to be upset. She reached for the wine bottle and poured herself a second large glass.

'So anyway, I'd fancied him for ages,' Ellie was saying. 'He was so gorgeous. I'd been flirting with him but nothing happened. Then there was this party off site. He was there looking fabulous and not with any girls hanging off him for a change. I had a few drinks for Dutch courage, then decided to approach him. I said something stupid like 'I really fancy you!' and he actually pulled me onto his knee. I thought 'Ey up! I'm in here!' Then, oh God, so embarrassing, I farted! Loudly! It makes me cringe to think about it, even now!'

'What did he do?'

'He pushed me off! I don't blame him. And that was the end of that.'

They all laughed. Neil glanced briefly at Kat, then said:

'I did something a bit similar once. I'd been going out with this girl called Anne for a couple of weeks. I was about sixteen I think. First girlfriend, I was dead keen to impress her. She was a bit posh, lived in a big detached house. Anyway she had a birthday party at her house, and her parents went out for a while. So we all got drunk, fooled around, listened to music and stuff. Then at eleven o'clock about, her parents come back. Her Dad switches the light on and everyone disentangles themselves and tries to look innocent. Anne pulls me up and says

'Neil, this is my Dad. Dad, this is Neil.' I went to shake his hand, and threw up all over him. She never spoke to me again.'

Neil looked again at Kat and she wondered if he was needling her with this story of a previous girlfriend. Was there a subtext?

'I'm not surprised she didn't speak to you! What an eejit!' said Sean. 'Ok, well since we're on the subject of bodily functions, get this tale. I've had a good few embarrassing moments, but this was one of my first. I'd got completely shit-faced out with my mates at the bar. Went home, got to bed like. Well my mam and da had bought this swanky new leather chair for their bedroom. White leather. Really pleased with it they were. So I gets up in the middle of the night needing a piss. Got the wrong door didn't I? Pissed all over their brand new leather chair. Did I ever get a bollocking for that!'

Gillian's story put her in a good light of course. She made sure everyone was listening before starting: 'I was on holiday in France, camping with my parents. The campsite had this amazing pool with slides and diving boards. I wanted to dive off the high board and I was wearing a brand new little bikini.' She stood, miming the size of her bikini suggestively, then mimicking a confident walk along a diving board, curling her toes around the imaginary end. 'I did a pretty good head-first dive, came up to the surface and, you've guessed, no bikini top. I had to climb out of the pool with my arms over my chest, with everyone watching. It was only when I reached my parents that I realised that I'd lost my bottoms too!' Great, thought Kat, as the others winced or oohed. All the lads will be imagining her naked now. Or picturing Gillian doing a graceful swallow dive into the water. Snotty cow.

Kat had been drinking fast to try and change her mood and catch up with the hilarity of the group. It wasn't working. She just felt nauseous. The argument still lingered in her mind, making her unsettled and insecure. She raked her memory for a good story but nothing came. Surely she could think of something that would make her feel included. Nothing. Wait, there was that one time. When she asked her friend Steve how his blind date had gone, not even thinking about the fact that his long-term girlfriend was sitting beside him. But that wasn't funny. She'd been mortified, felt like a complete idiot. She could only too well imagine Gillian's face if she told that story. Getting up to fetch another bottle, she lurched and fell against the sofa.

'Oops' she said, swaying, trying to right herself. Out of the corner of her eye she saw Gillian smirking.

'Come on, I think you've had a bit too much. It's bedtime for you,' said Neil. He stood up and placed her arm around his shoulders. Then, sweeping both her legs up behind the knee, he lifted her easily into his arms. Momentarily Kat felt the ecstasy his body close to hers. She didn't resist, instead letting her head fall against his warm neck. Breathing in his special smell. He carried her into the little bedroom, where he tenderly helped her get undressed and into her pyjamas. He fetched a mixing bowl from the kitchen and placed it by her head, just in case. Then he filled up a glass with bottled water and made her drink it.

'You'll be OK?' he asked, standing up.

'Yes. Stay with me! Don't go!' she asked, reaching for his hand. Even through the fog of alcohol, she was aware she was being clingy.

'Nah, you need to sleep it off. I'll come and check on you every couple of minutes.' And with that he was gone. Kat felt the tears slide down her cheeks. She cried silently for a while, then fell asleep.

Two hours later she woke with a tremendous thirst. She reached for the bottled water, but it was empty. She swung herself into a sitting position on the bed and waited for the spinning in her head to subside. Gingerly she got to her feet and made her way to the door. She paused again, feeling the nausea rise in her throat, then subside. She opened the door and made her way in the dark to the living room. The lights were out but the fire was still burning brightly, casting flickering shapes onto the windows. As she crossed the room towards the kitchen area she heard a noise. She looked again towards the fireplace. At first her brain would not let her register what she saw. She stood frozen, looked again. A pair of jeans, discarded in a heap. A sweatshirt. She recognised that sweatshirt. Buttocks rising and falling rhythmically, glowing orange in the firelight. Dark hair obscuring the face underneath. A hand reaching into the air, then falling to claw his back.

Kat was suddenly completely sober. She felt as if someone had punched her hard in the stomach. She stood there, rooted to the spot, numb, watching. Minutes passed. Kat's whole body felt as heavy as lead. Somehow she made it silently back to the bedroom and sat on the bed, head in her hands. There was no mistake: Neil and Gillian. It somehow felt inevitable. Of course they were doing it. What did she expect? She curled up into a ball with her fists pushed tightly into her eyes. When Neil entered the room several minutes later she pretended to be asleep.

21

Dusk was gathering as Kat and Ellie approached the chalet. They trudged up the hill on tired legs, carrying their skis, looking forward to the welcoming warmth of the elegant living room, a drink and a hot shower. They were surprised to find it in darkness, the big glass windows above black and lifeless. They dumped their equipment in the basement and went up the wooden stairs. The front door was open as usual – they never locked it, but the big central copper light had not been switched on and the stove had not been lit.

'We must be the first back,' said Ellie. 'Damn, I was hoping to just crash out for a bit in front of the fire with a G and T. I wonder where the others are? I bet they've gone to the bar.' She looked around the room hopefully. 'Maybe they left us a note to say where they'd be. We could go and join them. They could have lit the stove before they went though. I'd better do it now.' She lowered herself onto creaking knees and began to balance strips of kindling in cross-cross patterns inside the wood burner.

'Hang on,' said Kat, happily. 'There *is* a note, look, on the table. Cinderella, you *shall* go to the ball!' She fetched the note, read it quickly, then handed it over to Ellie, a puzzled frown on her face. 'That's really odd,' she said. 'It must be from Matt and Sean. Look!'

Still squatting by the stove, Ellie reached for the note, and read it aloud: 'Called back to the UK. Family emergency. Sorry.' She looked up at Kat. 'That is bizarre,' she said. 'It's a bit brief. It doesn't look like Sean's writing. Way too neat! Must be

Matt's. I wonder why Matt wrote it and not Sean. Sean's the one we all know really.'

'I guess it's Matt who's got the family emergency. Oh dear. Poor things. I wonder when they left?' She paused, thinking things through. 'We've still got about eight days of holiday left haven't we?' she did a quick count on her fingers. 'Maybe they'll be able to come back for the last couple of days. They might have left their stuff here. I'll go and check their room.'

She ran upstairs and pushed open the door to their bedroom. The cupboard doors were open but the contents were gone. A pair of ski socks lay abandoned on the floor. The bed was unmade, the sheets in a messy tangle. It looked like they'd had to pack up in a hurry. She checked the bathroom they shared with the next bedroom. The toothbrushes and shaving kits were still sitting on the shelf below the mirror. Very odd – they really had been in a hurry. She sat on the edge of the bath, trying to think things through. Then she heard the door open downstairs and Nigel's voice call out 'Halloo! We're back!' She rushed down the stairs to meet them.

'Hi. Did either of you see Sean and Matt earlier on today?' she asked.

'No, why?' said Neil, taking off his jacket and slinging it over a chair.

'They've gone back to London! They left this note, look.'

Neil raised his eyebrows as he read the note, turning it over as if hoping to see more of an explanation on the other side. Then he passed it to Nigel. 'How weird. I suppose they must have checked their emails at the restaurant and found out something. Hope it's nothing too awful. Sean's parents aren't in very good health, I know. His mum's got Parkinson's and his dad's got a heart condition. Maybe one of them's been taken to hospital.'

'Well, that's a real shame,' said Nigel. 'They were such good fun. It won't be the same without them. Funny though, I noticed their skis and boots are still downstairs. They didn't take them back to the hire shop.'

'Yes, I know, they can't have had time. And their tooth-brushes and stuff are still in the bathroom. It's as if they literally had just a few minutes to get ready and go.'

'But maybe they're coming back later?' said Ellie hope-fully. 'If they left their skis and toilet things here?'

'But why take all their clothes with them? You'd think they'd just pack a small bag.'

'Curiouser and curiouser. Well, there's nothing we can do for now. We'll send them an email tomorrow and find out the whole story,' said Neil. 'I'm off for a shower.'

Kat watched him go up the stairs, astonished that he didn't seem more concerned. She turned to the other two, and they exchanged puzzled looks.

'I don't get it,' she said. 'We all read our emails this morn-ing at breakfast. They didn't seem bothered by anything then. Sean's never talked about his parents being ill.' She looked at the note again. 'They didn't sign it, or put the time on it.'

Kat felt a creeping sense of dread. This didn't feel right. She tried to shake it off. She was probably making too much of things again. Then she noticed something that set all her senses tingling in alarm: A mobile phone was charging in the corner of the room. The protective cover was a garish riot of multi-col-oured shamrocks.

'That's Sean's phone! Why would he leave his phone? Even if you're in a hurry, that's what you always remember: wallet, passport, phone!' She turned the phone on, hoping to see some further clues, but it was password protected. 'Something bad's happened. I know it.'

Ellie was pragmatic. 'Look,' she said, 'There's no point worrying and trying to guess what's happened. There's usually a really logical explanation. Maybe they left in too much of a hurry, or maybe they're coming back in a day or two. Let's get on with life as normal tonight, and tomorrow we'll find out more.'

◆ ◆ ◆

It was a strange, quiet evening. None of them felt like playing board games. They sat around the stove, staring at the flames. Neil's fingers drummed lightly on his whisky glass.

Ellie broke the silence. She turned to her husband and asked: 'So anyway, how was your skiing today? Did you have fun? You were racing each other, weren't you? Who won most of the races?'

'Umm, about fifty-fifty. I held my own quite well. Neil's better on the smooth bits, in fact he's a bloody loony! Goes off like the bats out of hell. But I'm better on the technical bits when it's mogully. I'd say about honours even.'

'Glad you upheld the family honour, dear. How many runs did you do?'

'We did, what, about ten? Then we lost each other.'

'How do you mean, how did you lose each other?'

'I got to the end of the run, but no Neil. Where were you, mate?'

Neil looked up from staring into his whisky glass and said: 'You took so bloody long I thought I'd missed you and you were back on the chairlift. So I went back up to the top. We must have kept missing each other. I went down that run another couple of times, then I gave up.'

'So you both ended up skiing on your own?' said Ellie. Then to Nigel: 'You should have come and joined us at the restaurant. It was lovely on the terrace in the sunshine.'

'Where did you end up skiing?' Kat asked Neil.

'I went down the black a few times, had a late lunch, then went looking for Nigel again. I found him eventually.'

'So neither of you came back to the chalet this afternoon?' she asked.

They both shook their heads.

22

Back then

It was the last day of skiing. Everyone was hungover that morning. The talk was limited at breakfast as they filled their mugs with tea and tried to swallow mouthfuls of brioche. Only Silvio was behaving as normal, impatient to get onto the slopes.

'Come on then!' he chivvied. 'Get a move on you lot, let's get going.'

They looked through the small windows to see a sky heavy with cloud. An occasional small flake of snow drifted lazily to the ground. The grey weather matched their moods and no-one was in a hurry to face the day.

'Give us a break, Silvio. Kat and Neil aren't even up yet,' said Ellie. 'I'll give them a knock.' She got up from her chair, tapped on their door and said: 'Breakfast's on the table! Wakey, wakey!'

'Kat's not too well,' came Neil's voice. 'We'll get breakfast later. Don't wait for us.'

'I'll bring you two mugs of tea.'

'No, don't bother. I don't think we'll ski today. You go on without us.'

'Oh, OK.' Ellie was concerned. She'd nursed Kat through hangovers in the past and wanted to be there for her now. 'Are you OK, Kat? Can I come in?'

'I'm OK,' came a rather strangled voice. 'Don't come in, I look like shit.'

As if I care, thought Ellie. She paused, but didn't open the door and instead joined the others around the table. Neil was there with her after all.

Inside the little bedroom, Kat sat on the bed with her knees up to her chin. Silent tears fell in quick succession down her cheeks. Neil was hovering beside her, offering tissues and looking helpless. They listened to the sound of chairs scraping back and plates being stacked. Socks and gloves being lost and found. Feet clomping down the stairs. Eventually it was silent in the chalet.

'Please tell me what's wrong,' asked Neil again.

Kat couldn't speak. She shook her head, then rested it on her knees to hide her face.

Neil sat beside her and put his arm round her. They sat like that for several long minutes, sobs shaking Kat's shoulders. Neil patted her back awkwardly. More minutes passed. Then she grabbed a handful of tissues to blow her nose, and finally raised her head. Her eyes were red and swollen. She moved away from him, and his arm fell from round her shoulders. She shut her eyes tight for a moment, then looked at him directly.

'You had sex with Gillian. I saw you last night.'

Neil opened his mouth to say something, but nothing came out. He stared at her in dismay.

'I…. I….' he began.

'I saw you. I went to get a glass of water. You were on the rug. You fucked Gillian while you thought I was asleep.'

'Oh God. I'm sorry. I'm sorry.' Neil hung his head. He found it difficult to meet her eyes.

Kat looked at him, sitting there, staring at the floor. For a second she felt a flash or contempt which strengthened her. This wasn't her fault. It wasn't that she wasn't sexy enough or funny enough. This was all down to him. Neil had screwed up.

'Well?' she said. 'Haven't you got any excuses?'

He looked up, shame-faced. 'She err..' he began. 'She err… We were so drunk and she err.. she put her hand…' he couldn't finish.

Kat stared at him until he dropped his eyes again. She didn't need to hear any more. She could imagine only too easily.

'How could you?' she asked.

'I'm so sorry, I'm so sorry. It was nothing. It was stupid. I'm an idiot.'

'Yes, you are.'

After a long silence he asked: 'Can you forgive me? I don't want us to break up.'

Kat's emotions were in such disorder that she felt completely blank. 'I don't know,' she said, honestly. She felt exhausted, utterly drained. 'I don't know anything. I want you to go away now. I need to sleep.'

Neil stared at her. Then he nodded twice. He bent to fetch more tissues and put a stack on the bed beside her. He patted her shoulder tentatively, then he left the room, closing the door very quietly behind him.

Kat slept for several hours. When she woke and opened the bedroom door, Neil was immediately by her side. He made her sit on the sofa and bought her tea and toast. She drank the tea but couldn't touch the toast. He fetched the duvet and tucked it round her carefully, then sat on the floor by her feet.

'Kat, look at me.'

She flicked her eyes towards him briefly, then turned away to look through the window. The snow was falling steadily. She found she was crying again, big slow tears, and thought distractedly that her tears were almost in sync with the snowflakes outside.

'I'm sorry. It was a mistake. I'll never do anything like that again. Please, Kat.'

She didn't react, but continued to stare through the window. Neil began to rub her feet. 'God, your feet are freezing.' He got up from the floor and started to make a fire. Kat watched his back as he broke twigs for kindling and chose small bits of wood to lay on top. She felt as if she was floating above the scene, watching two people in a play or on TV, two people completely unconnected to her. Two strangers.

When the others returned that afternoon, they found Kat and Neil still sitting around the fire. Neil was reading a thriller, the ashtray beside him full of dog-ends. Kat was still in her pyjamas, wrapped in the duvet. Her eyes were small and pink-rimmed in her pale face. Ellie rushed over to sit on the arm of the sofa.

'Oh my goodness, are you OK? You look terrible! What's the matter?'

Kat tried to smile. 'I'm OK,' she said. 'I think I've got some sort of bug. Been throwing up all day.'

'Well I hope Neil's been looking after you. You need to drink plenty of fluids. Have you taken any medicine? Do you want some tea?'

'No it's OK, I've had loads of tea. I just feel worn out.'

As Ellie sat beside her, Kat looked up at the others. They stood in a semi-circle looking down at her with sympathetic expressions. But as she caught a glimpse of Gillian leaning against the wall, she thought she saw a small smile playing on her lips.

23

It was as if the soul had gone out of the chalet. It felt too big for the four of them. Neil was taciturn, frequently going out onto the balcony to smoke alone. Even Kat and Ellie were quiet. It seemed that Sean and Matt had been the glue holding the group together with their amiable stream of chatter. Now the four remainers all seemed a little self-conscious and conversations were stilted.

They went to the restaurant the next morning, where they composed a joint email to Sean using the free Wi-Fi. They expressed their sympathy, asked if everything was OK, and if the couple planned to stay in London, or come back for the last few days. They asked Sean if he wanted them to post his phone on. Neil checked Sean's Facebook page but found no updates there. He left a Messenger text asking Sean to contact him.

'There's nothing else we can do really,' said Neil, as he put his phone away. 'We've got another week of skiing. We might as well enjoy it.'

They walked back to the chalet without enthusiasm. The weather had indeed changed. A solid layer of thick cloud hung oppressively overhead, blocking out all but the bottom of the mountains. There wasn't a breath of wind to sweep the clouds away.

'I hate this type of weather,' said Kat. 'It's that flat light again. You can't see any of the bumps in the snow until it's too late. It makes me ski like a total plonker.'

'I'm not that keen on it either,' said Ellie. 'Maybe we should have a day off?'

'We should do something, we can't sit around moping about Sean and Matt all day. We could take the cable car down the valley, see if there's a bowling alley or something?' suggested Nigel.

'What about snow-shoeing?' said Ellie. 'Has anyone tried it? I've always wanted a go. I had a bit of an obsession with Red Indians when I was young – I used to literally tie tennis rackets to my feet and clomp about the garden if there was a centimetre of snow. It looks so cool!'

So it was decided. They stopped off at the ski hire shop and got four pairs of snowshoes for the day. Ellie picked up a map of the local trails and asked which ones were suitable for beginners, relishing the chance to show off her rusty German and making Kat smile fondly. Ellie was making some atrocious grammar mistakes, but was communicating just fine. Then they went back to the chalet to make up a picnic of ham sandwiches and boiled eggs.

An hour later they found themselves at the start of the circuit, in front of a little green sign with a picture of a snow shoe and the number one on it. They struggled a bit to put on the snow shoes, adjusting them to their different shoe sizes and figuring out how to tighten the straps. Then they set off. The trail crossed a wide, snow-covered field before branching off steeply downhill into the forest. The metal spikes gripped the compacted snow and they gradually gained confidence, trusting that they would not fall. Then the track veered left to stepping stones across a river; each stone covered with icy compacted snow. This was quite a challenge. Nigel went first, placing his poles in the river for balance as he swung his feet awkwardly from stone to stone. Ellie went next and got stuck half way. 'Help!' she said in a feeble voice, making them laugh. With everyone advising and encouraging she made it over to Nigel's outstretched hands. Kat and Neil followed, and they continued uphill, through the trees, stepping over roots and under low-hanging branches still heavy with clumps of semi-melted snow. They went in single file, their snowshoes making satisfying crunching noises, the effort making talk impossible. Then suddenly they came out into a clearing which seemed quite magical. It was totally quiet. A rare beam of sunlight caught the snow and made it sparkle. The trees formed a black, dense circle around them. They could see the tracks of birds and animals – hares maybe? Or foxes? But very little trace of humans. It was so beautiful, still and serene that they all stopped to take it in.

'This is better than skiing,' Kat said. 'You really notice what's around you. And it's so peaceful! We haven't met a single other person so far.'

'And it's way better exercise,' said Ellie, always more prosaic than poetic.

Neil looked at the little map they'd been given. 'We're about halfway round,' he said. 'Shall we eat?'

They found a stout fallen tree, wiped off the snow and sat on it to eat their picnic in an almost reverential silence. After a while they started to feel chilly, so set off again, onwards through the forest and up to an open south-facing hillside. Here the snow had partly melted, and the track was mud and stone in places. They clattered over the bare patches noisily. Over the crest of the hill they saw the first sign of human habitation; a little farm with a barking dog and tractors in the barn. A thin plume of smoke rose up from the chimney. They passed the farm, crossed a tarmacked track and then found themselves back in the forest, the snow once again thick and crunchy under their feet.

It was four hours later and the sky was beginning to darken when they finally saw the welcome lights of the village below. They were physically tired, but somehow the circuit had bound them together again as a group, as they helped and encouraged each other over fallen trees or through gates. They were all beginners, all learning at the same speed. Their legs ached but they were happy.

Back in the chalet, Nigel and Ellie went upstairs to soak in the bath. They took a bottle of wine and two glasses with them. Kat watched them go up the stairs, winking suggestively at Ellie, then went out onto the balcony to join Neil, who was lighting up a cigarette.

She leant against the railings and gazed at the view. The cloud cover was still thick, and had taken on a purplish hue as the sun set.

'You smoke way too much, you know,' she told him. 'You're one of the last people I know who still smokes.'

'I know,' said Neil. 'Old habits die hard.' He contemplated the cigarette in his fingers for a moment, then took another long draw. 'It was a good day today, wasn't it?'

'Yes, really good. The best thing we could have done with the day.'

Neil looked at her for a long moment, then said: 'We haven't spoken about what happened before. You know, that night…'

Kat didn't turn to look at him. Her hands gripped the railings a bit more tightly. She remained silent.

'I said sorry so many times back then and I'll say it again now. I was a stupid drunken idiot. I've regretted it ever since. I wasn't thinking. I don't know if you've forgiven me. Have you?'

Kat threw him the quickest glance, then looked back over the valley. 'I'm not going to just say 'oh it's fine, water under the bridge, blah blah blah.' You really hurt me. You made me distrust men for a long time afterwards. If it hadn't been for Peter…' She broke off with a sigh. 'I was in love with you. I believed in the whole romantic happy ever after stuff. I thought we'd be together for ever. What a naive idiot I was.'

'I'm the idiot. I didn't realise what I had. Gave it all away for a quick shag. Christ, I really need to know that you forgive me now.'

Kat finally looked at him. 'You were an arse, but you made me grow up. I got more independent, more determined. And if we hadn't split up I'd never have met Peter. So,' she paused. 'I still think you're an arse but life's too short to bear grudges. Come here and give us a hug.'

Ellie looked out from her bedroom window, a thick white

towel wrapped about her body and another covering her hair. 'Uh oh. Come and have a look at this, Nigel,' she said. He came to join her at the window and they both looked down at the pair below. Kat's nose was pressed into Neil's chest and they were both rocking giddily from side to side. 'I thought this might happen. She's falling for him again.'

24

Back then

Kat stared out of the window as the dramatic Swiss scenery passed by. She watched it change from oppressive, craggy mountains to lush green hillsides covered with still-bare vines and picture-perfect villages, each with a steep-spired white church at the centre. Then the deep blue of Lake Geneva, dotted with sailing boats. She registered the changes with half her brain. The other half was dormant, lulled into sleep by the repetitive clickety clack of the rails. She willingly allowed her mind to empty.

Neil had been endlessly attentive and protective since the night before, never leaving her side as they packed their cases and cleaned up the chalet. He had carried her skis as well as his back to the hire shop that morning. He had held her hand tightly as they walked to the cable car. He asked her over and over if she was OK. Each time she'd replied 'Yes, I'm fine' with a distracted half smile. They'd parted company with Silvio, Sean and Gillian at the bottom of the cable car. They were driving back. Kat had found it almost funny to watch Neil hesitating as to how to say goodbye to Gillian, whether to ignore her totally or give her a brief kiss on the cheek. In the end he gave her an embarrassed little wave and Kat had snorted with another small flash of contempt. She herself had kept her distance from the three of them, saying 'You don't want to catch whatever bug I've got.'

Silvio had seemed happy to be rid of them. He'd given them all jobs to do the night before and had been exacting, demanding that the chalet be returned to its original state. Sean had taken several trips to the bottle bank. Kat had watched as Neil swept out the basement and washed the floor. Rob and Sue had scrubbed the stains off the cooker and emptied and bleached the fridge. Gillian had got the old-fashioned upright hoover out of the cupboard and run it round the rooms. Eventually Silvio was almost satisfied, but he'd made them all pay for the burn marks in the rug and the broken glasses. They knew they would not be invited again.

Now, as the train flew smoothly through the stunning landscape, Kat felt immensely glad to be going home. She needed a few days back with her parents in Yorkshire; a few days of normality, of boredom even. She didn't want to have to think. Neil sat opposite her, reading his thriller and looking up at her from time to time. Across the aisle, Ellie, Rob and Sue were playing a noisy game of contract whist. Ellie seemed to have accepted that Kat's quietness was due to a virus, much to Kat's relief. She knew that if Ellie had noticed her emotional state, she would have been there instantly with sympathy and advice, and Kat would have found it impossible to hang on to her composure. She would have broken down completely as soon as she saw the concern in Ellie's blue eyes. Kat listened to Ellie now, as she slammed her trick down on the little table, laughing with the simple joy of winning a round. Dear Ellie. True, loyal Ellie. A friendship much stronger than her romance with Neil. Ellie would never let her down, or lie to her. She knew that Ellie had never totally trusted Neil. Maybe she was the better judge of character after all.

The rhythmic clack of the rails began to lull her into sleepiness. Her eyes felt heavy. She closed them and let her mind shut down, blocking out everything.

❖ ❖ ❖

They parted company in London. Ellie was going to spend a

147

couple of days in the city with Rob and Sue. Neil was travelling on to Euston Station and then on to Scotland. Kat was heading off in the opposite direction to Kings Cross.

'Got time for a coffee before your train?' Neil asked as they walked through the station concourse.

'Not really,' said Kat. 'I want to leave plenty of time just in case.'

'Can I walk with you, carry your bag?'

'No, you'll miss your train. I'll be fine. You go on.'

'I don't mind; I can get a later one. Let's talk?'

'No, you're OK. You should go.'

'Oh. Well… OK. Promise you'll phone me tonight, whatever time it is?'

'OK. Bye Neil.'

They hugged briefly, then Kat pulled away and started to walk towards the exit. Then she felt a hand on her arm, slowing her down.

'Wait! Don't go yet! Are we still OK? I need to know.'

'I've got to go. I'll phone you tonight. We'll speak then.'

'Promise?'

'Promise.'

But Kat knew she would not call, and she would ask her parents to field any calls from Neil. She walked away from him as fast as she could and did not look back.

25

The next day dawned just like the previous one. Oppressive grey clouds hung over the mountains in a solid unmoving curtain. They had breakfast at the restaurant as usual, but there was no communication from Sean. Ellie and Kat had messages from their children. Kat was looking a bit worried as she read her text.

'Sarah's bought a car! I wanted her to wait and look for one with you, Nigel, but she's so impulsive. I hope she hasn't bought an old banger.'

'You're probably better off with a banger to start with,' said Nigel. 'Then you can do third party insurance. It's horrific for young ones to insure cars these days. Didn't she say anything about the make and model?'

'No, she just texted 'guess what, I've got a car.' I'll get her to send a photo, then you can give your expert opinion.'

'OK, will do. I've had a text from Dom too,' said Nigel. 'He's had another interview but he thinks he's messed it up royally. They asked him to improvise a sales pitch and he just went blank. He's had four interviews, and nothing to show for any of them so far.'

'At least he's getting the interviews,' said Ellie. 'One of them will come good.'

Neil was tapping his fingers on the table, looking slightly impatient. 'So what's the plan for today?' he asked. 'To ski or not to ski, that is the question. Whether 'tis nobler in the mind to suffer...' he gave up.

'The bumps and crashes of outrageous weather conditions,' added Kat.

'Or take the plunge into the sea of clouds,' contributed Ellie.

'To die, to sleep, no more,' Neil finished, rather ominously. 'So are we skiing or what?'

'I'd rather snowshoe again,' said Ellie.

'Me too,' agreed Kat.

They decided to split up. Nigel and Neil went off to fetch their skis, while Ellie and Kat bought pastries and drinks from the bakers and headed off to the hire shop again.

It was even more fun this time. They knew the route and trusted their new-found ability. They flicked the branches as they passed under them in single file to spray each other with snow. When they got to the clearing they messed about taking silly photos, posing in mock ballet positions with one snowshoe in the air. Near the crest of the hill they stopped and sat on a rock to eat their pastries.

Ellie gave Kat a shrewd look and asked: 'So I saw you and Neil in a clinch last night. What's going on there then?'

'It wasn't a clinch. We just hugged it out. He was apologising for...' She stopped, realising that she'd said too much.

Ellie was onto it like a hawk. 'For what? Spill the beans. What's he done?'

'Oh it's nothing.'

'Kat, come on, tell me. What has he done?'

Kat paused for a long moment, considering a lie and then discounting it. 'It was ages ago. I never told you before,' she began. 'I should have told you everything at the time but it was too painful and I couldn't face talking about it.'

Ellie waited, giving Kat time to collect her thoughts.

'It was when we came here before. Remember that girl Gillian? He slept with her.'

'Oh my God. Really? When....Oh! So that was... I remember. We all thought you were ill. You looked completely wiped out. Was that when....?'

'Yes, I'd just found out. They'd got drunk together and he

slept with her while I was in bed. That's why we broke up.'

Ellie looked away, pensive. Kat had expected more of a reaction.

'You don't seem very shocked.' She had a sudden thought. 'Did you know?'

'No, of course not. I was just thinking. People make stupid mistakes, you know. It happens all the time. You didn't ever think about giving it another try with Neil?'

'No, I...I couldn't.' They were silent for a moment. Kat looked at Ellie, who was poking little holes in the snow with her ski pole, avoiding her gaze. She had a sudden flash of insight. 'You say people make stupid mistakes. Do you mean... Has Nigel...?'

Ellie rubbed her face with both hands and exhaled deeply. Then she looked at Kat and said baldly: 'No, not Nigel. Me.'

Kat's mouth dropped open. This was not possible. Not Ellie. She felt her world begin to shift and slide. Ellie was the rock she clung to, the person she admired and envied most in the world. Perfect Ellie.

'Don't look so shocked, Kat. You're such an idealist. But life is messy sometimes.'

'What happened? Who?'

'It was ages ago. When I went to London for a conference when I first got the job. I went with Tom from the office. We went to a show in the evening, had a couple of drinks. I'd been feeling so out of it and mumsy for so long; it was so exciting to be wanted again.'

'But... but... Oh my God! Does Nigel know?'

'Yes, of course. I told him everything and we've put it all behind us.'

'Did you have an affair? How long did it last?'

'It was just the once.' Ellie sat up straighter and said, almost fiercely: 'People fuck up. It's not a perfect world.'

'But how come I never knew about it? I thought we told each other things like that?'

'It was when you and Peter were living in Manchester. I

didn't see you so much that year. Besides, you know me, I'm great at putting things in little boxes and closing the lid.'

They sat together in silence, digesting the information both had learned. Then Kat turned to Ellie and said: 'So do you think I should have forgiven Neil?'

Ellie shrugged. 'Maybe. But if you'd stayed together you wouldn't have met Peter, you wouldn't have had the children. Regrets are a waste of time. Life is what it is. We learn and we move on.' She slapped her hands onto her thighs decisively. 'Come on, let's go.'

She got up and pulled Kat to her feet. They strapped up their shoes and plodded on over the crest of the hill.

◆ ◆ ◆

This time the stove was lit and the lights were blazing when they returned to the chalet. Nigel and Neil were in the kitchen area with their backs to them, grating cheese to make fondue.

'Honey, we're home!' Ellie called from the doorway.

'Hey! How did you get on?' asked Nigel.

'Great. We took loads of photos. I'll show you later. How about you?'

'Good! Neil nearly wiped out some poor woman on a snowboard, but apart from that, great.'

'Do you need any help with cooking?' asked Kat

'No, we've got it all covered; you two go and relax, pour a drink, have a bath or whatever. It's going to be a while yet.'

Kat smiled briefly at Neil as she went up the stairs. She opened the door to her bedroom and lay on the bed, stretching her aching limbs in every direction. She was still trying to digest what Ellie had told her, to make it fit into her picture of her friend. Ellie had slept with another man! If Ellie had been unfaithful, maybe she herself was too naïve to expect people to stay on the straight and narrow. Was she living by quaint, old-fashioned standards while everyone else had moved with the times? Nigel had obviously forgiven Ellie. Their marriage was still really solid. How come she'd never guessed? Never noticed any tension between them? She sat up and started to take off her clothes to shower, then stopped dead. Something was odd. She'd kept a diary from the age of 14, writing a page every day. It had become a necessary routine. The diaries massed up and one year she'd thought 'this is stupid!' and not bought one. She'd lasted until February before she cracked and got one again, writing up as much as she could remember about the lost days. She found it very therapeutic to consign her thoughts to paper. When she closed her diary it was like putting a lid on her worries. Out of habit, she always put her pen diagonally across the hard cover, lining it up with the top right corner precisely. She'd started doing this to check if her mum was reading it when she'd first stopped writing about horses and schoolfriends, and started writing about boys. Now the diary lay on the bedside table, as before, but the pen lay neatly beside it. Someone had been in her room. Someone had read her diary. Not Nigel. He wouldn't be interested. Ellie this morning? Maybe she'd nudged the pen off looking for a hairbrush to borrow or something. Neil? Who else could it be really but Neil? Had he been so desperate to find out what she felt about him? What she'd written about him last night? Oh, God, what had she written? She looked at the last sentence of yesterday's entry and cringed. She read: 'We had a massive hug. It actually felt pretty good to be in his arms again!'

26
Back then

Ellie knocked on the door of Kat's campus room and said: 'It's me! Are you awake? I can't sleep!'

'Me neither, come in.'

They'd been revising together all day, ready for an exam on post-war German history, and their brains were full of dates and quotations. It was the last exam. The other exams had been a mixture; some awful (translation into German) and some easy (Urban Studies). They had spent the whole week cramming together and doing post-mortems after each paper. Just one more exam. The last stretch. After that life would become a little easier. The rest of the term would be taken up writing their dissertations. Kat was writing about the squatters movement in Berlin, having interviewed both town planners and squatters during their year out. She knew her viewpoint was a little too socialist to please her supervisor, but she had tremendous sympathy for the students, anarchists and ordinary people who wanted to preserve Berlin's historic tenement blocks from the developers' bulldozers. Ellie was writing about Berlin's city planning policy, which was to build all prestigious new buildings as close to the wall as possible, as a show of confidence that the wall would come down one day. Secretly both she and Kat thought this policy was ridiculous. The wall would never come down! It was a fact of Berlin life, solid and permanent. This was just political posturing! They had both applied and been accepted to work a few shifts in the university cafeteria, washing up, cutting chips, diluting orange concentrate and wiping tables. It would give them a little bit of extra money to help pay off their overdrafts.

Ellie came into the room and threw herself onto the bed with a dramatic sigh: 'Every time I close my eyes I see my revision notes with the dates highlighted. Thank Christ this is the last one!'

'I know. Just think, it might be the last exam we ever have to take! Ever! Do you realise, we're going into the adult world soon. Jobs! Flats! Paying taxes! I'm not sure I'm ready for all that. I should have applied for a PhD or something. Three more years of irresponsibility.'

'Oh, not me, I can't wait to have a job. It's the next stage, it's exciting!' Ellie was full of optimism as always.

'When's your interview again?' asked Kat.

'Thursday next week. You can help me decide what to wear.' Ellie had an interview with an international road haulage company to work as a logistics planner. Kat was very impressed that Ellie had the confidence to work in such a masculine field, telling big-muscled truck drivers where to go and what to load. She could imagine her small, slim friend with her crazy hair sticking out from under a hard hat, a clipboard in hand, directing trucks across the continent like a conductor with his orchestra. Kat herself had already had one interview with an advertising agency, which hadn't gone well. She realised she didn't have the necessary imagination and she'd decided to concentrate on marketing instead. She knew she wanted to move to London, to push herself outside her comfort zone and try to recreate some of the excitement she'd felt in her year out in Berlin.

'Difficult to know what you should wear really. You could go for walking boots, high viz jacket and flat cap maybe?' she teased. 'Yep, that should do it. Definitely not something too sexy, you don't want the lorries to crash.'

'Fat chance of that!' said Ellie. 'No, I want to look really professional but a bit, you know, asexual.'

'Trouser suit, definitely. Low heels, dark colours. But just a touch of something vivid – red shoes or a small bright green scarf. I'll go shopping with you after the exam if you like.'

'That would be great! You know I can't be bothered thinking about clothes. I really want this job. I'll be able to use my languages and tell people what to do all day. Perfect.'

She's bound to get it, Kat thought. How could she not? She'd beat all the guys on the shortlist hands down.

'So anyway, we're both young, free and single!' Ellie continued. 'How great is that? You can invite me to parties in London and we'll go to all the cool night spots. Covent Garden. Comedy clubs. Then when you need a break you can come and see me in deepest Norfolk. We can have weekends walking on the beaches to get the smog out of your hair!'

'We won't lose touch will we?' asked Kat, suddenly worried.

'No, never. Don't be daft.' Changing the subject, Ellie asked: 'Have you still not run into Neil?'

'No. Thank goodness.' Kat kept her tone light and breezy. 'I really don't want to see him. I've been avoiding the Upstairs Bar like the plague. I did see Sean the other day. He said Neil spends all his time in the library these days. Can you imagine? So anyway, not much chance of us running into him there, we never go!'

Ellie was curious. Happy to have Kat back all to herself again, she nevertheless wanted Kat to dish the dirt, to prove her right. But each time she'd asked what had happened, Kat was evasive and changed the subject.

'But why did you split up?' she tried again now. 'You never really explained. It all seemed to be going fine in Switzerland, then suddenly you come back to Uni and say you finished with him.'

'We had some rows,' Kat was vague. 'We were just on different pages. I wanted a proper relationship. I don't think he ever did.'

'So who split up with who in the end?'

'It was my decision.'

'Was it?' Ellie was surprised. 'How did you do it?'

'Oh God, you'll think I'm terrible. I really took the coward's way out. I couldn't face him. I got my dad to say I was out when he called. Then one day I answered the phone and it was him. I told him I'd got back together with Kevin.'

'You didn't! That was a bit vicious, wasn't it? What did he say?'

'He just put the phone down. And didn't call again.'

'I'm not surprised. Crikey! What did he do to deserve that?'

Kat straightened her shoulders and said rather fiercely: 'He turned out to be a wanker like all the rest. We're better off without them. Besides, why are you sticking up for him? I don't think you ever really liked him, did you?'

'Umm, well I can admit it now. No, he gave me the creeps. But anyway, it's not about what I think. But you were a different person when you were with him. I didn't feel you were being yourself.'

'Yeah, maybe.. But I did kind of like that person...Anyway. Water under the bridge, plenty more fish and all that. When did you finish with Roger, by the way?'

'Last week over coffee. Neither of us was really bothered so there wasn't any drama. So, here's to the single life!'

Ellie looked at her watch. 'It's past midnight and I still don't feel like sleeping. Have you got a book I can borrow?'

'Here, take this.' Kat passed her Graham Green's 'The End of The Affair'. 'It's brilliant, I've just finished it. A bit sad,' she warned.

Ellie went back to her room, clutching the book. When Kat called for her the next morning to walk to the exam hall she found her still in pyjamas, tears pouring down her cheeks.

'I couldn't stop reading it,' she sniffed. 'I read all night. Thanks very much for that; you could have lent me something light and happy!'

Kat laughed. 'You daft idiot!' she said affectionately. 'Come on, you've got about ten minutes to get dressed and out of here! Hurry up.'

27

There was still no word from Sean the next day at breakfast. Even Neil had to admit this was strange.

'Is there any other way of getting in contact?' asked Nigel. 'Do you have his work number or anything?'

'No, I don't,' Neil replied. 'I don't even know the name of the accountancy firm they work for. Did he tell any of you?' They shook their heads. 'All I have is his email address and his Facebook page. We've tried both those. I don't think he's got a Linkedin account.'

'We could do friend requests to all his Facebook friends and see if anyone accepts, then ask them if they've seen him,' suggested Nigel.

'What about Matt, what's his surname? I'm sure we can find him somehow,' said Ellie. But no-one knew his surname. They hadn't thought to ask him.

Kat had a sudden idea: 'Maybe he took Sean's surname when they got married. If women do that, why not men? Let's look up Matt Delaney on Facebook – he might be there!'

There were dozens of Matt Delaneys on Facebook. They spent almost an hour checking profile pictures and countries of residence, but didn't find their Matt.

'This is hopeless,' said Neil finally. 'Let's not waste any more time. It's snowing at last, the snow will be fantastic for a change. Fresh powder. Let's make the most of it.'

It had started snowing the night before, and the little resort was quite transformed. A fresh layer covered the rooftops. The streets, which had previously been alternately icy, then slushy, as the thin snow cover froze, then melted, were now several inches deep in crisp pure white. It looked once again as a ski resort should do. Gazing out of the window, Kat had a vivid flashback to their first holiday, all those years before. Following Neil's figure through the silence of falling snow.

'OK,' she said. 'It might be fun to ski today. We won't be able to see much though. Let's do the short blue run that we all know. If we stick to the piste markers it should be fine.'

They collected their equipment and made their way to the ski lift. It was very quiet. The lift hummed and clanked as usual as the chairs swung round the bull wheel. Just a couple of lone figures sat hunched up and solitary ahead of them, their uncountered weight making the chairs tilt crazily. Kat wondered for a moment if this was really a good idea, but the lift operator smiled happily enough as he checked them into position for the next chair. There was a pause while he made Nigel take off his backpack and hold it in front of him, then the chair swung round and they were off. Neil pulled the bar down, having a bit of difficulty getting it over the backpack. Kat rested her skis on the footrest but Ellie let her skis dangle, enjoying the slight pull and stretch in her calf muscles.

'Aren't you scared your skis will fall off?' asked Kat.

'I never thought of that,' said Ellie, swinging her skis back and forth exuberantly, knowing this would get on Kat's nerves. 'If they fall off, one of you will have to go and fetch them.'

'Fat chance! If they fall off we'd never find them! They'd be buried instantly,' Kat retorted.

They could see almost nothing on the long, slow ride to the top of the run. Just the occasional dark outline of trees, which disappeared the higher they climbed. When they skied off the chair, the deep snow was a shock, acting like a brake to slow them to a standstill. Huge flakes swirled around them insistently as they made their way to the start of the run. They could just make out the first piste marker through the fog, a couple of metres away, but nothing more.

'OK! Here we go!' said Neil. 'We've just got to stay together and go slowly. The first bit will be tricky but when we get to the trees it'll be a doddle. Shall I go first and Nigel last?'

They adjusted their goggles, tightened their boots and looped the pole straps around their wrists. Then, with a thumbs up sign, Neil set off slowly towards the first marker. Kat followed, enjoying the feel of the thick snow spraying out as her skis cut into it. At the first marker Neil paused, checking everyone was together, then set off again. But after a while Kat began to feel odd. The old dizziness came back. She could hardly tell up from down, and when her skis were so covered in snow, she was not even sure if she was moving or at a standstill. She began to feel really nauseous, sure she was going to throw up. 'This is horrible, this is horrible,' she thought, as she struggled to keep Neil in sight. When they stopped at the next marker she said: 'I'm sorry, I can't do this anymore, it makes me feel really sick. I'm so dizzy. I think I might faint.'

'OK, let's have a pause,' said Neil. He lifted his googles and shuffled up to put an arm round her. 'Look, we're nearly at the trees. You'll have no problem there, you can get your bearings off them. If we go really, really slowly to the trees, do you think you'll be able to make it?'

'Yeah, I think so. Got no choice really. Don't you guys feel sick at all?' she asked.

They shook their heads. 'No I actually quite like this,' said Ellie, a little apologetically. 'It's like skiing on a cushion; you know you can't hurt yourself.'

'Well, if I ever get to the bottom I'm packing in for the day. I must have a dodgy inner ear or something 'cos I just can't hack this at all.'

Going as slowly as it was possible to go, they made their way down the slope until at last the vague, smudged outline of trees began to appear. This made all the difference, and Kat was able to ski with some semblance of style to the end of the run.

'That's it for me,' she said. 'I'm definitely packing in. You guys carry on though.'

'I'll come back to the chalet with you,' said Neil. 'We can

get some lunch together. I might join the others later.' He turned to Nigel and Ellie. 'Are you guys going to stick to this run?'

'Yeah, at least for a bit. We might try that one down to Hindenalp too; that's mainly through the trees and should be OK.'

'Well, I'll hopefully catch up with you at some point,' said Neil.

He and Kat skied as far as they could to the chalet, then walked uphill the rest of the way. Neil jammed his skis into the thick snow that had piled up outside the door but Kat was not going to venture out again that day – she put her skis on the rack in the basement, changed into her shoes and together they went up the stairs.

'Are you feeling OK now?' asked Neil.

'Yes, fine. It's a kind of motion sickness I guess.'

'I think you should have a whisky – purely for medicinal purposes!'

He poured them both a good measure of Highland Park and they sat down opposite each other, leaning back into the leather sofas. They sipped their drinks in contented silence for a while.

Then Kat gave Neil a direct look and said: 'Did you read my diary yesterday?'

'No! Of course not!' Neil was indignant. 'Why ever would you think I did?'

'Oh, nothing. Someone moved it, that's all.'

'Well it certainly wasn't me. That's not my style.' He thought for a moment. 'Why? Did you write something embarrassing in it?'

Kat felt the blood rushing to her cheeks again, treacherously. She looked down into her whisky glass, silent, not knowing what to say.

'You did didn't you?' He grinned. 'Come on, spill the beans. Did you write about me?'

'Only about what a total arse you still are.'

Neil laughed. 'Yeah, I can imagine. You've kept a diary for

all these years? I remember you used to write it every night, before. What do you find to write about?'

'Oh, these last few years it's been absolutely fascinating. What I had for dinner. What I watched on TV. Which birds I saw in the garden. You really should read it actually, it's riveting!' She paused. 'I was going to burn all my diaries in a huge bonfire one year, but now that Peter's gone, I'm glad I didn't. One day when I'm up to it, I'll re-read them and remember all the things we did together.'

'Yeah, that's good.' They were silent again for a while. Then Neil leant forward to pour himself another whisky. Still leaning forward he looked at her, his blue eyes direct and searching. 'When do you think you might be up to it?'

Kat hesitated. Was there a double meaning here or not? What was he suggesting? 'Are you asking about the diaries or about life in general?'

'I suppose I'm asking about moving on. I'm sorry, it's such a horribly overused expression.' As Kat remained silent, not knowing how to reply, Neil rushed on: 'I'm sorry, I'm sorry, I'm being insensitive. I don't want to make you uncomfortable. Let's change the subject. What shall we eat for lunch? Something here, or shall we go to that pizzeria?'

As talk returned to the mundane subject of food, Kat was left wondering what was left unspoken. Was he interested in her again? And if so, how did she feel about it?

◆ ◆ ◆

A couple of hours later, Neil walked her back to the chalet. They had shared a pizza and a bottle of red wine, and reminisced a little about the old days – safe subjects like the music they used to listen to and the pinball machines they used to play.

'Do you remember that Kiss machine?' asked Kat. 'I can

still picture it now, it was so garish. Red and white with all the faces on the bumper things.'

'Yeah, and the noise it used to make when it hit them. I can still remember that. Christ, we must have spent a fortune on that machine.'

'Not really, we used to win all those replays, remember? We used to get up early the next morning just to play all our replays!'

'Crazy times!' said Neil. 'Here we are, home again, home again. Do you mind if I ski some more, see if I can find the others? There's still a couple of hours before it gets dark.'

'No, I don't mind; but Neil, you've had two whiskies and half a bottle of wine. And it's still snowing. I don't think you should go. It's dangerous.'

'Don't worry, I'll be fine,' he said. He gave her a light kiss on the cheek and went to fetch his boots.

28
Back Then

Kat stifled a yawn as the Vice-Chancellor droned on. It was supposed to be an inspiring speech, urging the hundreds of bright young minds in front of him to do great things in the future, but he had a terrible voice; flat and toneless. Kat's mind began to wander. She looked around her. Rows of black-gowned students, fresh faced, eager, sitting on pews at the back of the cathedral. In front of them the parents and family members, dressed in their most respectable clothes, some filming the dull speech with camcorders. On the stage the lecturers sat in a semi-circle behind the lectern, their faces impassive and their hand folded solemnly in their laps. Their multicoloured robes provided the only splash of colour. A small group of musicians below the stage had rested their instruments and were looking as bored as she felt. Suddenly her attention was caught by a movement. A butterfly had made it into the cool, dark cathedral and was trying valiantly to land on the music stand in front of the chief violinist – a small, balding man with a red face. He, in turn, was trying to discourage it with repeated flicks of his bow, without drawing attention to the movement. The butterfly would not give up, rising into the air, only to settle again a few seconds later. Ellie was sitting in the row in front. Kat poked her lightly in the back and pointed at the violinist. They began to giggle. Then snort. Ellie's shoulders were shaking and Kat felt tears coming into her eyes as she tried to supress the laughter.

The Vice-Chancellor was into his stride. 'The milestones of life… we reflect on… it's not an ending, but a beginning. You have emerged from the chrysalis and will now take wing…'

This was too much to bear. Kat and Ellie bent double in their seats and shook with the effort of remaining silent, making their respective pews bounce. Their classmates looked round in surprise, not sure if they were crying or laughing. Someone passed Kat a tissue, assuming she was overcome with emotion at the prospect of leaving the university. This only served to set her off again.

'As Nelson Mandela said, education is a weapon that can change the world. Sitting here today are the very people who will shape a better world.'

A round of applause broke out, and Kat and Ellie were able to bring themselves under control. Row by row, the graduands ahead of them stood up and filed up the aisle to receive their scrolls, shake hands with the Dean and be quickly caught on camera. Kat sat up, hoping her mascara had not run too much for the photographer. As she waited her turn, she wondered which of her classmates were going to shape a better world. They did look wonderful today – shining and pure, a different breed entirely from the bleary-eyed students who had stumbled into lectures and grumbled about impossible assignments. Would Ellie shape the world? She would make a good politician. She had the human touch, immense common sense and a strong streak of stubbornness. But Ellie had accepted her logistics job and was bound for deepest Norfolk, buried away in the country. Miles away. She was going to miss the daily contact with her friend so much. What if Ellie made other, better friends? She made friends so easily!

Kat realised for the first time that she loved this place and didn't want to leave. Maybe the last three years hadn't been as exciting or challenging as she'd expected, but they had been a comfortable cocoon, a secure environment. She was unexpectedly felled by a wave of premature nostalgia, and felt a lump rising in her throat.

Then it was their turn. She stood up and followed her classmates into the aisle, with Ellie a dozen people ahead. Ellie turned round and grinned at her, lifting one leg and showing off a shoe. That had been Ellie's idea – and a very good one; they had gone clothes shopping for graduation outfits together in a Leeds department store. Kat had originally been looking at dresses and trouser suits, but Ellie had overruled her: 'No-one is going to see what you're wearing under the gown. It's stupid spending money on that. I think we should buy some really fun shoes instead.' So that's what they did. Ellie's high-heels were a bright, sunshine yellow, and Kat's court shoes were a violent lime green.

Their moment passed quickly. A name, a handshake, a smile, 'Congratulations', the flash of the camera. The next name. Ellie's parents had cheered loudly as the Vice-Chancellor read out 'Eleanor Rose Bradshaw', and Ellie had given them a thumbs up, a huge grin on her face. Kat was relieved to see she'd made it up the steps without mishap in the unaccustomed heels. Then her turn. 'Catherine Louise Williams.' She found herself also grinning widely at the Vice-Chancellor, and almost tempted to curtsy.

Then it was over. They filed out of the cathedral to the accompaniment of the little orchestra, and milled about on the steps outside. Kat found her parents and hugged them. Her mum was in her Sunday best: a red two-piece suit, her white-gloved hand clutching a small square bag. Her dad looked stiff and uncomfortable in his dark suit and tie. Dozens of photos were taken, amidst shouts and laughter. Kat found Ellie and asked her dad to take several shots of them together, in front of the cathedral, arms slung around each other, the fabulous shoes raised, can-can style. The German class were called onto the steps by the official photographer to take the classic photo, throwing their mortar-boards into the air. Dozens of fathers got into position just behind the main cameraman, and Kat was pleased to see Ellie's dad there, Kodac Instamatic at the ready. 'One, two, three,' they tossed their anachronistic black hats skywards. Click, click, click.

One by one, families started to stroll down towards the

marquee below, where there would be drinks and music. As Kat looked around for her parents, she saw a familiar figure hovering a little way off, watching her. Her heart thumped in spite of herself. Neil. Why did he still have this effect on her? She thought she was over him, but she was annoyed to find she couldn't look away. He made a gesture with his head and she walked towards him.

'Hi,' he said.

'Hi. What are you doing here?'

'I came to say congratulations.'

'Oh…Thanks. When's your graduation?'

'Thursday morning.'

'Is your mum coming down for it?'

'Nah. It's too far. I told her not to bother. So… what are you doing next? Have you got a job?'

'Yeah. In marketing. In London.'

'Right. Cool.' They looked at each other, Kat keeping her face impassive, but Neil seeming preoccupied.

'Umm, I wanted to ask you something…' he began.

'OK.'

But just then Kat's parents came up behind them, her father looking at his watch and her mother looking straight at Neil.

'Who's this then?' asked her mum with false brightness, in a voice that made Kat cringe. 'Are you going to introduce us to your friend?'

Kat knew that her mum would be taking in Neil's ripped jeans and sweat-stained t-shirt, would be disapproving of his unkempt hair and hunched-shouldered posture. She in turn was embarrassed by her mother's going-to-church outfit and her upper-middle class vowels. She felt caught in the middle, desperately uncomfortable.

'Oh. Mum, Dad, this is Neil. You remember? Neil, this is my mum and dad.'

'Oh. Yes.' They shook hands awkwardly and made stilted small talk about the beautiful June weather and the peculiar architecture of the cathedral.

Neil turned to Kat again, and was about to say something, but at the same time her father said: 'Everyone seems to be moving off. Perhaps we'd better go too?'

Neil's eyes bored into hers, trying to convey something, but all he said was: 'Well, good luck I guess. Bye.'

As he walked off, Kat's mother snapped her handbag shut decisively and said: 'So that was Neil. I must say, I'm glad you're not going out with him anymore. You can do better than that. He seems very working class.'

Kat bristled, instantly defensive and furious, but bit back a retort about snobbishness. This was her parents' day as much as hers, after all. Pick your battles. This one could wait. She watched Neil walk off in the other direction, with his familiar loping stride and hunched shoulders. Then, with a mental shrug, she put on a bright smile worthy of her mother and said 'OK, let's go before all the canapes and drinks run out!' The three of them followed the trail of flapping black gowns down the hill to the marquee.

PART 2

29

Ellie was having fun skiing with her husband Nigel. Just the two of them. Nobody else to worry about. She loved the softness of the snow, the way you could send great arcs of white shooting behind you as you made a turn. The runs were almost empty and it felt as if she and Nigel had the whole resort to themselves. She was happy to have a moment away from Neil, if she was honest. He was OK, but so intense! So competitive. Not really her cup of tea at all. But Kat obviously still liked him. If they got together, would he pull Kat away from her, as he'd done once before? 'Oh bugger Neil,' she thought, and concentrated on keeping up with Nigel.

Her thighs were beginning to really ache and she was cold. At the bottom of the run she said to Nigel: 'I need a break and a hot chocolate. Do you want to come too or are you going to carry on?'

'I'll just go down twice more, then I'll come and join you. I'm loving this powder. Will you be in that café over there?' He pointed to the little bar on the right of the ski lift, it's terrace optimistically lined with deckchairs, which were now sagging under the weight of accumulated snow.

'Yep, I'll be inside, by the fire if they've got one!'

'Okey-doke! We'll get something to eat when I come back. See you in a bit.'

'Be careful, it's still pretty foggy at the top!'

'I will, don't worry.'

Ellie stuck her skis in a drift, loosened her boots and pushed open the door. The warmth and the smell of cheese hit her immediately and she realised she was starving. She decided to have a couple of gruyere tarts with her hot chocolate. That wouldn't spoil her appetite too much.

An hour and a half later, Ellie was still sitting at her table, a second hot chocolate now empty. She spooned up the thick chocolate which was glued to the bottom of the mug and licked her finger to pick up the few pastry crumbs that remained on the plate. Nigel should have been here by now. It was a short run, he could have done it four or five times by now. The bar was beginning to close up its hot food counter – Nigel was missing out! Where the bloody hell was he?

Ellie was not a worrier. She always assumed things would come out right, and usually they did. Maybe Nigel had just forgotten the time; he was having too much fun.

After another ten minutes though, Ellie had to admit to the possibility that something might have happened. She looked out of the window again towards the bottom of the run. Hardly any skiers were coming down it – she had counted three in the last half hour.

'I'd better go and look for him,' she thought, getting up reluctantly and putting on her jacket. She left the cosy warmth of the bar and went out into the cold. The sky was just beginning to darken slightly and she shivered. Snapping on her skis, she glided over to the chairlift and pushed herself up to the lift attendant with her sticks.

'Haben Sie meinen Mann gesehen?' she asked, 'Er hat eine rote Jacke.' Oh God, what was the German for backpack? He would remember Nigel's troublesome backpack surely? Oh yes, Rucksack of course wasn't it? Bloody hell, of course. Noun, masculine. 'Er hat einen grossen Rucksack. Schwartz.' She worried for a second that she was getting her endings all wrong, then told herself not to be stupid. What did grammar matter now? But the lift attendant shook his head apologetically. He hadn't seen him.

Ellie decided to go and look for him. She didn't panic. As she sat on the chairlift, she went through the possibilities.

Nigel was the most sensible, the best prepared, the most well-informed person in the world when it came to safety. If he'd fallen, he'd have taken all the necessary measures to be found. He would have stayed on the piste, put his skis into a cross shape and waited for a skier to find him. But knowing Nigel, he could also have completely lost track of time. Or got into conversation with someone. Or was helping someone out who was struggling. Lots of possibilities.

At the top of the run, Ellie skied slowly down, making huge turns to cover as much ground as she could. There was no sign of Nigel.

She decided to go up again. Maybe she'd missed him the first time. As she positioned herself to receive the chairlift, holding out a hand ready to grab and slow the seat, another person skied up smoothly beside her. They took the lift together and Ellie pulled down the bar. She glanced across at the figure in the seat beside her, glad to have a bit of company.

'Ich habe meinen Mann verloren,' she said. There was no reaction from the figure next to her. She tried again in English: 'I've lost my husband. I think he's on the run somewhere.' This time the man turned his head slowly to look at her. His eyes were impossible to distinguish beneath the goggles, and most of his face was covered by a black woolly hat pulled down low, and a black scarf pulled up over his nose and mouth. He seemed to stare at her for a second or two, then turned his head away again, not saying a word. 'How rude!' thought Ellie. She wasn't going to let him get away with that. Must be a young guy, they have no manners at all these days. She would make him talk if it killed her.

'J'ai perdu mon mari. Vous êtes français? Mais enfin! Sprechen Sie Deutsch? Sagen Sie doch etwas!' But the man stared resolutely ahead and Ellie gave up, fuming silently to herself. She looked down instead to see if she could see any people on the slope below, but all was swirling mass of white.

The lift seemed to be taking a painfully long time today. Ellie was impatient. They must be about three quarters of the way up by now, she calculated. Then, suddenly, she felt her hands slipping off the bar as her silent chair-mate lifted it and pushed it behind them.

'It's too soon!' she yelled at him. 'Zu schnell! We're not at the top yet! It's dangerous here, there's a bloody ravine to cross!'

Still she was indignant, furious with this rude and anti-social yob; it didn't occur to her to be scared. When he grabbed her shoulders in a lightning fast movement and flung her off the chair with ease, she found she was falling, falling, though the cloud of white. 'Oh! What? No! This is not really happening. It can't be!' Her brain was incapable of accepting the reality, even as her body plummeted downwards. She hit the rocks below with a sickening thump and Ellie thought no more.

30

Kat pottered about the chalet on her own, not knowing how to fill the time. She lit the fire in the wood-burner. She read for a bit, but couldn't get into the story. She went upstairs and peeped into Neil's bedroom, looking for clues that would help her understand him better. It was neat. The bed was made with military precision. 'Must be the boarding school effect,' she thought, looking at the hospital corners. Feeling a bit guilty, she opened his wardrobe. Lots of warm clothes, dark colours. His wallet sat on the shelf next to his phone; for a minute she was tempted to look through the contents, but then she stopped. 'Don't be a hypocrite,' she reprimanded herself. 'You can't give him a hard time for reading your diary and then go through his wallet.' She closed the door and went back downstairs.

'I know, I'll cook something!' she decided. She pulled on her coat and boots and walked down to the village. Before she got to the little supermarket, a sudden impulse made her turn and search out the path towards the old chalet. Everything was slightly different. New shop fronts. Different signs. But the deep snow was just the same as it had been back then, making her memory kick in. Yes, that was it. You turned just before the ski shop. She waded through the snow, trying to make out which building they had stayed in all those years ago. Surely that one wasn't it... was it? It couldn't be – or could it? The little chalet looked defeated and desolate. One downstairs window was boarded up. Through another window, she could see the red and white curtains, still drawn, but badly faded. The wooden balcony around the first floor showed frightening gaps in the floorboards. One of the prettily carved shutters was hanging loosely from a broken hinge. Kat shivered. The whole place had an atmosphere of long abandon. A little path had been cleared through the snow to the front door. Was there someone living there? It looked unlikely. Maybe the footsteps had been made by the postman delivering junk mail.

As she walked slowly up to the door, she was assailed by vivid memories. Silvio sitting under the lamp, reading his book. Rob telling horror stories, his face glowing and animated in the firelight. And Gillian, leaning against a wall, glossy and self-assured, with a slight smirk playing on her lips.

She wondered what had become of Silvio. Had he inherited that great estate in Italy? Had he managed to save his home? Or had he turned his back on everything, escaped his destiny and let the castle fall into ruin? She remembered how he'd kept himself apart from the others, as if he'd been from a different generation. How she'd ended up feeling sorry for him. She hoped he's found a way to make things work. She'd lost touch with Rob and Sue. She knew that they'd married, but had they opened their pub together? Were they still married? And Gillian. I bet she's married to some Tory politician, with a London townhouse and a country retreat in Surrey. Or maybe she's a politician herself, or something high up in the civil service. God help us.

She peered through a crack in the boarded up window and could just about make out some furniture. As her eyes adjusted to the gloom inside, she recognised the same squashy sofa and threadbare rug. God! The whole place has been frozen in time! That rug. She pictured it clearly. A red and orange rag rug, a bit musty even then, with a couple of blackened patches where embers had fallen onto it from the fire. She saw again the two naked bodies, entwined and oblivious. She expected to experience a glimmer of the anger she'd felt at the time, but instead she just felt sad. My God, she'd been so naive back then. Would she react the same way if it happened now? People were much more casual about sex these days. Not many young folk believed you stayed faithful to one person all your life. These days it was all Tinder and open relationships. Even Ellie had been tempted away. She walked back to the door and was about to try the handle when she stopped. 'No, I don't want to know,' she thought. 'It will be damp and dingy inside. Bound to be mice or rats. Too depressing. No point hanging about here. It's all ancient history.'

Instead, she made her way back to the supermarket and bought pastry, cheese and eggs, then back in the beautiful, luxurious and modern chalet, she started to make her speciality quiche. It was one of the only things she could make with complete confidence; it never failed. Even Ellie said Kat's quiche was better than hers. It was a total cheat; bought flaky pastry, crème fraiche from a tub – but she hadn't told Ellie that! As she beat the eggs and cream together, she was suddenly felled by an intense longing for Peter. He had loved her quiche but always wanted to eat it lukewarm, whereas she liked it straight from the oven. It was an argument they had every time. 'But the cheese tastes so much cheesier when it's cooled down.' She could almost feel him beside her now, watching her busy fingers, preparing to win the battle of the quiche. Such little things they had argued about. Who's turn it was to drive after a night out. Who forgot to set the video recorder for the last episode of a Swedish thriller... The predictability of their bickering had been comforting. She had really known Peter. Known him through and through, so she could guess what he was going to say before he said it, could finish his sentences when he couldn't be bothered to do so. She'd known exactly what do when he said 'Can you thingy the whatsit?' What did she really know about Neil? He gave so little away, gave a strong but silent impression, but then suddenly surprised her with some fact that she struggled to make fit. He was still a mystery. Did she really want that?

The quiche was just the temperature Peter would have loved by the time Kat heard the door open. She looked up from her book, expecting to see the three of them come in, but it was just Neil.

'Hi there. Are the other two still taking their boots off?'

she asked.

Neil looked puzzled. 'Are they not back here then?'

'No, you're the first. Did you ski with them?'

'No, I tried to find them but no luck. Actually it was almost impossible to find anyone in these conditions. They should be back soon; the lifts have closed now.'

He took off his jacket, came over and kissed her on the top of the head. 'How you feeling?'

'Absolutely fine. I've had a lovely lazy time. And look! I've made dinner!'

'I can smell it! Smells wonderful. I'm just off for a quick shower. Do you want to open a bottle of wine? There's a nice Viognier in the box out the back.'

An hour later, Kat started to get a bit concerned. 'If they'd gone for a drink I'm sure they would have told us! And you'd think they'd dump their skis here first. It's really dark outside now.'

Another hour passed and Kat was now really anxious. 'It's nearly half past seven! Neil, something must have happened.'

'Maybe they just wanted a bit of time on their own – or wanted to give us time on our own,' he suggested.

'No. First Sean and Matt. Now Ellie and Nigel. I don't like it.'

'Let's think. If they were doing the Hindenalp run, they might have missed the last lift back up the mountain to get back here. They might be stuck in Hindenalp for the night.'

'What if they're stuck on the mountain somewhere in the dark?'

'Nigel knows what to do. He'd keep them safe and warm. Don't worry. But I think I should go and alert the patrol people. See if they know anything. You stay here in case they come back. I'll be as quick as I can.'

He threw on his jacket, stepped into his boots again and made for the door. Opening it, he turned and said: 'Try not to worry!'

Kat paced about the chalet, not able to relax for a second.

She went to the big glass windows again and again, although it was too dark to see anything but the lights in the village windows below. She was talking to herself: 'Come on Ellie, come on Ellie!' She looked at her watch: half past eight now. Oh God, if they were stuck outside all night in this... No, they must be safe. They must have missed the last lift. They would be back with a story to tell in the morning. Surely!

Neil came back at last, shaking the snow from his coat before coming inside. 'I've put out a missing persons alert. It's too late for the patrols to do anything tonight. They asked us to report to them first thing tomorrow if they're still missing. They're going to phone the hotels in Hindenalp to see if they checked in there tonight. If they don't come back on the first lift tomorrow they'll do a full search. Don't worry. They'll find them. Nigel's got all that gear; if he's stuck on the mountain he's probably built an igloo by now and skinned a rabbit for dinner.'

His attempt at humour did nothing to make Kat feel any better.

They spent a silent mealtime together, sitting opposite each other at the massive oak table. Kat could only pick at the quiche. She hadn't touched her wine. She looked at the door every time she heard a slight noise from outside. Neil tried to make light conversation a couple of times, but she was distracted and barely responded. He knew she was thinking about Ellie, so changed tack and asked about their friendship.

'Have you been friends with Ellie since you were in first year?'

'Yes. First term actually.'

'And did you stay in touch all the time, after we left Uni?'

'Yeah. Those first couple of years after Uni were brilliant. Ellie used to come up to London for the weekend. She had a little 250cc motorbike and didn't think anything of riding it up from Norfolk in all weathers. She's much braver than me. We used to go shopping in Camden Market, go drinking in Covent Garden, then go on to a nightclub like Heaven, and dance till the early hours. We thought we had the world at our feet.' She smiled at the memory.

'Then you both ended up moving back up north?'

Yes, eventually. Ellie got a bit bored of Norfolk. And for me, well London was great for a while. I think everyone should experience it. But long term it gets too frenetic. And too expensive.'

'Who got married first, you or Ellie?'

'Me. Ellie brought Nigel to our wedding. That was a surprise. It was the first time I'd met him. You can hear his laugh all through the wedding video, its unmistakable. So loud and infectious. I could tell she'd found the right man. Someone as joyful as herself.'

'Hm. Yes,' said Neil, nodding in agreement. 'She was such a happy person.'

Kat's head snapped up. She looked across at Neil, puzzled and alarmed. 'Why did you say 'was'? Why use the past tense? Do you think she's…?'

'Oh God, no! I didn't mean anything,' interrupted Neil quickly, raising both hands and looking aghast. 'I just meant when I knew her at University. In the old days.'

Kat continued to stare at him.

'She will be fine!' insisted Neil. 'They both will be. Everything will work out in the morning. You'll see.' He smiled reassuringly. 'Shall I top up your wine glass?'

'No, thanks. I think I'll have an early night.' She got up and pushed her chair back. 'Goodnight. See you tomorrow.'

'Goodnight.'

Neil watched her walk up the stairs. Then he refilled his own glass and sat back in his chair, a thoughtful expression on his face.

Kat lay in bed, mentally exhausted, but sleep refused to come for several hours. When at last she fell asleep, her dreams were fractured and nightmarish. In one dream she was alone in her own house, back in Yorkshire. She stumbled on a door that she had never noticed before. She opened the door and discovered, delighted, that her house was twice as big as she had previously thought; there were many other doors to open and rooms to explore. One room was full of treasures from a previous occupant. A doll's house, jewellery, exquisite paintings. Another was stacked high with boxes. A third door was difficult to open, the wood having expanded into the doorframe. She shoved it with her shoulder until it creaked open. A dark room, musty and damp. As her eyes adjusted she saw a figure in a rocking chair, looking at her, smiling. It was Peter. She ran towards him, overjoyed to find him again, but then noticed it was not Peter at all. It was Ellie. She was concentrating on knitting a long scarf that pooled in a spiral round her feet. When she looked up, Kat saw that half her face was missing. She put down her knitting and started to rise from the rocking chair.

Kat woke up with a start, heart thumping, trying to work out what the nightmare could have meant. She often had that recurring dream of a house with unexpected hidden rooms. Sometimes the dream turned out to be delightful, and other times frightening. She had once asked a psychologist acquaintance what she thought it could mean, and been told that it might be something to do with her own personality, being stuck in the same space, wanting to open up new avenues but unsure if that would turn out well or not. But why had she dreamed of Peter? And why, when she dreamed of Ellie coming towards her, had she been repulsed and terrified?

31

When Nigel felt his consciousness returning, the first thing he was aware of was the cold. His eyelids felt stuck together under his goggles. His fingers and toes were numb and his teeth were chattering uncontrollably. Gingerly, he tested his limbs, slowly moving both arms and legs, trying to make his fingers and toes unclench. He didn't think he had broken any bones, but his whole body felt battered. He knew that his shivering was a good sign. His body was fighting to keep him warm. If he wasn't shivering he would be near to hypothermia, and that could be fatal. He then tried to work out exactly where he was. He seemed to be hanging from something. Painfully slowly, he clenched and unclenched his hands until he could feel a little life returning to them. Very carefully he took off one glove and held it protectively in the other hand. After several attempts he eventually manged to unzip his jacket pocket. He found the little torch he kept there and quickly put his glove back on, almost dropping it in his hurry. The effort of this small movement had made him feel weary and he fought to keep himself awake. Finally he switched the torch on and swung the beam of light in a big circle around him. All he could see were the black shapes of trees, spaced out, descending down steeply below. He pointed the beam upwards and saw that he was dangling from a branch. It looked as if a strap of his backpack had been caught in the tree, stopping his fall. He pointed the beam down and saw he wasn't far from the ground. He needed to somehow unhook his backpack. He had handwarmers, food and water inside.

 He tried to find a foothold on a branch, but again and

again his heavy ski boot slipped off. He stopped for a moment. Just don't panic, keep calm, keep trying. Once more he fought to find a foothold, kicking some of the ice off the branch. This time his foot stayed there. Holding the torch in his teeth, he reached for a higher branch and gradually raised himself until he was standing on it, praying it would hold his weight. Again he paused. Any mistake now and he could freeze to death. Carefully he slid one shoulder and then the other out of the backpack. Released from his weight, the branch snapped upwards and the pack danced, showering him with snow. For one awful moment he thought he had lost it. But no, it was swinging happily from the branch above, still attached. He looped one arm round the tree trunk and stretched the other up towards it. Not high enough. He paused, once again moving his toes and fingers to keep the circulation going. Then, hugging he trunk tightly, he kicked the snow off a higher branch and raised himself up onto it. He tried again to reach the pack. Almost there! Arm outstretched, he was inches away. He loosened his vice-like grip on the trunk so that he was just clinging to it with his forearm, and leaned further towards the pack. Yes! He had it. He tugged. Nothing. Just another shower of snow. He was almost overcome with frustration, but forced himself to calm down and think rationally. Again he took off his glove, shoved it in his inside jacket and reached into his top pocket. Yes, the Swiss army knife was there. Still holding the torch in his mouth, he once again reached out towards the pack. This time he made his frozen fingers cut again and again at the strap. At first it seemed to make no impact on the strong nylon but then at last it started to fray. He sawed and sawed at the strap until there were just a couple of threads holding it together. Finally he yanked it sharply and the pack fell to the ground. Once again he rested, exhausted, beating his chest with his free hand to keep warm. Then he slowly felt his way down the tree, testing each branch before trusting his weight on it. He let himself fall the last two metres and landed in soft snow, the pack beside him. Yes! He was on the ground, no bones were broken and he had his emergency gear. He was not going to die, not tonight.

He cast the thin torch beam around him and saw that the mountainside was thinly wooded with large drifts of snow between the stunted trees. This was good. He could build a snow hole. He'd seen it on a survival programme - Bear Grylls probably, or Ray Mears. He remembered pretty much what to do. Dig upwards into a drift, line the hole with branches. Poke something through the top for an air hole. First he had to get warm though. He pulled the pack towards him and found the ten-pack of handwarmers. He put two inside his jacket, and one in each hand. Then he undid his boots and put one inside each before putting them back on. At first the pain was excruciating as the sensation came back, but then it started to feel really good and his optimism returned. He found an energy bar and ate it quickly, then drank a few sips of water. Ready at last, he made a snowball to test the snow. Luck was with him; it wasn't powdery, it compacted easily. He looked around for the largest drift, tested the wind direction by licking his finger, then putting his gloves back on, he started to dig.

A good hour later he was satisfied. The hole was just big enough to take his body and the walls had started to freeze together to make a solid structure. He crawled into the hole feet-first, judging this safer in case it collapsed in the night, and finally pulled his backpack into the entrance to block out the cold wind.

At last Nigel was able to take in what was happening to him. He momentarily felt a twinge of pride in his achievements. 'I built a snow cave! I can't wait to tell Ellie' he thought. 'I'll be able to dine out on this story for years'. His weary brain tried to remember how he had ended up falling down the mountain. He was so tired. He thought back with difficulty. He had been at the top of the run. He'd just skied off the chairlift and was pushing himself towards the start of the run. The fog had been dense and the snow swirled around him. That's right, he could picture it. But what had happened then? He forced himself to remember. He had been about to start the run when he'd thought he heard someone call his name. It had been a high voice, and came from the right, above the lift. He'd stopped and listened again.

'Nigel! Help me!'

'Bloody hell!' he'd thought. 'Who's that? It wasn't Ellie was it? It didn't sound like Ellie! She was safe in the restaurant. Could it be Ellie? Was she in trouble?' He'd unclipped his skis and used his poles to climb upwards towards the voice.

'Hello? Who's there? Where are you?'

'Over here!' came the voice, from higher up. Nigel had struggled on through the knee-deep snow. He came to a rocky outcrop and stopped. He looked around but could see nothing but snow and rock.

'Ellie? Ellie? Is that you?'

Now Nigel remembered with a shock. Jesus, there had been someone there. But not Ellie. He had turned round in time to see a dark figure swinging a ski towards him, aiming at his chest. He'd turned away from the blow instinctively, but the force of the impact had knocked him off his feet and sent him crashing downwards.

Slowly it dawned on Nigel. Someone had tried to kill him. This was no accident. The person knew his name. Had lured him to the edge of the cliff. Oh God, Ellie! Was she safe? What had she done when he didn't show up? Had she come looking for him, or had she returned to the chalet? Fuck, fuck, fuck! He had to get back to the chalet and warn her. Warn the others. Christ, Sean and Matt! Maybe they hadn't gone back to London. Were they dead? Oh sweet Jesus. Was there was a killer in Felsenalp?

32

Kat woke up with the sun streaming through her bedroom window. She'd forgotten to close the blinds the night before. She felt a joyful surge of energy. Yes! Good weather at last. Great skiing today. Then reality caught up with her. Ellie and Nigel were missing. As her brain finally registered the fact, her body reacted. Her chest tightened, as if someone had it in a stranglehold, and her throat felt as if a massive air bubble was trapped there. She remembered these feelings from two years ago. A panic attack would not help now. She forced herself to do her breathing exercises, inhaling and then exhaling as slowly as she could for five minutes, and the symptoms subsided.

She got out of bed and padded across to Ellie and Nigel's room, hoping against all probability that they had returned in the night. The bedroom was empty. She threw a jumper over her pyjamas and went downstairs, where Neil was making coffee in the kitchen area.

'Any news?' she asked.

'Nothing. It's too early though. It's only half past eight. If the lifts open at eight, even if they made it onto the first lift, they still wouldn't be up and down again by now. I reckon we should wait 'til about ten before we contact the rescue team again.'

'Really? That long? Isn't there anything we can do?'

'Let's go and check our emails again – if they stayed in a hotel overnight they might have emailed us.'

'No, I don't think they took their phones with them. Digital detox, remember?'

'Shit, yes, you're right.' He paused, then added: 'But they could have borrowed a phone. Or used the hotel computer. Let's go and get breakfast as usual and check. There might be something from Sean too, you never know. Here, have a coffee then we'll get dressed and go.'

At ten o'clock they were back in the chalet, and there was still no sign.

'You wait here,' said Neil. 'I'll go and tell them to start the search.' He gave her a quick hug, then quickly left.

Kat was left alone in the chalet again. She wandered around the big open space, randomly picking up objects and examining them with unseeing eyes before replacing them. Her mind was on Ellie, creating image after image of her, lost on the mountain, or injured, suffering. For some reason she kept returning to a clear mental picture of Ellie lying amongst jagged rocks, her legs at a strange angle. 'For God's sake,' she scolded herself. 'Don't be so negative. She'll be OK. She has to be.' She closed her eyes tightly to stop tears coming. Ellie was more important to her than anyone, apart from her children. She wasn't sure how she'd cope if Ellie was no longer there to push her along, tease her, make her laugh at herself. The tears started to fall and Kat wiped them away angrily. 'Snap out of it!' she said aloud. 'This isn't helping anyone.'

Almost without thinking, Kat found herself keeping busy in the best way she knew, as she had done so many times in the past when life was difficult. She gathered together all the cleaning products she could find and threw herself into giving the bathrooms and the kitchen a thorough scrub. She focused with utter intensity on making the tiles and shower glass sparkle, getting rid of the cooking stains on the hob, even cleaning out the cutlery drawers.

Then she looked at her watch. An hour had passed and Neil was still not back. She supposed he must be providing the rescue patrol with details of their clothing, their possible whereabouts, their ski levels. At least the weather was good today – the patrol would be able to see easily. Maybe they'd send out a helicopter too. Come on Neil! Tell me what's happening! Come on!

She looked around for something else to do, and decided to build a fire in the stove. She saw that the log basket was almost empty and went down the stairs to the lean-to to fill it up. 'We'll need more kindling too,' she thought, hoping that splitting a couple of logs would help calm her jangling nerves. She was good at splitting logs, having done this job on holidays in Scotland. She was much more adept than Peter had been. She chose a couple of logs that were not too heavy, and which showed already the beginnings of a separation in the grain. She balanced one carefully upright on the large round chopping block and looked around for the axe. Normally it was left wedged lightly in the chopping block. Where had it got to? She looked around, hoping it was on top of the wood pile. No luck. Not on the ground. Then she saw it. It was embedded deeply into one of the thick posts holding the lean-to up. She examined it more closely. It must have been swung into the post with some force; the blade was only half visible. How stupid! It would take her some effort to get it free again. She gripped the wooden handle with two hands, ready to give it a good heave. Then she paused. She looked more closely. The back of the axe was strangely discoloured at the top. A reddish-brown stain covered the metal head and some of the wood. It looked a bit lumpy. Was that…? Was that hair? She let go and jumped back, horrified. Jesus Christ! What the hell? Her heart started thumping again, far too fast, and she felt the panic rising. She took several steps back and turned away, forcing herself to take the deep breaths, hold and exhale slowly. At last she felt her heartbeat slowing. She took another look at the axe, searching for some logical explanation. It looked like blood. Had it been used to dispatch a rabbit? Cut the head off a chicken? But who would borrow their axe to do that? And if not an animal…

She went slowly up the stairs and sat on one of the heavy oak chairs, her elbows on the table and her head in her hands, trying to think. Her thoughts were flying in a million directions and she fought to control them. Be logical. What are the facts? Six people had arrived at the chalet. Only two were now left. Sean and Matt's note had been strange – too brief. Sean had not taken his phone. It was not normal that they hadn't been in touch since. Had they really left? Or had something happened to them here and someone was covering up? Someone had been in her room, she was fairly sure, and had read her diary. Nigel and Ellie were missing. They had been on one of two easy, gentle blue runs. Admittedly the weather conditions were terrible, but they were neither of them risk-takers. If they had been forced to spend the night in Hindenalp they would have been back by now. This was all adding up to something terrifying. 'There's just me and Neil left,' she thought. What did that mean? Did it mean that Neil was involved? She tried to remember where Neil had been when the others had disappeared. She racked her brains. She thought he had been alone each time, with no alibi. She shook her head. No! What on earth are you thinking? It's not Neil! You know Neil. A creeping doubt entered her mind. Did she really know him? He had a dark side. He was fascinated by violence – at least in theoretical form. What was it he'd said? That he loved blood and gore? His father had been blown up – had that had some terrible psychological impact? He knew how to use guns. He'd killed an animal when he was younger. Didn't they say that psychopaths always started with animals? But no, he was tender, affectionate. He was a loner, but his emotions were sincere and normal, weren't they? It wasn't Neil. Impossible. Should she tell him about the axe? Would he help her figure things out? But what if... If he was somehow involved, then she should get the hell out of here, grab her passport and money and take the first cable car out of here. Go, go now!

At that moment the door opened and Neil walked in. He looked tired. Kat noticed the dark circles under his eyes and the grim set of his mouth. He gave her a half smile as he took off his jacket. Her Neil, familiar and solid and reassuring. How could she ever have thought him capable of murder? She jumped up and ran towards him.

'What news? What's happening?'

'Sorry that took so long. They're getting the ground search team together and they've contacted the helicopter base in town. They'll find them, they're experts in this terrain.' He looked at her, taking in her paleness, her unwashed hair, the lack of make-up. 'Are you OK? You look terrible. You're shaking.'

She shook her head dismissively. 'I'm OK. But what should we do? Did they give us any instructions? How can we help?'

'There's nothing to do. We've got to leave it up to the experts. They will find them, I promise.' He put his arms round her and enveloped her in a massive hug. Kat felt some of her doubts slip away as she relaxed into his comforting embrace. She breathed in his familiar smell and felt the tension easing from her neck and spine. He stroked the hair at the back of her head for a few minutes, murmuring softly: 'It's going to be OK, it's going to be OK.' Then he drew apart, putting his hands on her shoulders and looking into her eyes. 'You look bloody terrible. Sitting around here worrying is not doing anyone any favours. Go and get a shower. Then we'll get out for a bit. You need some fresh air. We'll take the lift to the top of that run with the res-taurant. We'll eat a good lunch in the sunshine. When we get back, there'll be news.'

Kat looked into his concerned blue eyes, seeing only love and protectiveness in them.

'OK,' she said.

33

Nigel spent a restless night in the snow hole, sleeping fitfully for a few minutes at a time before waking up, on the edge of panic. His dreams were full of weird ghosts and omens. When he was awake he was aware of the intense silence, the darkness. It was total sensory deprivation. He wished he could sit up, look around, talk to someone, hear another human sound. The night was the longest he had ever spent. Eventually he saw a glimmer of light around the backpack at the entrance of the hole. Dawn at last. His body was aching and stiff, but he was not too cold. The branches he'd been lying on had insulated him from the snow below. Slowly, he crawled headfirst out of his cave. He stood up and stretched painfully before relieving himself.

'Don't you eat that yellow snow, watch out where the huskies go.' His brain crazily remembered the old Frank Zappa song and he started to sing. 'Dreamed I was an Eskimo, don't you eat that yellow snow'. The noise broke the silence and sent a couple of rooks cawing into the air from a nearby tree. Squatting down, Nigel pulled another energy bar out of his backpack and chewed it carefully, making sure to eat every crumb. He took another swig of water, then got out his map and compass. He had to work out where he was. He knew that in winter accidents, the advice was to stay where you were, create some kind of sign that was visible from the air, and wait for help to arrive. You should never try to get yourself out of a dangerous situation - you could end up somewhere worse. But he had to get back to Ellie. He had to warn the others. He looked at the map, locating the top of the blue run and trying to work out where he might have fallen from. Jesus, the contour lines were close together! He was on a really steep slope which continued right down to the glacier. As the sky lightened, he could just see the top of a peak above the trees behind him. The shape of it seemed to correspond to the map. He estimated he was about ten or fifteen metres from the top. But it looked impossible to climb back up – the rock was bare and overhanging in places. He would have to traverse across the slope. If he headed off to the left it looked less steep. There seemed to be some buildings marked on the map – maybe a farm? Or a refuge of some sort? If he could reach that, he might be able to get help.

First he gathered the branches he'd cut to make his mattress, and dragged them to a small clearing in the trees, where he shaped them into a rough SOS. That way, if help came from above, they could follow his trail. Then, taking a last look around, he zipped his map into a front pocket, hung the compass around his neck, put on his backpack and started off. The snow was deep but irregular. With one step he was on solid ground, but the next he sank up to his thighs. The ski boots were heavy and awkward. Jesus, this was going to take a long, long time. But the weather was on his side, the sun warming his face and the visibility good. He could do this.

On and on he plodded. He was forced to take frequent rests as his bruised body cried out in protest. Eventually his mind settled into a kind of numb acceptance. He blanked out all thought and trudged onwards mechanically, concentrating only on putting one heavy foot in front of the other. Eventually he picked up some animal tracks. Not just a bird or a hare, but something heavier. Maybe an ibex or chamois? They were going in the right direction, heading diagonally down the slope and he decided to follow them.

After many, many hours, Nigel was beginning to lose hope. Just a bit further, just a bit further, he told himself. He was exhausted, battered and bruised. He'd fallen many times and each time it was getting more difficult to force himself to get up again. Think of Ellie! Keep on! Once again he fell, land-ing heavily. He rested his face in the snow and thought 'I'm just not fit enough, who am I trying to kid?' He lay there for several minutes, then dragged himself to his knees. The sky was starting to darken. Oh God, not another night in the snow? Would he have to build another shelter? He knew he didn't have the energy to do it properly. No, press on. He got to his feet with excruciating slowness and stumbled a few more metres along the track. Then he paused. He could smell something. Was it his imagination? Was his mind playing tricks like someone in the desert who sees an oasis that isn't there? No, this was real. Wood smoke! And where there was smoke there was fire, and where there was fire there were people! With a fresh spurt of energy, he stumbled on, determinedly, head down, following the smell. It became stronger. He saw what looked like a light. The trees began to thin out. There was a fence! Oh God, habitation! He climbed over the barbed wire, not caring as it put another rip in his expensive Gore-Tex ski jacket. He saw the outline of a farm building against the indigo blue sky, the smoke rising from its chimney in a thin grey line. Two dogs began to bark excitedly as he approached, pulling madly on their chains. The door of the farmhouse opened, letting a burst of orange light spill out onto the snow. Nigel half ran the last few paces to the door. His heart began to beat uncomfortably, painfully. He stopped, held out a hand and opened his mouth to speak. The old farmer looked on in astonishment as the crazy, dirty, dishevelled person lurched towards him again; he was tempted to shut the door in his face. This looked like trouble. But as he stepped back, about to shut the door, Nigel crashed to the ground, unconscious.

34

Kat and Neil sat opposite each other on the restaurant terrace, two huge dishes of spaghetti Bolognese steaming on the wooden table in front of them. They had skied the short distance from the top of the lift to the restaurant and Kat now found, to her surprise, that she was starving hungry. The view was stunning in the sunshine. The sky was cloudless and the snow sparkled. The jagged peaks surrounded them and enclosed them, but today they looked benign. Again Kat was reminded of tourist board images of Switzerland – a perfect vision of the peaceful, beautiful, fresh and healthy Swiss Alps. How could anything bad ever happen here? She watched a couple of skiers glide gracefully down the slope below them, then sprinkled a generous spoonful of parmesan over her plate and started eating hungrily. She looked up, aware that Neil was watching her.

'Better?' he asked.

'Much.' she replied. 'It's just… I can't get this picture of Ellie out of my head. I keep seeing her lying on some rocks, all twisted. I keep coming back to it.'

'Well, it's probably just your imagination working overtime, I should think. Or do you think it's more? Have you ever had any psychic experiences in the past? You know, premonitions or anything?'

Kat thought back. 'No… I don't think so. Wait a minute, yes, once. Ages ago. It was when me and Peter first started going out. We were both still smoking back then. We'd just gone to bed. I was asleep and I had this dream that there was a cigarette burning down in the ashtray. It was balanced on the rim, you know, and as it burned lower and lower it fell onto the bed and the sheets started to smoulder, then caught fire. The whole bed was soon burning and we were on fire - and that's when I woke up. I shouted 'Where's the ashtray!' in a panic. Peter woke up, and we both saw that there was in fact a cigarette still burning in the ashtray on the windowsill, looking like it might fall at any moment. Perter felt awful about falling asleep and leaving it burning. He got really paranoid after that about his cigarette butts. He used to grind them to nothing, or keep them in a little tin. He never, ever put them in the bin, in case the bin caught fire! We both stopped smoking soon after.'

'Sounds like a genuine premonition though. Did it never happen again?'

'No I don't think so. Well, maybe a bit when my mum died. I knew something was going to happen that day. A bird crashed into the window and killed itself. Then the electricity kept going off and on. It was really windy outside so it could have been the power lines, but in my heart I knew something bad was going to happen.'

'Was she ill? Were you half expecting it?'

'Not really, she had dementia, but she was physically pretty healthy.'

'Tell me more about your vision of Ellie. Maybe we can work out where she is.'

Kat looked at him, astonished that he seemed to be giving credence to the premonition idea. Was he humouring her? No, he looked deadly serious. She closed her eyes and emptied her mind, waiting for the image to reappear.

'OK.... It's quite dark, as if it's in shadow. The sun isn't reaching her. The rocks are sharp and pointed, sticking out of the snow. She's face-down and her leg is at a funny angle. And... there's red on the snow."

'Jesus. That sounds specific. Do you think... do you think she's breathing?'

Kat's eyes flew open in surprise and she gulped for air. She locked eyes with Neil. He was staring at her with such intensity that it made her confused. 'I don't know, I don't know,' she whispered.

Neil's face suddenly relaxed into a smile. 'Sorry,' he said. 'I should be cheering you up, not making things worse. Look, let's eat our meals and talk about something else. I want to know all about your children. Do they take after you or Peter?'

Kat made an effort to answer, but her mind was elsewhere. Soon conversation ran dry and they finished their spaghetti in silence.

Neil pushed the two plates to the end of the table and leaned back, searching in his pocket for his cigarettes. He flicked the bottom of the pack to tap one out, and put it in his mouth. Then he reached into the pocket again for his lighter. He flicked the top open and struck the flint, cupping the flame with his other hand. An old-fashioned butane lighter. Not his usual plastic one. A heavy silver lighter. Kat's muddled brain suddenly clunked into gear and she saw with perfect clarity. Matt's lighter. Neil was using Matt's lighter. That was without a doubt Matt's beautiful lighter – expensive and sophisticated, reflecting its owner. Had Neil borrowed it? Or had he taken it? And if he'd taken it, where was Matt? Had he…? Oh my God, Ellie!

Suddenly Kat was calm and focused. She knew what she had to do. She immediately dropped her eyes so Neil wouldn't see her staring at the lighter. She looked again at the skiers carving their paths down the slope below. She forced her shoulders to relax, then looked up at Neil with a smile and said: 'I could sit here in the sun all day. I don't want to go back and face reality yet.'

'Well, there's no hurry. I'll fetch us a couple of coffees and we can sit here as long as you like.'

'There's quite a queue at the counter,' said Kat, glancing through the restaurant windows at the line of people waiting to pay, their trays loaded with food. 'Are you sure you don't mind?'

'Of course not,' said Neil, grinding out his cigarette in the glass ashtray. 'Long or short coffee?'

'I'll have a long milky one please.'

196

'Be right back,' he said, with a smile. He stood up and Kat watched him make his way unhurriedly through the tables, enter the restaurant and join the queue. 'Don't look round at me,' she prayed, but he had his back to her, focusing on taking a tray from the metal trolley.

Quickly, Kat zipped up her jacket and hurried across the wooden terrace to the rack where she'd left her skis. They sat beside Neil's longer ones, and on impulse she grabbed one of Neil's skis and threw it onto the snow a good three metres away. That should slow him down a bit. She snapped her boots into the bindings, grabbed her poles and took off down the slope.

35

She remembered this run. It was the one they'd done all those years ago. It started as a nice easy blue, winding gently all the way back to the village. But there was another option – the black, veering off to the right, steep and dangerous but direct, fast. Neil would never expect her to take the black. If she could do it, she'd be back at the chalet in minutes. She could grab her things and go before he was even aware she'd gone. Take the cable car down to the town, find the police station. But if she fell… She skied quickly to the start of the run and stopped on the ridge where it dropped away invisibly below. She remembered the last time she'd been in this spot. She imagined she could hear Silvio, standing behind her, advising her to follow the fall line for greater speed. 'I can do this. I can. I've done it before' Her heart was hammering in her chest. But adrenalin was good, it would help her. She was aware of the tension in her shoulders, the rigidity of her arms. She needed to make her body loose if she was going to absorb he shocks of the bumps below. Make your mind up, quick, quick. Still she hesitated. A cloud passed over the sun, and she looked up, surprised. The weather was changing. The breeze had stiffened, whipping little crystals of ice into her face. The sky was turning grey. Shit, shit, it would make the run more difficult. Think, think! Blue or black? She looked around, desperately searching for a group of skiers she could attach herself to. There was no-one. Silence. As she struggled to make a decision, she heard a noise; the swish of skis cutting through the snow behind her, coming closer. Was it him? It couldn't be, could it? Had he seen her leave the restaurant?

Followed her? If he knew that she knew, he would kill her. He'd killed the others. Just go! Go now!

Without looking back, she pushed off with her poles and launched herself onto the run. She navigated the moguls well, turning on the top of each one to save time and effort. Round a bend the run evened out into a wide, gentle slope. She flew down it at speed, barely making any turns. Another steep bit, then the dip. She knew she had to tuck into position and fly down as quickly as possible to make it to the other side. She went into the schuss, her skis together, her knees taking the shock of the uneven snow. She made it to the top and for just a second felt the sheer exhilaration of speed. She paused, looked back. There was a figure on the other side of the dip, just starting to go into a tuck. It was hard to make out details. Was that Neil's black ski suit? Oh God, it could be. She turned and looked down the slope. The next bit was really steep. She could see patches where the snow had been scraped bare to reveal the blue ice below. She could do it. She had to. She set off, following the track made by others.

It started well. Then half way down she felt one ski slipping away from under her. She fought to control it, to bring it back parallel but it was no use. She fell heavily and rolled over and over, one ski flying off and continuing alone down the hill. She came to a stop and lay face down, winded, trying desperately to get her breath. Then she heard it. Swish, swish. The sound of skis from close by. She struggled to get up but one leg lay awkwardly underneath her, ski still attached. The noise stopped. A shadow fell over her. For a second she thought 'This is how I first met him. I fell on the dry slope and he came to help me.' She remembered looking up and seeing his blue eyes, his smile. There was a certain symmetry to things. It ends how it all began. Inevitable really.

Slowly she raised her head and looked up. But it wasn't Neil standing over her. A friendly face, brown eyes and a wide mouth. A woman. Oh thank God, thank God! Kat's breathing started to return to normal. She put one hand to her chest and forced herself to take deep breaths. She looked up at the woman again. She was peering down at her with a worried expression, holding her sunglasses in one hand. She wore a black ski suit and a cheerful red and white striped bonnet with an enormous pompom. Nice hat, thought Kat, irrationally.

'Hi, are you OK? Can I help?'

Kat struggled to speak. 'I'm... I... my ski...'

'I'll get your ski. You just get your breath back,' she said, and skied smoothly down to where Kat's ski lay abandoned. She picked it up, placed it over her shoulder, then side-stepped easily back up to where Kat lay and dropped it beside her.

'Here you go. Did you hurt yourself?'

Kat shook her head and tried to order her thoughts. 'No, I... I've got to go. He's... my ex-boyfriend... I think he's... a murderer.'

The woman laughed, her wide mouth showing even white teeth and her brown eyes crinkling. 'I think you've had a bang on the head!' She had a beautiful voice, melodic and warm. 'Sit up and put your head between your knees.' She reached out a hand and helped Kat to a sitting position, then squatted down in front of her.

'No. No time. I think I'm in danger.' Kat scrabbled for her ski and tried to haul it parallel to the other. She tried to stand up on shaky legs but fell back again.

'Let me do it,' said her saviour. She pulled Kat's leg into position and dug the ski into the snow so it wouldn't slide away. She placed the runaway ski next to it, and did the same, making a little flat ledge for it. Then she took her pole and knocked the snow off Kat's free boot, before hauling her to her feet. She supported her weight while Kat snapped her boot into the binding.

'OK?'

'Yeah, thanks.'

'You're still shaking. Look, I'm going to follow you down to the bottom of the run, make sure you get down it OK. Is that alright?'

'OK,' said Kat. She didn't want help; she just wanted to

get down to the bottom as quickly as possible, but some innate politeness made her accept.

Together they made it down the slope. The pompom woman was an graceful skier. She stayed behind Kat on the gentle parts, but when it became steep she passed in front, showing Kat where to turn, smiling her encouragement.

At the bottom of the run, Kat didn't stop to thank her, but continued as far as the gradient of the slope allowed, to the centre of the village. There she pushed down on the heel levers with her sticks to release her skis and abandoned them where they lay, continuing on foot towards the chalet.

'Wait!' called a voice behind her. Pompom woman. Kat was surprised she was still there. She turned, impatiently.

'You said you were in trouble. You look like you need help. What can I do?'

Kat was exasperated and just about to turn away again when she had a second thought. She might be useful as a lookout. 'Come on then. The chalet's up there. Quick.'

They struggled uphill, digging the toes of their boots into the snow to get a grip. When they reached the chalet, Kat turned, panting, and said:

'You wait here. If you see a guy in a black ski suit, yell as loud as you can.'

'OK, got it. Go!'

Kat raced up the steps and into the chalet. She yanked her boots off and ran up the stairs to her room. There she found her handbag and stuffed her passport, purse and phone inside. She put on her fur-lined boots and took a quick look round the room. No, that's all I need, she thought and ran down the stairs.

At the foot of the stairs she stopped, surprised.

'What are you doing?' she asked.

Pompom woman was standing in the living room, smiling. She had dragged two of the heavy oak dining chairs away from the table and placed them side by side against the back wall.

Kat suddenly noticed the long, sharp kitchen knife that

was in the woman's hand. She knew that knife. She'd chopped onions with it. It was really good; German steel, sharp. A proper chef's knife.

'What the hell…'

Then realisation hit her. She was alone with a killer.

36

'Please sit down,' the woman said, gesturing towards the nearest chair with the knife.

Kat started to run towards the door but the woman was faster, cutting off her route and holding the knife out. She walked slowly up to Kat and sliced upwards into her ski jacket, making a long tear, following the path of the zip from hem to collar. There she rested the knife against Kat's throat and said again:

'Please sit down.'

This time Kat obeyed. She was numb with shock and terror, convinced she was going to die. But against this thought fluttered another one: It's not Neil! Neil isn't a murderer.

The woman pulled off her bonnet, shaking her head and letting loose a cascade of curly red hair.

'You're Anna,' breathed Kat.

'That's right. Clever you.'

'Where's Ellie? What have you done with her?'

Anna rolled her eyes and sighed. 'All in good time. Let's get comfortable first. Now, take your jacket off, slowly. That's right. Now, catch this.'

She threw a small object to Ellie, who caught it. A cable tie.

'Put it around your right ankle and the chair leg. Then pull tight.'

Kat stared at her without moving. Anna took three steps towards her, the knife gleaming in her hand.

'Look sweetie, do as I say. Or it won't be just your jacket I cut.'

This time Kat didn't hesitate. She put the tie around both her leg and the chair leg and pulled the pointed end through the clasp. The teeth clicked as she pulled it tight. But not too tight. By moving her leg slightly, she was able to give the impression of tightness while leaving a good couple of centimetres of slack.

'Good girl!' said Anna, and threw her a second cable tie. 'Same again, other leg.'

Kat complied, then looked up to see Anna giving her a brilliant smile. 'Terrific!' she said. 'Now, I was going to tie your hands behind the chair, but these chairs are so huge I don't think you'd reach. So it will have to be in front. Put your hands out. Inside wrists together.' Kat did as instructed, flinching as Anna came towards her, the gleaming knife in one hand and a third cable tie in the other. She put it around Kat's wrists and pulled it viciously tight.

'OK. Great! Now all we have to do is wait for my darling Neil to get here.'

'What do you intend to do then?'

'Patience my dear, you'll see. Now, no more talking. I don't want to have to cut your tongue out.'

Kat's mind raced. She had an idea how to escape from the cable ties – she remembered a video she'd seen years ago while randomly checking stuff on YouTube. She searched her memory. Yes, that was it; you use your shoelace. But how could she distract Anna long enough to do it? And was it worth the risk? Should she instead play for time, wait for help? Neil would be here soon, and the rescue team would surely come round after dark with news of the search.

Anna had taken off her ski suit and was now walking about the room, looking around, humming to herself happily. She picked up various objects – a paperback, a camera, the whisky bottle - examined them, then replaced them. Kat watched every move, trying to assess the situation. This woman was undeniably beautiful. In her early forties perhaps. Slim and fine-boned. She had a long straight nose covered in freckles and a generous, mobile mouth. Her brown eyes were lively and expressive. So this is who Neil had been married to, thought Kat. She could understand the initial attraction only too easily. But the woman had to be mad, completely insane.

Kat watched as Anna went up to the big glass windows and looked out. 'Please, someone notice her! Let Neil see her!' thought Kat. But Anna then pressed the switch to activate the electric blind. The room gradually darkened. She then tested the light switch near the door, walked up to the central light and removed the bulb. Next she opened the fridge door, took out a half-full bottle of white wine and a jar of olives. She fetched a glass and poured herself a big measure, then pulled out a another chair and sat facing Kat, glass in her left hand. In her right, the knife, around which she absent-mindedly twirled a lock of red hair.

'Cheers!' she said. 'Your very good health.' She took a long, appreciative gulp of the wine. 'Oh, that's good. Neil always did have good taste in wine.' She looked at Kat, head to one side, a puzzled expression on her face.

'Whatever did he see in you? You're so much older. You look so... ordinary.'

Kat couldn't help the retort from bursting out: 'Well I'm not insane for a start.'

'Oh shit, oh shit,' she thought, as Anna got off her chair slowly and came towards her, tapping the flat of the knife against the palm of her other hand. 'I've gone too far. Stupid!'

'Now, now, that was a bit bitchy. I'll let you off this time, but two strikes and you are out. We are going to wait for Neil, and you are going to keep your filthy, wrinkly old mouth shut. OK?' Once again she gave that brilliant smile, sending a shiver down Kat's spine.

They waited in silence for what seemed like hours. Eventually Kat heard the sound of ski boots clomping hurriedly up the wooden stairs outside. The door burst open and she called out: 'Neil! Get out! Run! Run!'

But Neil didn't move. He stood stock still, then came into

the room, flicked the useless light switch again and again and peered into the darkness.

'Kat? Where are you?'

'Neil, sweetheart,' said Anna. 'I'm so glad you could join us! Do come in! Sit down.'

'What the... Anna? Oh God! Is that you? For fuck's sake! What are you doing?' His eyes had adjusted to the dim light and, horrified, he could now see Anna standing over the chair, holding a knife to Kat's throat.

'Anna, please, no! Stop!' He came towards her, his hands stretched out in entreaty.

'Whoa, slow down. Now listen carefully, Neil. Come forward really slowly and sit on this chair here. One sudden move and I cut her throat.' Neil did as she said. 'Good. You'll see two cable ties on the floor next to the chair. I want you to tie them round each leg and the chair leg.'

Neil looked questioningly at Kat and she gave him a slight nod to do as he was told.

'OK, great.' Anna moved the knife away from her throat and Kat released her breath, unaware she'd been holding it. She shut her eyes for an instant, weak with relief, then opened them and locked eyes with Neil, sending a silent message that she was OK. Neil gave her a shaky smile of reassurance. Neither of them reacted in time as Anna reached for the wine bottle and with incredible speed, smashed it into the side of Neil's temple.

'No!' yelled Kat, as Neil slumped in the chair, motionless.

'Oh for God's sake!' snapped Anna. 'He'll be unconscious for a minute or two at the most. I not going to kill *him*.' The emphasis she put on the 'him' was ominous. She gently placed Neil's arms behind his back and secured them fast. Then she went over to the kitchen and switched on the small spot above the worksurface, casting a feeble light over the room. Finally she went back to her chair and took another long drink from her wine glass.

'Now we wait'.

37

They sat in silence for several minutes. Kat thought furiously. She had to distract her somehow.

'Your glass is empty,' she said at last, cursing herself for this a feeble attempt. But amazingly it seemed to work.

'So it is. Where do you keep the white wine?' Anna's tone was light and pleasant, as if she was a guest chatting to a host at a dinner party.

'In a crate round the back, behind the woodpile.' Kat shivered as she mentioned the woodpile, once again seeing the axe embedded in the post. She thought now that it must have been human blood she'd seen on it. Was it possible Anna had killed with it?

Anna cupped her chin in her hand for a moment, thinking. She stood up and tested the weight of the oak chair she'd been sitting on, holding the seat and trying to lift it. It moved only slightly.

'I don't think you're going anywhere. But I warn you, if I see you try to escape I will cut you.'

With that she left the room.

Kat didn't hesitate. Her boots were fur-lined and zipped up the side, but they had decorative laces all the same – thin laces but nice and strong. She bent down and with her wrists still awkwardly pressed together, managed to work one lace out of her boot. She fed it behind the cable tie on her ankle and worked her bound wrists up and down in a see-saw motion, sawing against the plastic. Come on, come on! Desperately she continued to saw, but the range of movement in her hands was severely restricted. It wasn't going to work, was it? Just as she heard footsteps coming back up the steps outside, the cable tie finally snapped. Kat quickly kicked it behind her and sat up straight as Anna came into the room. The small victory had given her hope. If she could do the same with the other leg she there was a chance she could do something. It was possible this madwoman had killed Ellie. But she was damned if she was going to kill her too. She was going to get out of this. She was not going to let her children lose another parent.

Anna lazily searched in the drawer for a corkscrew and began to open the bottle she'd brought up. Lavaux, nice dry Swiss wine. Good choice, thought Kat, bizarrely. Anna poured a glass, and with an ironic 'Santé', sat down again.

'Can I have a glass of water?' asked Kat.

'No.'

'Please tell me where Ellie is!'

'She's dead of course,' Anna snapped. 'What did you think? Ah, look who's waking up at last!' Her voice had changed again to silky-smooth. She moved over to look at Neil more closely. She ran her finger tenderly along his cheek and brushed the hair back from his forehead.

Neil's eyelids fluttered. He lifted his head, then winced in pain. Suddenly his eyes shot open and he stared at Anna, an incredulous expression on his face.

'Anna. What the fuck are you doing here?'

Anna laughed. 'I followed you here of course. I've been following you for a while.'

'What do you mean? What have you done?' Neil's voice was shrill. He made a huge effort to sound calm and reasonable as he continued. 'Listen, you need help. Let me help you.'

Anna smiled and continued, her voice soft and gentle: 'Darling, you're the one who needs the help. I've been keeping an eye on you, you know. Silly thing, you never changed your email password or your Facebook login. I've been keeping up with all your movements. I followed you to Edinburgh, did you know that? I used to stand outside your little flat in Morningside.

Didn't you ever feel me watching out for you?' Neil's expression of shock and horror made her giggle. 'I used to come up for the weekend and watch you leave the flat in your trainers to go running, or get in the car to go shopping. I followed you to that bar you loved – the Canny Man's wasn't it? I sat at the next table once and you never even noticed.' She sat down again, taking another sip of wine.

'This is crazy. You've got to stop this. We were not good together. We divorced. Let go of this!'

'And then you moved down to Shropshire. A new job. You didn't seem to have many friends there. You got the big promotion but you didn't celebrate with anyone, did you? I drank champagne in your honour that night. You see, I cared, I was really glad for you. You had that girlfriend for a short while didn't you? What was her name? Barbara wasn't it? She wasn't right for you. I had to put a stop to that.'

'For fuck's sake Anna, what did you do? Did you kill her?'

Anna laughed again, her pretty, tinkling laugh. 'No, of course not. Well, maybe I should have done really. No, I just told her I was your ex-girlfriend and that you'd given me AIDS. She couldn't run away fast enough. What a light-weight. No match for you! You deserve the best.' She shook her head sadly and tutted.

'I went into your house once or twice. Didn't you smell my scent there? You should really lock the door when you work in the garden, Neil. Anyone can get in. I could have been a burglar. But your house, Neil! There's no soul to it. Just a shell. I looked through your drawers, your bookshelves but there was no personality anywhere. It could have been a holiday home. I could tell you weren't happy. You needed saving; you needed me.'

'Anna. What have you done? Where are the others? Sean, Matt, Ellie, Nigel?'

'Well, they're all dead.' Anna smiled happily, as if she was imparting wonderful news and Kat shivered. 'I did it for you!'

Neil struggled wildly against the chair, his eyes full of

panic. 'What? What? Oh Christ!'

'Sweetheart, you were living in the past. You were obsessed with the old days. You used to go on and on about how good university was, how great your friends were. About that *whore* there.' She spat out the word, pointing her knife at Kat. 'When I found out you were getting back in contact with those people I knew I had to act. Don't you see? Darling, I've liberated you! I've freed you from all that. Now you can move on, you can have the future you deserve. You never gave our marriage a chance really, did you? There were too many ghosts. Well now you can. We can start again with a clean sheet.'

'Anna, listen to me. This is not what I want. It's not what you need either. You need to get help. You're ill. I can help you. Don't do anything else, please. Look, untie me and we can talk properly.'

'Maybe. In a while. There's so much more I want to tell you first. I want you just to sit and listen. Just a bit longer. Then we'll decide what to do.'

Anna stood and went over to Neil. She lightly touched the tender spot on his temple. 'I'm so sorry I had to hit you. Does it still hurt? Poor baby.' She went to drop a kiss on his head but he recoiled in revulsion. For a moment a look of pure hatred flashed in her eyes. Then it was gone. 'Silly boy'.

As she turned back to her chair, Neil looked at Kat and mouthed 'OK?' Kat raised the leg she'd managed to free, and quickly replaced it as Anna sat down. Neil nodded his head almost imperceptibly. He had a glimmer of an idea.

'Anna,' he said, 'You're right. We need to talk. Bring your chair closer. I want to look at you. Tell me everything.'

Anna raised her eyebrows in surprise. She glanced at Kat, considering, then dragged the heavy chair nearer to Neil's. She refilled her glass, then sat down, leaning forward. She could still see Kat from her peripheral vision, but her attention was now completely focussed on Neil. As she started talking, Kat bent down as slowly as she possibly could, the shoelace hidden in her hands.

38

'Well,' Anna began, 'there's another reason I killed them. I did it for your book.'

'My book? What book?'

'You remember! Don't tell me you've forgotten, silly! That first year we were married. You said you wanted to be an author. You wanted to write a thriller set in a ski resort.'

Neil forced himself to smile. 'Yes, I remember. I even started a chapter or two.'

'Yes, and you told me the plot. It was original and so marketable. How there was a madman on the loose, killing a group of friends one by one. We used to sit in bed together and you'd tell me how you planned to kill them off. I could visualise it all so clearly. You had a real talent, Neil, but you doubted yourself too much. You should have stuck with it at the time, but I know you've still got it in you! You are a writer! When we get home you can give up your job and just get down to it. I can be your agent or your publicist. I'll do everything in the house so you can concentrate on just writing. And I've made it easy for you. Really easy. I've been testing out your murders for you!'

Anna beamed at Neil, delighted with her revelation. Neil struggled to keep the disgust out of his voice as he asked: 'So how did you do it? How did you kill them?' Out of the corner of his eye, he saw Kat threading the shoelace behind the cable tie on her left leg. He had to keep Anna talking.

'You would not believe how easy it is! Let me tell you, once you've done one, it just gets easier and easier. You know, sometimes I used to think about killing you. If we'd had a row and I was cooking. I often used to think how very easy it would be just to turn round and thrust the knife under your ribs, into your liver, little twist. But something always stopped me. Thank goodness! But anyway. I digress. First I killed your two gay friends. Don't think I'm homophobic, I could have started anywhere. But the chance came up and there they were.'

'Go on.'

'They both stayed in the chalet that day while the rest of you went skiing. Do you remember? I watched them. They got up really late – goodness knows what they'd been doing!' Again that pretty laugh. 'After they had breakfast I went up to the chalet, knocked on the door and said I was the owner's daughter. There'd been a problem with the boiler and I wanted to check it. I asked if they minded if I went to the basement. No problem, they said, go ahead. I took the axe from the woodpile and put it next to the boiler. Stayed for a few minutes, then went upstairs and said to the tall one, Sean, that was his name: 'It seems to be working OK, but there's something I need to show you. If it stops there's a trick to get it started again.' Poor lamb, he didn't have a clue. Followed me down to the basement, meek and mild.'

Kat was sawing away at the cable tie desperately. It didn't seem to be working. Was it a different type of plastic? Stronger? She renewed her efforts but suddenly the shoelace broke in two. Shit, shit, shit! She sat back, despair threatening to overwhelm her. Luckily Anna chose that moment to turn round and check on her.

'Are you enjoying this?' she asked. 'I'll get round to your fat little friend soon.' She turned back to Neil and Kat worked up her courage again. She had a second shoelace. She had to get it free.

'So anyway,' Anna continued, 'I said 'See that knob under the boiler? You just turn that a quarter turn… Have a go!' Clever wasn't it? He was so tall I'd never have reached him otherwise. So he bent down to look. I got the axe and smashed it into his skull. He dropped like a stone. Dead as a doornail.' She clapped her hands in delight and beamed at Neil.

Kat had been reaching down to her foot but she couldn't help a moan escaping from her lips when she heard this. She froze. But Anna wasn't looking.

'Next I ran back upstairs and said to the other one: 'Come quick, I think your friend's had some sort of attack. He's fallen over'. Of course, he came running down the stairs with me, bent over his man to see and whack! Same again with the back of the axe. I didn't use the blade, you see, too messy. There would have been blood everywhere. So there they were, both dead. You see how easy it is? They looked like such a nice couple. I lay them side by side and put their hands together as if they were just sleeping, holding hands. They did look cute. I'm surprised you didn't see them; I thought one of you would have gone into the boiler room to do washing or something.'

'So they're still down there now?' asked Neil, struggling to keep the emotion out of his voice.

'Yes they must be. Don't worry, it's so cold down there, they'll still be quite fresh. Then anyway, after that I went upstairs, found some paper and wrote the note. I worked out which their room was, and packed their cases. They're down in the boiler room too. If you'd have looked you would've seen them. So what do you think? I know it's not in your original plot, but could you build that into the book? It's quite clever don't you think?'

Neil opened his mouth to answer, but could think of no reply. All the time he was aware of Kat trying to undo her second shoelace with slow, careful movements. 'Keep looking at me, Anna!' he thought.

There was a sudden noise outside, a shout and some words exchanged in German. 'Thank fuck for that!' thought Neil. 'It must be the rescue team. At last.' He looked over towards the door, expecting it to burst open. Nothing happened. He looked back at Anna, to find her smiling knowingly at him.

'You expecting someone?' she asked.

'No.'

'Don't lie to me, Neil. You thought that was the rescue patrol you alerted this morning, didn't you? You see I followed you there too. I heard you speak to them. I waited for half an hour, then, when they were getting the team together I went up to them and said 'I'm so sorry! It's a big mistake.' I said I was Nigel's sister and we'd just found out they were safe and sound down in the town. They'd left us a note to say where they were going but we'd only just found it. So the search party got cancelled I'm afraid. Oh dear, I can see you're disappointed.'

Neil swallowed back his anger and said, his voice hoarse with supressed fury: 'Tell me what you did to the others.'

To his despair, Anna stood up and moved her chair back to where it had been. Kat sat back, quickly, straightening up just in time as Anna turned to her. 'You'll want to hear this too,' she said to Kat. 'They were your special friends weren't they?'

Anna sat down, took another big mouthful of wine and began.

'I really wanted to do the killings in the way you described, you see, Neil. All very well offing your gay friends, but whacking them over the head with an axe wasn't in your plot. Then, hey presto, a foggy day yesterday! Perfect. You see, it was meant to be! The Gods were on my side! I followed you all in the morning. Your ex-girlfriend here is a really shit skier isn't she?' she sent Kat a condescending glance. 'You had to keep stopping for her. Poor Neil, you must have been so frustrated. Anyway, after you split up I stayed with the other two, Nigel and his fat little wife. Then they split up – how lucky can you get! When Nigel got to the top of the run I was waiting by the edge, a few metres above. I called to him. You couldn't see a thing. He must have thought it was Ellie and he came charging up the slope. I crouched down behind some rocks, then, when he stopped and searched around, I hit him across the back with my ski. He went over the edge. All the way down to the glacier with any luck. Wasn't it perfect? Do you like it?'

Neil's face was grim. He shook his head. 'No, Anna, not perfect. He was a good bloke. You don't know what you've done.

Oh Christ.'

Once more that flash of anger crossed Anna's face. Her body stiffened and she gripped the knife harder, the knuckles of her hand showing white. Then she relaxed, smiled that sweet smile again.

'OK, maybe that was not quite the same as your book. But this is the one I'm really proud of. Wait till you hear this one Neil, it is exactly as you described it. You'll love it! So after a while, the fat one came looking for her husband. The fog was still really thick and no-one else was using the lift much. I followed her as she went down the run, looking for him. Then when she went up a second time, I made sure I was next to her on the chairlift. Your little friend was a real chatterbox, wasn't she?' she addressed this remark to Kat, who was sitting, mesmerised, tears pouring down her face. My Ellie, she thought, so positive, so trusting. She would never have guessed she was in danger. She could visualise the scene so easily. Ellie would talk to anyone. She would be trying to make conversation, sitting innocently next to this – this twisted, psychopathic monster. She wanted to turn back the clock twenty-four hours, to stay with Ellie, to reach out and warn her. Don't go! Don't ski today! This couldn't be allowed to happen. Not to her Ellie!

Anna continued, relentlessly, enjoying herself. 'She tried to talk to me in all sorts of languages, stupid woman. And you know, she never put her feet on the footrest, did she. It was as if she was purposely making it easy for me. I put up with her chatter until we got to the ravine. Then I simply lifted the safety bar and pushed her off. Voilà!'

'How do you know she's dead?' asked Neil. 'Maybe she survived.'

'It was a whiteout.' Anna shrugged. 'When she went, she just disappeared into the fog. I couldn't see or hear anything. But if she didn't die in the fall, she'll be dead now. It was easy, Neil. So easy! Just like you thought it would be.'

Kat could bear it no longer. Huge sobs wracked her body and she found herself wailing loudly, hardly able to gulp for air between sobs.

'Oh do shut up, for God's sake!' spat Anna. She pointed the knife at Kat, menacingly.

'So what now?' asked Neil, hurriedly, turning her attention back to him. 'You've killed four people Anna. Isn't that enough? You've made your point. You've shown how it can be done. Bravo. But let's stop there.'

'But there's one more to go, isn't there?' She looked over at Kat and laughed. 'I'm not quite sure how to do this one. Have you got any good ideas? Maybe if I'm really clever I can make it look like suicide, then blame the killings on her? But I'm not sure I can be bothered. I thought about burying her under the woodpile but that's a lot of effort. So I'm just going to kill her now, Neil, in front of you. Then you'll know you're free. We can set fire to the chalet. Then we'll go.'

'Anna, no! No! No! Wait. You don't have to kill her. She means nothing to me! Nothing! It's always been you!'

'Yes, I know that, darling. I mean, just look at us both. That snivelling middle-aged hag with her dyed hair, her eye bags and her wrinkles! How could you find that attractive? And she's such a pathetic wimp too, she's got no backbone. It's just nostalgia that made you think you liked her. Look at her, Neil, really look at her. She's nothing. Certainly not good enough for you. But you have been leading her on a bit, have you not? There's a passage in her diary that's very revealing.'

Neil had an idea. 'You've read her diary? What did it say? I'd really like to know.'

As he'd hoped, Anna leapt up with a grin. 'Oh, just you wait till you hear it. It'll make you laugh.' She got up, walked over to Neil and planted a kiss on the top of his head, then began to walk up the stairs, knife still in her hand.

'Quick!' whispered Neil to Kat. She glanced at the stairs, then quickly bent down, finished undoing the second lace and fed it behind the cable tie with trembling fingers. Once more she began to saw at the plastic. Come on, come on, come on! It was taking too long! It must work!

'What are you doing?' came a voice from behind her. Kat froze, looked round. Anna was halfway down the stairs, diary under her arm. 'Stop that!' She hurried down the remaining stairs, throwing the diary aside and clutching the knife tightly. Kat continued to saw at the plastic faster; there was nothing to lose. She sensed Anna coming nearer and nearer and frantically redoubled her efforts. It wasn't going to work! Then she felt her head being yanked back as Anna pulled her viciously by the hair. Once more she felt the knife at her throat. This is it, thought Kat. I'll be with Ellie. With Mum and Dad. At least it will be quick.

But Anna took her time. 'Are you watching, Neil? Look! Look at her!'

Neil refused to look. Instead he said in a low voice: 'I never loved you Anna. It was a mistake to marry you. You are mentally ill. You are deranged. I can't help you. I don't want to help you. You're too sick. I wish you were dead.' He spoke these last five words slowly, forcefully, and finally he looked up, his eyes cold and determined.

Kat felt the pressure of the knife ease as Anna took a step back.

'Neil, darling,' she said with a shaky laugh. 'Don't tease.'

'I'm not teasing.'

'You don't mean it!' she said in a small voice. 'You can't mean it. After everything I've said and done for you.' She shook her head repeatedly. 'No, no, no, no, no'.

'I mean every word. I wish you were dead.'

Then, everything seemed to happen at once. Anna made an inhuman noise, a roar of pain. Her face showed disbelief, confusion, then twisted and froze into a mask of intent, of fury. Suddenly she was ugly. She started to move slowly towards Neil, her movements jerky.

Kat screamed 'No!' and stood up, one leg still attached, trying desperately to drag herself and the chair towards them. There was an audible snap as the plastic finally gave way. With hands still tied, Kat lunged for the bottle and, grasping it by the neck, she broke it against the edge of the table. It wasn't like the movies: instead of a knife-sized weapon, she was left with just a few jagged inches around the neck, but it was a weapon of sorts. 'Don't you fucking dare!' she screamed, pointing the make-shift knife at Anna.

The red-head hesitated, then gave a snort of derision. 'Oh, will you look at you! Have you gown a pair all of a sudden? But really, what do you hope to do with that thing?' She looked from Neil to Kat repeatedly, as if unsure who to deal with first, hate gleaming in her eyes. She lurched towards Kat. Then there was another noise: 'Police, freeze!' Bodies crashed into the room. A warning shot was fired. 'Throw down your weapon! Hands in the air! Now! Now!'

Anna looked around in confusion. She saw three blue-clad policemen, their guns trained on her. 'Oh!' she said, simply. The expression on her face slowly changed. As Kat watched, fascinated, her eyes softened and her mouth relaxed. She smiled again, charmingly, wistfully, once more calm and beautiful. Then she carefully laid the knife on the floor and put her hands up. She was tackled to the ground roughly by two burly officers, then handcuffed and pulled none too gently to her feet. As she was being marched to the door she said: 'Stop. Wait!' The two policemen took no notice, so she twisted her head round to look back at Neil and said, sadly: 'I did it for you, Neil. I loved you. Don't forget that. She'll never love you like I loved you.' Then she allowed herself to be led away, meek as a child.

Kat felt drained of all emotion. She dropped the bottle neck and slumped back onto the chair again, shutting her eyes. Then she started to shake, uncontrollably. She felt the ties binding her wrists being cut. Someone threw one of the sheepskin rugs around her shoulders and put a glass of whisky in her hand. Finally she opened her eyes and looked over at Neil. He looked suddenly ancient, grey and drawn, as if he's aged twenty years. The skin around his cheeks looked unnaturally tight and his eyes were blank.

Two more men entered the room. The first held a radio in

his hand and was speaking into it in fast German. Kat looked at the second man, taking in the bruises and cuts on his face, her mind slow to make the connection. Was that…? Was it really?

'Where is Ellie?' asked Nigel.

Kat staggered to her feet and ran towards him. 'Oh thank God! You're alive.'

'Where's Ellie?' he repeated, his eyes darting around the room wildly.

Kat put her hands either side of his face and forced him to look at her. Tears were running down her own face once again.

'I am sorry, I'm so sorry.'

PART 3

39

Nigel was taken away to a nearby hospital. He would be kept in overnight for observation and checked for broken ribs and possible frostbite. Kat had hugged him hard goodbye but he'd barely responded, his expression dazed and uncomprehending.

The man who had come in with Nigel identified himself as Detective Gerber of the Kantonspolizei Bern. He was a short man with a stiff, upright posture and an intimidating air. 'Napoleon complex' thought Kat, distractedly, as she watched him strut about the room. He told Kat and Neil to pack a few things together quickly, as the chalet was now a crime scene and they would have to leave.

'I've booked rooms for you at the Gasthaus Alpenrose,' he said briskly, when they came back downstairs with their bags. 'It is in the centre of the village. Please stay inside all day tomorrow. I will need to take statements from you. And do not leave the village until I give permission. My colleague here will escort you to the Gasthaus now.'

They nodded wordlessly and followed the officer down the hill, still numb with shock. They stopped outside a little guesthouse with walls painted an inappropriately cheerful yellow. A warm glow emanated from the two downstairs windows. The name Gasthaus Alpenrose was painted above the wooden door in Germanic script. As they entered the small reception area they could glimpse a little bar-restaurant to the right, with half a dozen tables, low beams and ugly, old-fashioned round glass lampshades. A murmur of conversation could be heard coming from the handful of guests there. The officer spoke a few words to the guesthouse owner in a low voice that Kat couldn't catch, but it was easy enough to guess what he was saying from the expression on the owner's face. He was looking over at them with a mixture of surprise and open curiosity. Luckily he did not try to make conversation. He took two heavy keys down from nails on the wall behind the bar and said: 'Folgen Sie mir, bitte.'

The policeman wished them a polite goodnight, and they followed the proprietor up the narrow staircase. There were just four rooms on the first floor. The owner unlocked a first door, then a second, leaving the keys in the locks. He said in heavily accented English: 'If you want food, you come down.' Then he left them.

Kat and Neil were alone. They stared at each other for a long moment. Then, as Neil made a move towards one of the rooms, Kat put out a hand to stop him.

'No,' she said. 'Come here.' She pulled him by his coat into the nearest room and shut the door. There was only one thing she wanted right now. She had seen enough death. Enough sorrow. Enough fear. She urgently needed to prove that she was still alive and that a future was possible. To drown out the past with new sensations. To feel an embrace, warmth, a heartbeat. To feel something stronger than the hollowness that filled her.

They stumbled towards the bed, pulling clumsily at each other's clothes and fumbling with buttons. They fell together onto the hard mattress, their mouths locked together. Pulling at their underclothes with one hand and gripping each other with the other hand, they acted with mindless urgency. He entered her quickly, powerfully, thrusting with a kind of desperate energy. She responded equally, pushing her hips to meet him, wanting his body to fill the void and make everything else disappear. The bed rocked noisily but she didn't care. They gasped and moaned. She sank both hands into his hair and pulled his head up so she could look at him as they came.

It was over quickly. Neil collapsed onto her, sinking his head face-down into the pillow next to her head, breathing fast.

She watched the rise and fall of his shoulders. 'His heart still beats faster than mine', she thought. She stroked his back and arms, surprised at the weight of him. Her fingers once again found the v-shaped scar where he'd fallen off a bicycle as a child, steering his bike with one hand and holding a precious glass bottle of Irn Bru in the other. The broken bottle had nearly cut his tendon in half. She found the little raised mole on his back. She remembered nagging him to get it checked. She bet he never had. His body began to shake and she realised he was sobbing.

'Shh… it's OK. It's over now. You're OK. It's finished,' she said over and over.

Eventually the shaking stopped. He rolled onto his back beside her, reached for her hand and held it tight.

'I love you,' he said, hoarsely.

'I love you too.'

She pushed herself up onto her elbow to look at him. They stayed that way for several minutes, he holding her hand tightly, as if fearing she would disappear. She stoked his chest with her free hand, tracing the little trail of chest hair that was new to her. She ran a hand over his stomach, still flat. His hip bones didn't protrude the way they used to. The leg muscles were solid and tight. She wanted to re-learn every inch of his body with her eyes and her hands.

'I should have known,' he said at last, breaking her out of her reverie.

'About Anna? How could you have known what she'd do?'

He closed his eyes, shook his head. 'There were signs right from the beginning that our relationship wasn't normal. Even when we met, at the conference, I got the impression she knew about me already, that she'd researched me. For example, she'd read some of my stuff in medical journals. I was flattered. She said 'You're more famous than you think, you know.' She really fed my ego, told me how great I was, how she admired my work.' He paused and Kat waited for him to continue, still gently stroking his chest, trying to provide a little comfort.

'When we got married it was fantastic at first. She

couldn't do enough for me. She'd cook amazing stuff when I got home from work. She'd buy me all these things I mentioned I liked just in passing. She used to phone me at work – she said she just wanted to hear my voice. And she was so beautiful – everyone thought I was punching well above my weight.'

Kat couldn't help feeling a tiny stab of jealousy, even after all that had happened.

'Then it got a bit suffocating. She'd surprise me by meeting me out of work more and more often. Saying stuff like 'It's such a lovely day, I thought we could go for a drink before dinner' or 'Let's go for a walk by the river.' It was nice, but at the same time, sometimes I just wanted to do other things. I found out she was neglecting her own work – she'd turned down some conference somewhere because she didn't want to be apart from me. Her boss phoned to persuade her to change her mind and I heard them arguing.

'Then the weird stuff started. We were in the street one day when a work colleague, Claire, just came up and said 'hi' to me, chatted for a minute or two. She was perfectly friendly to Anna. But Anna got it into her head that there was something going on with us. She'd ask about her obsessively. 'Did you see Claire today?' 'Did you have lunch with Claire?' 'What was Claire wearing today?' It got annoying, wearing. I tried to reassure her but it was like a stuck record, it kept coming back all the time.

'She'd ask questions about you, too. I told her a bit about university days, and she got a real bee in her bonnet about you. She wanted to know everything. How we met, what you were like. She'd say 'Am I prettier than her?' and 'Did you love her?' and 'Do you love me more than you loved her?' I just put it down to insecurity at first.

'She started texting me several times a day with little messages, asking what I was doing just at that moment, who I was speaking to. It used to happen in meetings and it was embarrassing. It dawned on me gradually that it wasn't just her missing me and feeling insecure – she was checking up on me.

Making sure I was where I should be. Eventually I got angry, told her she was being paranoid. We had a big fight, vicious, then afterwards she was so sorry, so repentant, trying to make it up to me, begging me to forgive her. Then we'd have great sex and, you know, I put up with a lot of shit because the sex was great. Stupid, stupid idiot.'

'What about her family, did they not notice anything was wrong? Or her friends?'

'She didn't get on with her family. I think her Dad was an alcoholic, she didn't even invite him to the wedding. She had a big group of friends when we first met, but one by one she started to cut them out, to find fault with them. She'd make excuses for us not to go to parties we were invited to, or not to hang out with her friends at weekends. Everything was all about me. And she wanted me to cut ties with my friends too. There was a guy at work I used to play squash with regularly. She couldn't stand that. Wanted me to stop. I refused, I put my foot down. Another big row, then make-up sex.'

'It must have been exhausting.'

'It was. It was such a roller-coaster. One minute it was all normal and sweet, then she could literally change in a heart-beat, yelling, accusing me of all sorts. Then the next minute weeping and clinging to me, telling me how much she loved me. I wanted her to get help. I thought we could stay together if she sorted her shit out, saw a therapist. But she refused. Things got worse and worse. I started not coming home till late. I'd go drinking after work. Alone usually. She began following me in her car. I started to really dread going home. But I never realised... I mean, I was never scared of her. I felt ... drained, I suppose. Tired out with it all. When I said I wanted to leave her, she went mental. Said she'd kill herself. She promised to see a therapist, said she would change, but never did. Oh, I don't know. I stayed far too long. Things were escalating instead of improving. In the end I started to really hate her. I left. I just upped and left everything. I made a clean break. Or, I thought I did. God I've been so stupid! How could I not have guessed? Of course she wasn't going to leave it there. Bloody hell, I should have changed the fucking passwords, at least! She didn't contact me after the divorce. I didn't hear from her at all for all those years. I thought the problem was solved. That she'd found someone else to obsess over. I suppose I began to forget about it, block it all out. But she was following me all that time. Reading all my emails. When she found out I was in contact with you again, that must have really sent her over the edge again. I led her straight to you. And to Ellie.'

'Still, you couldn't have known what she'd do. It's not your fault. You can't take responsibility for someone with a mental problem like that.'

Neil just shook his head sadly, screwing his eyes tight shut. She squeezed his hand, then gave him a little shake. He opened his eyes and looked at her. They stayed, gazing at each other, without speaking, for several minutes.

'Why did you run away?' he asked suddenly, breaking the silence.

'What?'

'Why did you leave me at the restaurant? God, it was only today. It feels like it all happened days ago.'

'I thought it was you.'

'What do you mean?'

'I thought you were the killer.'

'You thought…? Good God! But why?' He sat up and stared at her, astonished and clearly upset.

'You had Matt's lighter.'

'Oh…' He took this in. 'Yes. We ended up with each other's lighters by accident. But surely… that wasn't enough to make you think… How could you imagine I could…'

'There were other things. There were only the two of us left. You were never around when someone went missing. And you admitted to me yourself that you loved blood and gore.'

'Yes, but surely…'

'I found the axe with blood on it but I didn't know whether to tell you. I didn't think it was you until I saw the lighter. I panicked. I'm sorry. I'm so sorry I doubted you.'

The hurt look gradually left his face and he pulled her close into a tight embrace. 'No need to apologise.' He kissed her again lightly, then said: 'I'm hungry. Shall I go down and see if they can rustle us up some sandwiches?'

'OK.'

He pulled on his clothes and left the room. When he came back half an hour later with a tray of food and a couple of bottles of beer, she was fast asleep. He pulled the covers over her gently and left one of the sandwiches and a beer on the bedside table. He stroked her hair tenderly for a moment or two. Then he left the room, closing the door quietly behind him, and walked a few steps along the corridor to the other room. He sat on the bed and stared at the ugly picture on the wall blindly. He didn't see the crudely painted alps and badly proportioned cows. He was thinking. He knew he had decisions to make.

40

Kat woke up feeling refreshed after a good sleep, but then reality caught up with her and her mood plummeted. Ellie was dead. Her closest friend for over thirty years, her crutch, her sounding-board. What was she going to do without her? Ellie had simply made her life better. She had brightened up a mundane existence. She allowed herself to wallow in self-pity for a long moment, before realising that there were bigger issues. Nigel and the children. Hannah, Dom and Nick. How would they cope? There were horrible times ahead for them. She had gone through it herself, with her own John and Sarah. There would be anger, disbelief, bitterness. She would have to shape up now, pull herself together and be strong for them. She would be their rock now. She owed it to Ellie.

Sean and Matt – were they really gone? Two of the sweetest, gentlest, funniest people she had ever met. She imagined the reaction of Sean's parents in Ireland. Maybe they would blame themselves for wasting precious time with them, not being more open to the marriage. Or maybe they would see this as a kind of heavenly justice. No, surely no parent would ever think that.

She reached out to feel for Neil beside her, but the covers were flat. He wasn't there. She looked at her watch and saw with surprise that it was after nine o'clock. She showered and dressed quickly and went downstairs.

Neil was sitting at a table in the bar area, drinking coffee. He looked up and smiled as he saw her approach, but his eyes looked tired and the smile was forced.

'Have you had breakfast yet?' she asked.

'No. I was waiting for you.'

They ordered the standard breakfast and were served a plate of roschti with eggs and bacon, with yoghurts to follow. It was delicious. Kat thought how strange it was to be enjoying the food. She felt guilty for being able to taste and smell and appreciate this breakfast. Ellie would have loved it. But she would never cook or eat again. She paused with a forkful suspended in her hand.

'Don't feel bad about eating, 'said Neil. He had read her thoughts. 'You've got to eat.' Again that tired smile.

They finished their breakfast without talking much. Then, when another pot of coffee arrived, Neil asked: 'Are you OK. I mean, stupid question. But are you OK?'

Kat said what was on her mind. 'I'm desperate to phone the children. I just want to know they're OK. It's irrational I know, they're fine, safe and sound in England, why wouldn't they be? But, God I really wish I could talk to them.'

'Why don't you phone?'

'I don't think I'd be able to sound normal. They'd know something was wrong. I can't say anything about Ellie until we know for sure what's happened – and not until Nigel has told his family.'

'Yes, I see. Why don't you send them a neutral text – or just send them one of the photos you've taken. Then when you get a reply you'll know they're fine. They've got WiFi here; the code's on the bar, look.'

'Yes. Good idea.' Kat tapped in the code and got a weak signal. Then she scrolled through her photos to find a suitable one.

Tears started to fall, slowly at first, then increasingly fast. Here was Ellie, posing with both arms arced above her head, one leg in crossed awkwardly in front of the other – and snow shoes on. Ballet position 'relevé' – Ellie had told her that, as they'd fooled around that day. Her daughter Hannah had done ballet when she was very young. The next photo showed Ellie with her knees bent and her snow shoes pointing ridiculously outwards. Her arms were rounded in front, as if she was hugging in invisible tree. 'Plié,' she'd said. And finally Ellie with one leg stretched behind her, one arm stretched out in front, her gloved fingers beautifully extended: 'Arabesque'. The last photos I'll ever take of Ellie, thought Kat. It was unbearable.

Neil watched as she scrolled back and forth. He passed her one serviette and then a second. Eventually Kat blew her nose and gave him a feeble smile. 'Maybe I'll send the text later,' she said.

The Gasthaus door opened, letting in a blast of cold air, and Detective Gerber came in, stamping his feet on the mat, followed by a younger officer. He came directly over to their table, his face unreadable.

'Good. I see you have eaten. I will interview you both separately. Mr Adams, you first I think. Let us find a quiet room somewhere.'

Kat watched the three of them leave the bar. She felt very alone and vulnerable all of a sudden. She decided to go to her room and wait there.

It was an unbelievably long wait. Kat wondered absently if Neil was able to take cigarette breaks. She hoped so. He would find it a struggle if not. She tried to imagine what questions they would ask her. Her mind felt like mud – she was not sure she could remember anything accurately. What day had they arrived? When had she found the note she'd thought was from Matt? She tried to establish the sequence of events, but was unable to think logically.

After three hours there was a knock on the door. The young officer said, politely: 'Would you come to give your statement now please?' She followed him down the stairs and into a cosy sitting room. It must be the guesthouse owner's personal space, she thought. Detective Gerber stood up as she entered the room, and indicated the armchair opposite his own. The young officer took a chair near the door.

'Do you mind if I record our conversation?' the detective asked.

'No, of course not.'

He switched on the recorder, confirming the date and place and his rank, opened up his notebook and was about to ask his first question when Kat interrupted.

'Can I ask if Nigel is alright?'

'He is alright. There are no serious injuries. He has been released from hospital and has given his statement at the police station.'

'Did you find Ellie?

'I cannot say more. Our searches are ongoing.'

'What about Sean and Matt?'

'I can confirm that two bodies were recovered from the chalet this morning.'

Kat's heart sank. She had been hoping against hope that Anna had been lying.

'And Anna. Where is she now?'

'She is in police custody.'

'What will happen to her? I'm scared she'll come after us again.'

'She has given a full confession. She will go on trial for murder. I cannot say with certainty what will happen after that, but I expect she will be confined to a mental institution rather than prison.'

'For ever?'

'That is not for me to say. Now, let us begin. First, can you confirm your full name and address please?'

The questions were easy at first: name, address, age, occupation. Who booked the holiday, and when. Her relation to the other five in the chalet. After that came precise questions about each day. Kat broke down often as she described the events.

Sometimes she got muddled: 'I can't remember if it was on the Tuesday or Wednesday we went snowshoeing, I'm sorry... If I had my diary I could tell you for definite.'

The detective regarded her coolly and said: 'We will check later. We have your diary at the police station. We will return it to you soon. Now, the following day. What did you do that morning?'

On and on the questions went. At some point a tray of tea and biscuits was brought into the room. Kat welcomed the break – this was exhausting.

Finally, after almost three hours, the detective snapped shut his notebook and switched off the recorder.

'Thank you for your co-operation. You are free to leave the room now.' He gave a short, rather false smile.

'Right. Thanks. Can we leave the guesthouse to go for a walk? I'd like to get some air.'

'You may. But be here tomorrow. I may have further questions for you.'

The young officer nodded to her politely as she left the room and ran up the stairs. She found Neil, sitting on his bed with one of the guesthouse's dog-eared novels in his hand. He jumped up when he saw her.

'How did it go?'

'Gruelling. Horrible. And for you?'

'Same. It felt as if I was the criminal.'

'Let's get out of here for a while. Go for a walk. I feel like my head's going to explode.'

They found their jackets and went out into the cold late afternoon. Neil took her gloved hand in his, rubbing his thumb against hers. They walked through the snow in silence.

That evening, as they were again sitting in the bar, looking at their phones in a desultory manner, Kat looked up to see Nigel walking towards their table. She stood up instantly, making her chair scape noisily against the wooden floor. Neil looked up in surprise, then stood in turn, his face drained of colour. Kat rushed to hug Nigel but his body was stiff in her embrace. They all sat again, not knowing what to say.

Nigel was slumped in the chair, eyes on the floor, his fingers splayed on the edge of the table as if he needed the support to balance himself. 'I've just identified Ellie's body,' he said, eventually.

'Oh Nigel!' said Kat, instinctively putting her hand over Nigel's on the table. Nigel left it there for a moment, then pulled his own hand away. He still hadn't looked up.

'She was in a bad state. Multiple broken bones.'

'I'm so sorry,' said Kat, inadequately.

Nigel exhaled - a short dismissive breath. 'Yes, well...'

Kat had never seen him like this. He looked as if he was fighting to control several emotions. Sorrow, anger perhaps, disbelief. His jaw was clenched and she could see that his eyes were flicking back and forth madly under his half-closed eyelids. She felt overwhelmed with sympathy.

'Tell me what I can do Nigel. Do you want me to call the children?'

'Done that,' he replied shortly.

Neil knew he had to say something, but all the words that came into his head seemed trite, false or clichéd. 'I am so, so sorry,' he began at last, simply. 'This is my fault. She was my wife. I didn't know how ill she was... I never would have invited... Oh God, I am sorry!'

Nigel looked up at last, straight into Neil's eyes. Kat was astonished to see the raw hatred in his expression.

'Ellie always said you were bad news.' He said, slowly and deliberately. Neil gasped and recoiled as if the words had hit him with a physical force.

Kat's mouth fell open. This was unjust, even if she understood Nigel's desire to lash out. 'Nigel, don't,' she said softly. 'You can't blame Neil! Blame me, if anyone. I was the one who persuaded you both to come!'

Nigel never took his eyes off Neil. He got up slowly, then leant forward until his face was inches away from Neil's. 'Because of you, my wife is dead.' As he pronounced the word 'dead' he poked his finger into Neil's chest. Then he turned on his heal and left the room.

Kat was appalled. 'He's not thinking clearly, it's just a natural reaction to try and blame someone. He doesn't mean it. Don't take it to heart.'

Neil sighed and shook his head sadly. 'But he's right.'

'No, he...'

'Come outside a minute. There's something I've got to say to you.'

'What? No, Neil, it was not your fault! He'll be OK in the morning.'

"*Come outside!*' Neil insisted, his voice raised, almost angry.

Kat was shocked by his tone. She followed him out into the night air. They walked a few paces away from the door, then Neil turned to face her, his expression determined.

'Listen to me. Let me talk. I've had time to think.' He took a deep breath, then continued calmly: 'I have brought you nothing but misery. I think I broke your heart the first time we were here. Now I've killed your best friend. I'm no good for you. I bring unhappiness wherever I go. I shouldn't be with you. I shouldn't be with anyone. You deserve someone who doesn't bring all this... crap with them.'

'But...'

'Please, just let me say this. I can't be with you. I can't do that to you. I love you but that's not enough.'

'It is, it is! What about last night, didn't that mean anything?'

'It meant everything. But it doesn't change my decision. You've got a good life, good kids. I won't let you risk all that on a loser like me.'

Kat was frantic. 'You just shut the fuck up and listen to me you ... you...argh!' She knew she had to find the right words now, before it was too late. She gesticulated wildly with her hands as she fought for the ability to convince him. 'You love me. I love you. That's all that matters. That's *all*! Let something good come out of all this... this... madness. It is *not...your...fault!*'

Neil shook his head. He put both hands on her shoulders and looked into her eyes. 'Think for a minute. How would your children react to me? Would they be happy to see you hook up with someone who'd been married to a murderer? What if she came after us again? Do you want to risk your children's safety if she ever gets paroled?' Kat opened her mouth to try and find an argument, but nothing came. 'No, I thought not. I am sorry, but what Nigel said is right. I am bad news. You are better off without me.'

She broke free from his grip, desperate, then came towards him again, thumping his chest with both fists.

'No! No! I'm not going to let you do this.'

He caught her hands and pulled her into a tight embrace. They stayed like that for several minutes, his chin resting on the top of her head. Then he pushed her gently away. He gave her a last, long look and she could see the unshed tears gleaming in his eyes.

'You'll be thankful for this one day.' He said, and turned back towards the Gasthaus.

Kat stared after his retreating back, her emotions in turmoil. What he had said about her children had hit the mark. But uppermost in her mind as one thought: 'Not again! Not again!' How could she lose him again?

EPILOGUE
Two years later

As cemeteries go, this one was beautiful. It was situated on the flank of a hill, enclosed by iron railings. Two imposing stone pillars marked the entrance. The lower gravestones were the oldest; the stone worn to a greenish-black with time and exposure, the carvings once intricate but now almost impossible to interpret. Some of the stones had fallen over. Others leaned drunkenly, as if bracing against the wind. As the graves progressed up the hill, the stones changed colour. Reddish sandstone gave way to pale marble. At the top of the hill, black granite headstones stood square and erect, the highest ones still decked with flower arrangements.

Nigel filled his bucket with water from the tap and made his way up the hill. He reached the headstone he knew so well, and thought again how much Ellie would have liked this spot, high on the hill, under a tall, winter-bare tree, with views over the frosty moors beyond. As he squatted beside the grave, a crow took off from the tree above, giving life to the stillness.

He wet his sponge and started to clean the dirt from the headstone, his fingers tracing the bronze lettering and making it shine again.

ELEONOR ROSE BRADSHAW

BELOVED WIFE AND MOTHER

No cross. No intricate carvings. No quote from the Bible.

Just her birth and death dates. Ellie had been an unwavering atheist and had always hated flowery prose. Nigel remembered with a smile how indignant she'd been at the 'outpouring of grief' that followed Princess Diana's death. She'd hated the over-blown tributes in the papers and the sight of mourners lining the funeral route, wailing in anguish over someone they'd never met. 'Sentimental clap-trap', she'd called it. Her own funeral had been simple and understated. The humanist celebrant had taken the time to get to know and convey her life and character. Friends and colleagues had packed the crematorium seats and massed in the aisles and even outside. The wickerwork coffin had been decorated with early spring wildflowers. There had been short speeches, a poem and Ellie's favourite song. Nigel had sat through the ordeal in a daze, his arms protectively around his three children either side of him. Later, much later, he, Dom, Hannah and Nick had come to this cemetery to bury the ashes next to Ellie's Mum, under this shiny new headstone.

Checking that there was no-one else around, and feeling slightly ridiculous, he traced her name again with his finger and began to talk, telling his dead wife everything that came into his head: news of the children, the dog, the house. He didn't think for a minute that she was listening, hovering nearby or up on a cloud, but it made him feel better anyway.

'Digby's getting a bit old and fat. The vet thinks he might have a heart problem. He's such an idiot dog, he still thinks he can chase about like a puppy. He's had a couple of fits. We have to keep him on the lead now to calm him down. He misses you.

'Your Dad's hanging on. He tried to run away from the nursing home again the other day. They found him in the pub in town; he'd cadged a beer off someone and was sitting there in his pyjamas, enjoying his pint, talking about the old days down the pit. He doesn't recognise me anymore but he still knows the kids on a good day. I'm glad he doesn't remember what hap-pened to you. That's a blessing.

'The children want me to get one of those big American fridges, the ones with double doors and ice-makers. I'm not so sure. I don't think you'd have liked them. Ugly things really. What do you think?

'We've had foxes in the garden again. A vixen I think. I want to get some sort of action triggered camera set up to see what they get up to. You'd probably say 'not another gadget.' But it gives me a project. I um.. I don't know what to do with myself some evenings.'

Nigel paused and turned as he heard a car crunching over the gravel driveway below. The car stopped and the passenger door opened. There was Kat, in jeans, boots and an anorak, scanning the hillside for him. He stood and waved to her, and she waved back and started up the hill, carrying a heavy-looking supermarket bag. When she reached him, she dumped the bag and they hugged tightly.

'Thanks for coming,' he said.

'Thanks for asking me! It means the world. I wouldn't miss this for anything.'

'What's in the bag?'

'Trowel, secateurs and a small bag of peat.'

'Great. I've brought some plants and shrubs.' He pointed to a green garden waste bag nearby. 'There's periwinkle and winter hellebore. I've got some mixed bulbs too. It's probably not the right time to plant them, but you never know, they may survive.'

They worked together in silent harmony, clearing out the plants that hadn't survived, dead-heading the hydrangeas and geraniums and planting out the new stock.

'It's really nice here. Peaceful,' said Kat. They both paused in their work, sitting back on their haunches, and looked out across the moors. 'Ellie would love this.'

'She would.'

'Did she use to visit her mum's grave a lot?'

'No. Almost never. You know Ellie. An atheist through and through. She didn't see the point of bringing flowers and all that stuff.'

They watched a kestrel hovering overhead, searching for

prey, it's body perfectly stable as its wings beat steadily.

'Do you ever get the feeling she's near?' Kat asked.

Nigel sighed. 'No, I don't. I wish I did. She didn't believe in the afterlife or ghosts or anything like that, so I suppose it's logical. She won't be trying to send me a message.'

'I dream about her quite often.'

'Do you? What kind of dreams.'

'It's usually that I find her, and she's alive and the same as normal, and I'm so happy – there's been a mistake and she didn't die after all. I feel wonderful, euphoric – until I wake up.'

'I'm glad I don't have those dreams.'

'No. They're half fantastic and half awful. It's like losing her all over again.'

'I did have one dream once. Ages ago. A few months after she was killed. I dreamt I was in a church, sitting on a pew and talking to a vicar, arranging the funeral. It was dark and gloomy inside. Then I became aware of a light behind the vicar, and there she was, in a dark corner of the church, but surrounded by a kind of white glow, standing really still, and smiling calmly, reaching her hand out to me. I reached my hand out, and the space between us contracted. She was there. I was filled with a sense of wellbeing.'

'Oh Nigel! But that's a wonderful dream!' Kat leapt on this, desperate for a sign that Ellie was still around in some way. 'What do you think it meant? A message surely?'

'At the time I thought that it was her telling me it was OK, and to stop being so angry. I felt so peaceful afterwards. It really changed me for a day or two. But then I did some research. These dreams are dead common. Bereavement dreams, they're called. You see the person illuminated. They are healthy and happy. They give you a message of reassurance. It's just wish fulfilment, pure and simple. Me telling myself what I wanted to hear. No. She's dead. She's gone.' Nigel shrugged and dug his towel into the earth one more.

Kat felt tears pricking her eyes and blinked them back. Tears still came at the most awkward moments. The other day she'd heard James Taylor's 'Fire and Rain' on the car radio and had to pull off the road until her sobs subsided. She mustn't cry now. This was about Nigel, not her.

'Anyway…how are the kids coping?' she asked.

'Really, not too bad at all. They're bouncing back. Hannah's busy planning her wedding. But you know that – they phone you as much as they phone me! You could probably fill me in on what they're up to.'

'They do phone often. I hope you don't mind. I don't want to step on your toes.'

'No, it's great they can talk to you. There's bound to be stuff they can't tell me. Women's problems. Love-life stuff. It's good they've got you. Kind of spare mum.'

'No, I'll never be that, but I'll always try my best to think what Ellie would have advised them. And what about you, Nigel? Are you holding up OK?'

Nigel paused, knocking out the sticky earth from his trowel. Then he looked at Kat squarely. 'I wanted to ask your opinion. I'm thinking of joining an internet dating site. Do you think I should?'

'Oh!' Kat was momentarily taken aback. How could Ellie be replaced? Then she reconsidered. 'Yes, I do. Ellie wouldn't want you to be alone for ever. And you can get second chances, you know. Just look at me!'

Nigel smiled. 'But what about the kids, what do I tell them? Or do I tell them nothing? Let them guess?'

'Play it by ear. You don't need to ask their permission or anything. But don't lie to them. See how it goes and if you find someone you really like, then you talk to them.'

'And what about John and Sarah? Have they accepted you've got a new man?'

Kat frowned. 'No, not totally. It was really sticky at first. Tense and awkward when he was there, and then shouting and sulking when he left. But they're coming round, gradually. It's hard for them.'

'Are you happy, Kat?'

'I am. Very.' She said this with total conviction, beaming up at him.

Nigel nodded, slowly. 'I'm glad.'

They began to clear up, brushing the soil off the path and putting the tools back in the bag. When they straightened up, both pairs of knees gave audible cracks. They laughed. Kat stretched her aching back muscles. 'We're not getting any younger, are we!'

They stood back to admire their handiwork. The grave looked beautiful in the late winter sunshine, the new plants waving lightly in the breeze.

'Anyway,' said Nigel, 'I want to hear all about your new house! Where is it exactly?'

'It's on the moors above Huddersfield. It is beautiful – it's an old stone-built farmhouse. It's still got all the traditional features – original stone flags on the floor, mullioned windows, oak beams. And the views, you wouldn't believe. Of course, the weather can be bloody awful. The kids call it Wuthering Shites. But I just love it. You've got to come and see it!'

'I will. You try and stop me! When did you move in?'

'Just a couple of weeks ago. We're still living out of boxes.'

They picked up their belongings and began to walk down the hill towards the car below.

'Did you get a good price for your old house?'

'Not great. I was in a hurry to sell. I suppose I should have held out a bit longer, got a bit of competition going. But we wanted to act fast to get the farmhouse.'

'No, I think you did the right thing. We both know you've got to grab a good thing if it comes up. Life's too short and all that.' He turned to glance back at the gravestone, then looked down at the waiting car.

The driver had emerged and was leaning against the bonnet, watching them, his eyes narrowed against the low winter sun. He was tall and lean, dressed in black jeans and a worn leather jacket. He took a deep draw on his cigarette, his cheeks hollowing, his cheekbones sharp. As they approached, he threw the cigarette onto the gravel and ground it out with the tip of his grey Converse. Then he picked up the stub and put it in his jacket pocket, carefully. He straightened up and took a tentative step towards them.

Reaching the bottom of the hill, Nigel clasped him by the hand and pulled him into a man-hug.

'Neil, you old bastard,' he boomed. 'When the devil are you going to give up that filthy habit?'

'Nigel, you plonker. Good to see you again, mate!'

They slapped each other's backs in the way men do when they're embarrassed by their emotions. Both were grinning like idiots.

'Oi' said Kat. 'That's enough of the bromance stuff. This girl needs a drink. Where's the nearest pub?'

But Neil and Nigel ignored her. The two men hadn't seen each other since Anna's trial. Nigel had been civil to them both at that time, but nothing more. They had avoided each other as much as possible. Now, she could tell a wordless message was being communicated as they stepped back and regarded each other, smiling.

'You could have come up and helped us with the planting, you know,' said Nigel. 'You didn't have to wait down here.'

'No, it's special for the two of you. I didn't want to intrude.' He hesitated, unsure of himself, not wanting to push the fragile friendship that was being re-established. 'I brought something though. I don't know if it's appropriate.' He went to the back of the car, opened the boot and pulled out big super-market bag. 'It's heather. It's from Sleat on the Isle of Skye. I re-member Ellie saying that was her favourite place. Am I right?'

Nigel was stunned for a moment. 'Did you go up there specially?'

'Yeah. Dug it up myself. And a real bugger it is to dig up, too.'

He shut the boot and made to hand the bag to Nigel, but instead Nigel took a step to the side. 'No. You go and plant it yourself. Here's a trowel. She'd like that.'

Neil looked from Nigel to Kat, questioningly. Then he nodded slowly. He took the trowel from Nigel and looked down as it lay in his hand, considering with awe, it as if it was a valuable antique. His face lit up with a big smile and he and began to walk away from the car.

Nigel put his arm round Kat's shoulder and gave it a squeeze. Together they watched Neil weave his way through the gravestones towards the tree at the top of the hill.

AFTERWORD

Thank you so much for buying and reading my first novel. If you enjoyed it, please leave a review!

ACKNOWLEDGEMENT

Thank you first of all to my wonderful proofreaders:
- Chris Sykes, for correcting numerous formatting issues and providing invaluable advice on the publishing industry.
- Cathy Shahani for suggesting which parts needed expanding, developing or cutting.
- Abigail Durling, for supporting a project which has emotional resonance for her.
- Joanne McCarthy for being absolutely bang on about the importance of hooks!

Thank you to Annie Leonard for her insights into the psychology of obsession and murder.

Thank you to Steve Wright, Nigel Cressey, Stevie Smith, Ian and Linda Tomlinson and all the gang who skied with me many years ago in Riederalp, and who played the murder game!

And finally, thank you to my patient husband, Gordon, for his encouragement and support - although he still refuses to read the book!